simply *divine*

Jacquelin Thomas

POCKET BOOKS
New York   London   Toronto   Sydney

POCKET BOOKS, a division of Simon & Schuster, Inc.
1230 Avenue of the Americas, New York, NY 10020

This book is a work of fiction. Names, characters, places and
incidents are products of the author's imagination or are used
fictitiously. Any resemblance to actual events or locales or
persons, living or dead, is entirely coincidental.

ISBN-13: 978-1-4165-2718-3
ISBN-10:   1-4165-2718-4

This Pocket Books trade paperback edition October 2006

10 9 8 7 6 5 4 3 2 1

POCKET and colophon are registered trademarks of
Simon & Schuster, Inc.

Manufactured in the United States of America

For information regarding special discounts for bulk purchases,
please contact Simon & Schuster Special Sales at 1-800-456-6798
or business@simonandschuster.com

This book is dedicated to the teens at
Wakefield Family Center Church.

It's confusing when you're too old to be considered a child and yet too young to be an adult. Regardless, enjoy your youth; you can't recapture these years once they're gone. Use this time to build wonderful friendships and create unforgettable memories that you'll carry for the rest of your lives. My prayer for each of you is that your teenage years are simply divine.

acknowledgments

Before I go any further, I have to thank my Heavenly Father for this gift. Without Him I can do nothing and I'm so grateful for this opportunity to write the type of stories I yearned to read as a teen.

I have to formally thank Jasmine Nicole Bradford for reading *Simply Divine* when the story was in its rough-draft stages and giving me valuable feedback.

I'd also like to thank Megan Goodwine and Christina Frazier for their helpful insight into what it's like to be a teenage girl in 2006.

A special thank-you goes to my husband for his never-ending support, and to my children, who I love with all my heart.

simply *divine*

chapter 1

"*Mimi*, I'm dying for you to see my dress," I say into the purple-rhinestone-studded cell phone. "It's this deep purple color with hand-painted scroll designs in gold on it. I have to be honest. I—Divine Matthews-Hardison—will be in *all* the magazines. I'll probably be listed in the top-ten best-dressed category."

Mimi laughs. "Me too. My dress is tight. It's silver and strapless and Lana Maxwell designed it."

"Oh, she's that new designer. Nobody really knows her yet." I'm hatin' on her because she's allowed to wear a strapless gown and I had to beg Mom for days to get her to let me wear a halter-style dress.

I make sure to keep my voice low so that the nosy man Mom claims is my dad can't hear my conversation. It's a wonder

1

Jerome actually has a life of his own—he's always trying to meddle in mine.

I can tell our limo is nearing the entrance of the Los Angeles Convention Center because I hear people screaming, and see the rapid flashing of cameras as diehard fans try to snap pictures of their favorite celebrities while others hold up signs. I'm glued to the window, checking out the growing sea of bystanders standing on both sides of the red carpet.

The annual Grammy Awards celebration is music's biggest night and the one major event I look forward to attending every year. Singers, actors and anyone really important will be present. Media coverage is heavy and I know as soon as I step out of the limo, the press is going to be all over me.

Settling back in the seat, I tell Mimi, "I'll talk to you when you get here. I need to make sure my hair is together. You know how these photographers are—they're like always trying to snap an ugly picture of celebrities to send all over the world. That's the last thing I need—some whack photo of me splashed all over the tabloids. See you in a minute. Bye."

Cameras flash and whirl as limo after stretch limo roll to a stop. I put away my phone and take out the small compact mirror I can't live without, making sure every strand of my hair is in place. A girl's gotta look her best, so I touch up my lips with Dior Addict Plastic Gloss in Euphoric Beige. I like this particular lip gloss because the color doesn't make my lips look shiny or too big in photographs.

I pull the folds of my gold-colored silk wrap together and blow a kiss to myself before slipping the mirror back into my matching gold clutch. I'm looking *fierce,* as my idol Tyra Banks loves to say on *America's Next Top Model.* To relieve some of the nervous energy I'm feeling, I begin tracing the pattern of my designer gown. This is my first time wearing what I consider a grown-up gown. I've never been able to wear backless before, but thankfully, my mom has a clue that I'm not a baby anymore. I'll be fifteen soon.

"Divine, honey, you look beautiful," Mom compliments. "Anya did a wonderful job designing this gown for you. It's absolutely perfect. Doesn't make you look too grown up."

My smile disappears. She just had to go there.

"Thanks." As an afterthought, I add, "You do too."

My mom, renowned singer and actress Kara Matthews, is up for several Grammys. On top of that, she's scored starring roles in three blockbuster movies, one of which will have her leaving in a couple of weeks to film the sequel in Canada. She can be pretty cool at times but then she goes and ruins it by going into Mom mode. To get even, I say and do things to wreck her nerves. Like . . .

"I hope I see Bow Wow tonight. He's so hot . . ." I can't even finish my sentence because the look on Mom's face throws me into giggles. My dad, Jerome, comes out of an alcohol-induced daze long enough to grumble something unintelligible.

He's never allowed me to call him daddy. Says it makes him feel old, so he insists that I call him Jerome.

Hellooo . . . get a clue. *You are old.*

It used to bother me that Jerome didn't want me calling him Dad when I was little. But after all the crazy stuff he's done, I'd rather not tell anyone he's related to me. Although I've never actually seen him drink or whatever, I've watched enough TV to know what an addict looks like. If I could sell him on eBay, I'd do it in a heartbeat. I can just picture the ad in my head.

Hollywood actor for sale. Okay-looking.
Used to be real popular until he started
drinking and doing drugs. By the way, he
really needs a family because he's on his
way out of this one. Bidding starts at one dollar.

Mom interrupts my plans to auction Jerome by saying, "Divine, I don't want you sniffing around those rap artists. You stay with me or Stella. *I mean it.* Don't go trying to sneak off like you usually do. I don't care if Dean Reuben lets Mimi run around loose. You better not!"

Mom and Jerome make a big deal for nothing over me talking to boys. Period. I'm fourteen and in the eighth grade. I'm not even allowed to date yet, so I don't know why they're always bugging whenever I mention meeting guys. I will admit I get a thrill out of the drama, so I figure giving them a scare every now and then can't hurt.

"You stay away from that Bow Wow," Jerome orders. "He's a nice kid, but you don't need to be up in his face. Don't let that fast tail Mimi get you in trouble."

This subject has so come and gone. All his drinking must be making him forgetful or something. Rolling my eyes heavenward, I pull out my cell phone, flip it open and call my best friend just to irritate him.

"Mimi, we're about to get out and stroll down the red carpet," I say loud enough for him to hear. "Where's your car now?" Mimi's dad is an actor too. He's always out of town working, which Mimi loves because then she can run all over her entertainment-lawyer mom. Her dad is the strict one in her family. For me, it's Mom. She's the only grown-up in my family.

Our limo stops moving. The driver gets out and walks around to the passenger door.

"We're here, Mimi. I'll see you in a few minutes." I hang up and slip the phone into my gold evening bag.

Cameras flashing, the media are practically climbing all over the limo. As usual, my mom starts complaining. But if the media isn't dogging her, her publicist comes up with something to get their attention, which isn't hard to do with my dad's constant legal battles. I just don't get Mom sometimes.

Mom claims she doesn't really like being in the spotlight and the center of attention, but me, I love it. I'm a Black American Princess and I'm not ashamed to admit it. I take pleasure in being pampered and waited on. Mostly, I love to shop and be able to purchase anything I want without ever looking at a price tag.

"I wish I had a cigarette," Mom blurts. "I'm so nervous."

I reach over, taking her hand in mine. "Don't worry about it. I hope you win, but even if you don't, it's still okay. At least you were nominated."

She smiled. "I know what you're saying, sweetie. And you're right, but I *do* want to win, Divine. I want this so badly."

"I know." Deep down, I want it just as bad as she does. I want Mom to win because then I'll have something to hold over that stupid Natalia Moon's head. Her mother is singer Tyler Winters. As far as I'm concerned, the woman couldn't sing a note even if she bought and paid for it. And I'm pretty sure I'm not the only one who thinks so, because she's never been nominated for a Grammy.

The door to the limo opens.

Leo, our bodyguard, steps out first. He goes everywhere with us to protect us from our public. There are people out there who'll take it to the extreme to meet celebrities.

Mom's assistant Stella gets out of the car next. All around us, I hear people chanting, "Kara . . . Kara . . . Kara."

A few bystanders push forward, but are held back by thick, black velvet ropes and uniformed cops.

"They love you, Mom."

Smiling, my mom responds, "Yeah . . . they sure do, baby."

I'm so proud to have *the* Kara Matthews as my mom. She's thin and beautiful. Although she's only five feet five inches tall, she looks just like a model. I have her high cheekbones and smooth tawny complexion, but unfortunately, I'm also saddled with Jerome's full lips, bushy eyebrows and slanted eyes. Thankfully, I'm still cute.

"Hey, what about me? I got some fans out there. They didn't just come to see yo' mama. She wouldn't be where she is if it wasn't for me."

I glance over my shoulder at Jerome, but don't respond. He's such a loser.

I have a feeling that he's going to find a way to ruin this night for Mom. Then she'll get mad at him and they'll be arguing for the rest of the night.

I've overheard Mom talk about divorcing Jerome a few times, but when he gets ready to leave, she begs him to stay. I wish they'd just break up because Jerome brings out the worst in Mom, according to Stella.

Stella turns and gestures for me to get out of the limo. It's time to meet my public.

Okay . . . my mom's fans. But in a way, I'm famous too. I'm Hollywood royalty. Kara Matthews's beloved daughter.

I exit the limo with Leo's assistance. Jerome will follow me, getting out before Mom. She is always last. Her way of making an entrance, I suppose.

I spot a camera aimed in my direction. I smile and toss my dark, shoulder-length hair across my shoulders the very same way I've seen Mom do millions of times.

Mom makes her grand appearance on the red carpet amid cheers, handclapping and whistles. We pose for pictures.

Here we are, pretending to be this close and loving family. What a joke!

I keep my practiced smile in place despite the blinding, flashing darts of light stabbing at my eyes. It's my duty to play up to the cameras, the fans and the media.

I can't imagine my life any other way.

After a few poses in front of the limo, we start down the red carpet. Whenever I can, I stand in front of my parents, grinning like the Cheshire Cat in *Alice's Adventures in Wonderland*. I love being photographed and I know how to strike a perfect pose.

America's next top model—right here. As soon as I turn eighteen, I'm auditioning for that show. Mom says I won't have to. She actually had the nerve to tell me that I could be working right now as a model. Only she won't let me because she's real big on education, so I have to finish school first. Talk about dangling a pot of gold in front of my face and snatching it away.

Stella and Leo march in front of us, leading the way to the doors of the convention center.

I'm walking in front of my parents, close enough to hear Mom's words to Jerome.

"Do you have to manhandle me? You nearly ripped off my arm back there when you grabbed me."

I notice that Mom is careful not to move her lips for fear some reporter might be able to read her words. She's always trying to keep up appearances.

"Just 'cause you up for some awards, don't start acting like you don't know me," Jerome warns. "I'm the man of the house. I run thangs . . ."

"You don't run nothing," Mom shoots back. "When is the last time anyone called you for a job?"

"Could you please stop arguing?" The words just rush out of my mouth. "You're embarrassing me."

We run into another group of photographers.

Mom stops and leans against Jerome, wrapping her arms around him and wearing what everyone in the industry calls her million-dollar smile.

Well, I'm not about to be outdone.

I insert myself between my parents, separating them while tilting my face just right so that my best side will be photographed—just the way Mom taught me.

Jerome places his cold lips to my cheek, trying to show off for the media. After a few more photos he breezes past us and into the convention center.

"I hate him," I mutter under my breath.

"Don't say that, Divine. He's your daddy."

Mom pauses to be interviewed, so I reach into my purse and pull out my cell phone. Pressing the talk button, I place it to my ear. "Mimi, where are you?"

I give Mom a big hug in the press room after the awards. "I'm sorry you only won the Grammy for Contemporary R&B Album."

Smiling down at me, Mom holds the coveted award close to her breast. "Sugar, I'm just thankful for this one. That album didn't do as well as my others, so I'm amazed *Living for You* actually won. This validates me personally."

Looking high as a kite, Jerome clumsily drapes his arm around her. "Okay, baby girl . . . it's time for you to go home. Mama and Daddy wanna party."

Pouting, I look up at Mom. "Do I really have to leave right now? I wanted to hang out for a little while longer."

"Well, you ain't doin' nothing but going home," Jerome rudely interjects. Like I was talking to him in the first place. "I don' want you hanging round these li'l dudes. You too young. I don' wanna hafta kill nobody 'bout my shorty."

Mom tries the diplomatic approach. "I know how much you want to stay, but your daddy's right, hon. Besides, you have to go to school tomorrow and you're not exactly a morning person. We girls need our beauty rest."

"Mom, I know you can come up with something better than that. I'm cute—losing one night of sleep won't hurt me. Why can't I just pop into one party at least? I don't have to stay long. Just enough to say I went. All the other kids at school will be talking about the parties they went to." I impatiently push away a stray curl from my face. "I'm not a baby. I'm almost fifteen."

Jerome bristles. "We know how old you are, Divine. We were there when you were born. Remember?"

I'm not ready to give up, so I keep pushing. "Then why can't I go for a little while? Mimi's dad is real strict but he's letting her go to the party with them at the House of Blues. Tomorrow's Valentine's Day. This can be one of my presents."

Mom places a gentle hand to my cheek. "Hon, we're not changing our minds. You're going home and that's final."

I release a long sigh in my frustration. My parents never let me have any fun. They're ruining my life.

Mom hugs me. This is her attempt to soothe me but the effort is totally wasted because I'm really mad at her.

"How about we go shopping tomorrow after school? We'll go to the Beverly Center and Rodeo Drive."

At the mention of shopping, my spirits lift some. If Mom insists on switching to Mom mode, then I plan to punish her by spending as much of her money as I can. This time it's really going to cost her big. "I want to go to Gucci and Louis Vuitton because I need to get a couple of new purses. Then I want to see the new collection at Iceberg."

"We can do that too," Mom promises. "Whatever you want."

"I don't have to go shopping with Stella, do I?" The last time we were to go shopping, Mom backed out to do a radio interview to promote her album.

"No, you don't," Mom assures me. "Tomorrow, you and I are going to spend some much-needed quality time together. I promise." She glances over her shoulder at Jerome. "Daddy's gonna join us if he's not too busy. Right?"

Jerome sends Mom a strange look I can't decipher.

I really don't want Jerome tagging along. All he ever does is complain about standing around while we try on clothes, or he fusses about how much money we spend. It isn't like we're spending any of his money. Mom is the one making paper.

"I might be able to make it but don't hold me to it."

I hope that Jerome's not able to join us. He's such a loser.

Stella comes over to where we're standing. "C'mon, Divine. It's time I got you home."

I glance over at Mom, giving her one last chance to change her mind. "I don't want to leave just yet. Nelly is right over there. Can I just go over there to meet him before I leave?"

"For what?" Jerome demands. "You better just take yo' lil fast tail home."

"You need to shut up. It's not even like that. I just want to meet him so that I can tell everyone that I met him." I don't include that my friend Rhyann and I have a fifty-dollar bet to see who'll meet him first.

He leans over and plants a kiss on my forehead. "You my baby girl. I'm just tryin' not to let you grow up too fast. You know I love you."

I push him away, no longer caring who's watching us. I don't need Jerome trying to act like a father now. "Leave me alone, Jerome. You are so not related to me."

"Sugar, don't do that," Mom whispers. "Remember, we've talked about this. Be nice to your daddy. There's a photographer in the corner watching us." Smiling, she adds, "Now give me a hug."

Embracing Mom, I feign a smile. This is really going to cost her big.

"I love you," she whispers.

Whatever. Right now, Mom's entering the loser zone in a big way.

Jerome purses his lips as if waiting for me to kiss him, but he'll turn blue and green before that ever happens. I walk off toward the nearest exit with Stella following. She makes a quick call to have our driver bring the limo around.

Without a word spoken between us, I climb into the limo, turn on the small television and settle back for the forty-five-minute drive home to Pacific Palisades.

Mom's face appears on the small screen.

"Could you turn that up, please?"

Stella turns up the volume.

It's a clip of Mom's interview after her Grammy win. I smile. "She looks real happy, doesn't she?"

"Yes, she does," Stella murmurs. "I believe her whole world is going to change after tonight."

I like seeing my mom happy. Lately though, I've noticed that she spends a lot of time in her bedroom with the door locked. The few times I've put my face to the door I've smelled the putrid odor of marijuana. I know Jerome has been smoking the stuff for years. But for Mom I think this is something new.

I've never told anyone because Stella and Mom are always saying, "What's done at home stays at home. You never betray family."

It really bothers me that my parents smoke marijuana, especially Mom. Just last year, she was the keynote speaker at my school's drug-awareness program.

What a hypocrite.

It's all Jerome's fault.

His constant legal battles and a recent paternity suit have taken a toll on my mom. At least that's what I overheard Mom telling Stella a few days ago.

"Do you think Mom will divorce Jerome?"

Stella put away her cell phone. "Divine, you don't need to worry yourself with grown-up matters."

"Well, I hope she does," I confess. "Mom would be much happier if she did."

"Let's not talk about this right now," Stella whispers. "Divine, you really need to be very careful about what you say in public."

A small sigh escapes me. The last thing I need right now is another lecture, especially one from a nonparent. Just because she and Mom grew up together, Stella thinks she can boss me around, but she's nothing more than the help as far as I'm concerned. She better be glad I halfway like her because otherwise she would've been fired a long time ago.

chapter 2

"*Why* didn't somebody wake me up?" I yell after practically breaking my neck running down the stairs. I hastily tuck the crisp white blouse into the waistband of my navy and green plaid skirt—all part of my school uniform. "I'm late for school and you know how Mr.—"

Stella holds up a hand to silence me as she speaks with someone on the telephone.

I glance over at Mom, noticing the dark circles beneath her eyes, her uncombed hair and the stack of crumpled tissues. She's been crying.

I feel a knot growing in the pit of my stomach and realize that something is terribly wrong.

My gaze swings back to Stella.

14

"Ms. Matthews has nothing to say, so please stop calling here." She slams the receiver down onto the cradle.

What's going on? I wonder.

"Thanks, S-Stella," Mom manages between sniffles. "I'm so s-sick and tired of reporters calling here. I don't know why they won't just leave us alone. We already have enough to d-deal with." Groaning, she rubs her temples with her fingers. "My head hurts t-terribly."

Stella pours a glass of water and hands it to Mom while I make myself comfortable on the plush sofa beside her, curious to find out what the heck is going on.

"Mom, what's the matter?" I inquire, anxiety spreading through my body. "What happened?"

Mom wipes her face with her hands. "Sugar . . . I need to tell you something. Last night after I left your father, he—"

"He's in jail again," I contribute, completely disgusted with Jerome at this point. Didn't the man have a clue how to stay out of trouble?

Mom hugs me. "Yeah, he's in jail, but this time . . ."

Seeing Jerome's face on television, I zone out on Mom and pick up the remote control with shaky hands. I turn up the volume so that I can hear the news report on Jerome's latest stunt.

"—taken into custody for the murder of Shelly Campbell . . ."

Although I grasp the meaning of their words, it's still not making sense to me.

No sense at all.

Jerome's been arrested many times before and I'm pretty sure he wasn't always innocent of the charges, but this time I totally believe the police have made a huge mistake. There is no way Jerome would've done such a terrible thing. He's stupid but he's not a killer.

Images of a dead woman rudely elbow their way into my mind. A devoted fan of *Law & Order,* I have a clear mental picture of a sheet-covered gurney being pushed to the morgue, of a woman stretched out naked on a stainless-steel table, surrounded by all kinds of weird-looking instruments.

I suddenly feel sick to my stomach. I put a hand to my mouth, trying to force the puke back down my throat.

Through the heavy fog in my brain, I hear Mom ask Stella, "Has Jerome's lawyer called back?"

"Not yet."

I pull my knees up to my chin and wrap my arms around them. I can't believe how quickly things have changed from last night.

From Mom and Stella's conversation, I piece together the events. Apparently the evening took a turn for the worse after I left. Jerome flirted with another woman. Mom got upset and came home. Jerome must have left the party and gone to see Shelly, the woman they were now accusing him of shooting.

I know that Shelly Campbell is the reason my parents have been fighting so much for the past week.

Stella's voice cut into my troubled thoughts. "Divine, why don't you go to your room? I'll have Miss Eula send up a tray."

I give Stella a defiant glare before responding, "You must be crazy. There's no way I'm leaving my mom."

Mom betrays me by siding with Stella. "She's right, hon. Go on up to your room. There's going to be a lot of people in and out of the house today. I really need you to stay out of the way."

I cling to her, promising, "I won't get in your way."

"Divine," she says in a voice that's low with emotion. "Do this for your mama, okay?"

I give a reluctant nod and rise up from the sofa, my lips sticking out as far as I can get them. I give Mom another chance to change her mind. When she doesn't, I protest by stomping up the steps of the curving staircase. I'm so tired of being treated like a baby.

Inside my room, I turn on the television, searching for more news on Jerome's arrest. Through tears, I eye the pictures of Shelly Campbell that TV stations are flashing all over the screen. I've seen her a few times, mostly in the tabloids when she filed a paternity suit against Jerome. She was claiming that he fathered her four-week-old son, Jason.

I'm sorry she's dead but that baby is not my brother.

The first time Jerome was arrested, my parents sat me down and explained how their celebrity status brought on all sorts of accusations. They warned me that some people would do and say anything for money.

I angrily wipe away my tears. Jerome's innocent. He's being framed.

This is all a big mistake. When the truth comes out, I hope Jerome sues the police department and the news stations.

My cell phone rings.

"Dee, I just heard . . . are you okay?" Mimi asks as soon as I answer.

"Yeah. I guess."

"I know you're not coming to school today, right? Everybody is talking about it here on campus."

"What are they saying?"

"They're just wondering if your dad really did it. I told them I didn't think so."

"No he didn't do it," I snap. "Jerome isn't a killer. He's being framed. You'll see."

"Hey, I'm on your side. I already told them that he's innocent. Rhyann and I have been saying it all morning."

"I can't believe people are tripping like this."

"People just like to have something to gossip about. A couple of reporters tried to come on campus, but security wouldn't let them get far."

"This is so crazy," I mutter. "I can't believe this is happening."

"I know. I'd probably just stay in bed for the rest of my life if it were me."

"I'm not worried. When Jerome gets through with them, we're going to own the entire police department—maybe even Beverly Hills too. Mom's been on the phone all morning talking to our attorneys."

A short beep cuts into our conversation, letting me know that I have another caller. I check the caller ID and say, "Mimi, I'll call you back. Rhyann's on the other line."

"I just got off the phone with Mimi," I tell her as soon as I click over.

"Girl, do you need me to come over? I know this has got to be stressing you out."

Mom would freak if Rhyann showed up on our doorstep. "I'm fine. I was just telling Mimi that this is such a big mistake. Jerome didn't do anything."

"I know. My uncles and my brothers get accused all the time of doing stuff. Just do like my mama does—she falls to her knees and prays. Then she runs out and gets a lawyer."

"We have several lawyers working for us," I announce. "Good ones."

"Well, I wanted to check on you, girl. But I need to get my tail back to class. I'll call you later."

We hang up.

A few minutes later, my cell phone rings again. I don't recognize the number so I just let it roll to voice mail.

I'll be so glad when Jerome comes home. Then this nightmare will finally be over.

When Jerome is still in jail that night, I can't deny that I'm worried about him. I thought he'd be home by now. Why are they keeping him in jail? What is his stupid lawyer doing?

Mom needs to take care of this right now.

Unable to bare the suspense any longer, I swing my legs to the edge of the bed and get up. I grab the gift I bought for my mom and slip down the back stairs, the ones that lead to the kitchen. Mom and Stella are in the kitchen talking softly, yet their voices are loud enough for me to hear their words.

I stay hidden from view, listening.

"Where's Divine?" Mom inquires. "I bet she's somewhere eavesdropping. That girl's too nosy for her own good."

I'm offended. How could she say that about me?

"She's in her bedroom," Stella responds. "That was Mr. Whitcomb on the phone earlier. He called to see how she was doing. He said that her teachers will email her assignments for the week."

Still standing on the stairs with my back pressed flat against the wall, I wince at the mention of the headmaster of Stony Hills Preparatory School. He's had it in for me from the moment I stepped on campus. Now he's got something to hold over my head. He always makes little comments about me being just like Jerome.

Renewed anger flows through my veins. If only Jerome had come home last night with Mom . . . The kids at school are going to wear me out with this one. They were already teasing me over the paternity suit.

"I tried to tell Jerome that Shelly Campbell was nothing but trouble," Mom says. "I could tell by looking at her that she was after money. But nooo, he wouldn't listen to me. If he won't consider my feelings, you'd think he would at least think about what he's doing to Divine."

"Surely you don't think that he . . ."

"No," Mom quickly interjects. "No, he didn't kill her, Stella. You know Jerome's not a murderer."

The telephone rings.

"Just let it ring," I hear Mom say.

I choose this break in conversation to enter the kitchen, acting as if I've just come downstairs.

"Mom, this is for you." I give her the Valentine's Day gift I purchased the week before. I'm hoping it'll salvage some of the holiday for her.

"Thanks, sweetie." She takes it from me and places it down on the counter without even looking at it.

I try not to be offended because Mom's got a lot on her mind right now. The present can wait, even if it did take me forever to find the perfect gift for Valentine's Day.

The telephone rings a second time. Then a third.

"Stella, just turn the ringer off." Mom puts her hands over her ears and walks into the family room. Sighing loudly, she drops down on the sectional sofa. "I can't stand all this incessant ringing," she moans. "Why won't they just leave us alone?"

"The lawyers . . . We need to answer just in case . . ." Stella says.

"They can call me on my cell phone. I really need a drink."

"Kara . . ."

"Okay. Never mind." Mom wipes at her eyes with the back of her hand as I join her on the sofa. "Last night started off great," she mumbles. "Your daddy just had to ruin it for me. If he'd just come home, none of this would've happened. We were supposed to have a nice romantic dinner tonight for Valentine's Day."

Mom doesn't say anything else, we just sit holding on to each other. Feeling Mom's arms around me like this makes me realize just how badly I need this hug. I'm able to share the loss and confusion I'm feeling with someone who truly understands.

"I bet Reed is getting a big kick out of this," Mom mutters. "He thinks my life is nothing but a big mess anyway."

I've never met my mom's brother, but from all my eaves-dropping in the past, I know the reason why. Jerome met Mom almost twenty years ago in Atlanta while she was attending Spelman College. He was down there filming his second movie—the one that made him a star.

Jerome heard Mom sing and convinced her to drop out of college and move to Los Angeles with him. He told her he knew some people who could make her a star. He was right about Mom. She's a big success. It's just too bad that the very thing he wanted for her is what he resents the most. He's hatin' on her because now she's more famous than he is.

Well, maybe not. It just seems like it because she's wanted

for music and movies and the only thing that Jerome seems to be known for lately is breaking the law.

According to Mom, he was always a troubled soul. She says that Jerome never felt comfortable around her family and took offense at practically everything my grandmother and Uncle Reed said. But it was Jerome's actions toward my grandmother that tore the family apart.

The way I understand it, Mom had gotten into an argument with her mother. Jerome jumped in to defend her, cussing out my grandmother, who then hit him with a frying pan. Jerome shoved her, knocking my grandmother to the floor.

When my grandmother died a couple of weeks later from a heart attack, my uncle blamed Mom and Jerome for her death.

He vowed that if Jerome showed up for the funeral he would be a dead man. I've heard Mom say that Jerome is the reason she couldn't attend her own mother's funeral. He wouldn't let her go without him and Mom didn't want to have drama at the service, so she stayed away. It's still a sore spot for her.

I sit here quietly observing my mom. Her auburn-colored hair is flared out in a wild, uncombed mess. Mom's clothes—a pair of stained sweats and a grubby, oversize sweatshirt that belongs to Jerome—make her seem thinner than she already is.

Mom shivers.

"You okay, Mom?"

Nodding, she reaches into her Prada handbag and pulls out her wallet—along with a little packet of white powder.

My mom's doing hard drugs?!

She quickly tries to cover up the contents with her hand and toss it back into the purse, but isn't quick enough.

Rhyann is always talking about the amount of drugs that get

passed around during some of Hollywood's biggest parties. She amazes me with how much she knows about stuff like that because she's really not one of us.

Rhyann is what my dad calls a hood rat. She attends Stony Hills Prep on scholarship. Otherwise her family couldn't afford it. I've never been to her house because my parents don't like where she lives.

Mimi says Rhyann knows a lot about celebrities because one of her uncles is a drug dealer to the stars. It's common knowledge that he was recently arrested on drug charges, but I don't know if the celebrity connection is true.

Mom gets off the couch, saying, "Stella, I'm going upstairs to lie down for a while."

I rise as well.

Mom turns to me, saying, "Hon, you don't have to babysit me. I just need to get some rest." She kisses my cheek. "I love you, sugar."

Together we make our way up the stairs to the second level. After leaving Mom outside the master suite, I head back to my own room.

I pick up the phone to call Mimi, then realize that she's in class. I'll have to wait until lunchtime, which isn't for another hour.

Time passes slowly.

I turn on my laptop and log on to the Internet, but the first thing I see is a news flash with a photo of Shelly in a corner of the screen and one of Jerome in the center.

I don't want to read another article filled with speculation and gossip about Shelly and Jerome. I'm already on information overload.

When the clock strikes twelve, I reach for my cell phone. Mimi should be getting out of class and on her way to the cafeteria with Rhyann.

"Dee, we were just talking about you."

"What's going on?" I ask Mimi. "Are they still talking about Jerome?"

"Yeah. It's the only thing on anyone's mind right now."

"Even Jordan? He's like the coolest guy in school. Even *him*?"

"Yeah, girl, even Jordan."

"Great," I mutter. "My life is so over."

At the end of the week, Jerome still wasn't home and I was going crazy. Mom wouldn't let me leave the house—not even to go to school or Mimi's house. Now she's finally letting me out of the house. She's finally running in Mom mode again.

I really dread going to Stony Hills this morning. I try every excuse to keep from having to face everyone at school, but she's completely heartless. I call Mimi first thing to have her meet me because I don't want to face the student body alone.

Being the good friend that she is, Mimi is right there, standing near the edge of the campus waiting for my arrival.

"I'll get out here," I tell Leo.

He parks the Mercedes, gets out and comes around to open the door for me.

I slip on my dark sunglasses before stepping out of the car. Even in a crisis, I'm determined to look good.

Mimi runs up to me, greeting me with a hug.

"Girl, thanks so much for meeting me. I hate my life right now."

My schoolmates are more ruthless than the media. Someone

yells out to me in passing, "Your dad really knows how to get a paternity suit dropped!"

Another person asks, "Did your dad really kill that girl, Divine?"

"No," I shout back. "Did yours?" No way am I letting people think they can just say anything to me or about me. So far, I haven't had to show out on anybody. I'm not the only one here with celebrity parents who get in trouble from time to time. I'll just have to endure a few weeks of teasing when it happens— same as any other kid in school.

I'm worried about Mom.

Since Jerome's arrest a week ago, she's been spending a lot of time in her room. I'm sure Stella's just as concerned. Instead of being home with her new husband, she's staying at the house with me and Mom.

"Where's my mom?" I ask Stella shortly after I arrive home from school.

"She's in her room resting," Stella responds without lifting her gaze from the computer monitor. We're in the office, which is where Stella handles all of Mom's business.

"Are you *sure* she's just resting?"

This time Stella raises her gaze to meet mine. "What do you mean by that?"

I remove my backpack from my shoulders and let it dangle downward. "She's high, isn't she? I know about the coke in her purse—"

Stella wouldn't let me finish. "Sweetheart, your mother is very tired, so I convinced her to go upstairs and get some rest."

"Uh-huh." I didn't believe her. "I'm not stupid, you know."

Stella gets to her feet, comes around the desk and takes me by the hand. "C'mere. We need to have a little talk."

I sit down on the couch, staring straight ahead. Stella and Mom grew up together. I know she'd protect Mom with her life, but right now I don't care much for her loyalty.

"Your mother is under a tremendous amount of stress. This . . . this thing with your father is taking a toll on her, Divine. Sometimes, adults need to take medication to help them handle the stress."

"What medication comes in a little plastic bag, Stella?" I question. "Because to me—it looks like coke."

Stella looks surprised by my words.

"I told you I'm not stupid." I fold my arms across my chest. "I have eyes and I know what cocaine looks like."

"How do you know what it looks like?"

"I've seen it before. Jerome's had some in the house."

"Have you ever used—"

I cut her off by saying, "*No* . . . no way. I don't do drugs. I'm never doing that."

Stella releases a soft sigh of relief. She wraps an arm around me. "Honey, your mother loves you so much. She really needs your support right now."

"I love her too. But look at how drugs have messed up Jerome's life. I just don't want Mom to get messed up too. I need her."

I propel my body off the couch. "Stella, I don't care what you say. I'm going upstairs to see my mom."

Standing up, Stella tries to reassure me. "Honey, she's fine— just really tired. Kara didn't sleep well last night. Can you just give her a couple of hours?"

I survey Stella's face, trying to discern if I'm being told the truth.

"I'll call your room when your mama gets up. Okay?"

Nodding, I mumble, "Okay."

I take the steps one at a time up to the second level and tip-toe down the hallway to my mother's bedroom.

I peek inside.

Mom lay curled up in a fetal position, sleeping.

I want to walk over there and climb into bed with her, but I resist the urge. Instead, I close the door and go to my own room.

Sitting cross-legged in the middle of my bed, I pick up the latest copy of *JET* magazine. I gasp when I read the article on my father's previous arrest. I'm pretty sure the next issue will contain a story on Shelly's murder and the fact that Jerome's been arrested for it—even if he's released by then.

Will they even remember to mention that Mom won a Grammy? Or that she is starring in an upcoming movie? Or will they focus all of their attention on Jerome?

I'm restless and not in the mood to do homework, so I decide to take a long walk outside. I love the park-like grounds of our gated estate. My most favorite place here is what I call my secret garden. Mom had a fountain installed and this is where we've shared many mother-daughter moments.

Last summer, my friends and I spent a lot of our time swimming in the Olympic-size pool, or playing tennis on our championship tennis court complete with its own pavilion, barbecue area and bathroom.

Our home boasts eight bedrooms, ten baths, a climate-controlled wine room, gourmet kitchen, a recording studio and a home theater. My room is even equipped with a retractable screen for watching movies with my friends.

I sit down on one of the concrete benches in the secret garden, pondering my future.

We'll get through this, I decide.

Jerome will be found innocent. He'll come home a changed man and insist that I call him Daddy. After this experience, our lives will definitely have to change for the better. I'll finally have a normal family.

chapter 3

I hide out in the limo while Stella and Leo escort Mom out of the Beverly Hills Police Department ten days after Jerome's arrest.

First Jerome ends up in jail and now Mom's been arrested. I can't believe this is happening to me. The media's really going to rip our family to shreds.

Mom was caught on camera beating down some female reporter and then swinging on a police officer when he tried to break up the fight. How ghetto is that?

Some of the kids at school still make jokes whenever I walk by, but they were dying down. Mom's arrest is sure to start things up again.

A tabloid photographer springs out of a bush, landing directly in their path and snapping pictures of my mom.

Leo takes off after the guy while Stella practically drags my mom to the car.

I release a thankful sigh that I'm inside the limo. I'd die from humiliation if my face ended up plastered all over a trashy newspaper with the jail in the background.

Mom tries to kiss me, but I move out of her reach.

"How can you do this to me too?" I want to know. "The kids at school are still making jokes about Jerome. My life is so over, thanks to you. The last time I got in a fight you gave me this long lecture and punished me. But it's okay for you to do it?" I look at her in disgust. "I can't believe you."

"I'm sorry, sugar. I didn't mean to embarrass you."

Oh yeah. Like I really believe that. I turn my back to her, pretending I'm real interested in the scenery outside. I'm actually trying to see if our limo is being followed by reporters.

"It's just that Ava Johnson kept baiting me." Mom is still trying to explain but I really don't care.

"She had the nerve to say that Jerome was planning to leave me for Shelly and that she had on a seven-carat engagement ring when she died. *Can you believe that?* I just couldn't take her any longer. Ava needs to get herself a real job and stop working for that supermarket trash. She's the main reason the whole world is in my marriage in the first place."

I glance over my shoulder at Mom. "No, that would be because you're always on TV telling everybody how happy you are. And how you're always saying the media's giving you and Jerome a bad rap."

Mom uses her fingers to comb through her hair. "You're too

young to understand, Divine. Ava's had it in for me since Jerome dumped her. They were together when he met me."

I turn around in my seat. "Are you going to jail? They just said on the afternoon news that she pressed charges and is going to sue you."

"Ava's decided to drop the charges against me, but I still have to go to court because of the marijuana and cocaine charges." She reaches for bottled water.

I glance over at Stella, who is trying to look busy by going through a stack of papers she just pulled from her briefcase. *What can be so important?* I wonder. I think she's just trying to act like she's not listening to us.

I'm not falling for it. I know she's soaking it in. Just like a sponge. Besides, Mom tells her everything. They have been best friends forever, as my mom likes to tell everybody.

"You know everybody's going to say you're a big drug addict," I blurt out.

Stella's head snaps up, and she gives me this weird look.

What?

Mom says a few choice words that she'd kill me for if I ever repeated them.

Fuming, I settle back against the seat, too angry with Mom to talk to her. It's so unfair. Why can't my parents act like normal ones? Why do they always have to end up in trouble?

Why don't she and Jerome realize that they're ruining my life?

Later that afternoon, I crack open the door to Mom's office so I can listen to the telephone discussion she's having with her lawyer, Marvin Goldbloom. I'm so glad she has him on speakerphone. It makes it much easier on me.

"I'm in a lot of trouble, right?"

"Yes, you are," Mr. Goldbloom confirms. "Not only did you assault a police officer, but you had thirty grams of marijuana and two grams of cocaine in your possession when you were booked. Just the simple possession of any quantity of powdered cocaine is a misdemeanor offense that can get you one year in prison as a first-time offender."

I put a hand to my mouth. How could Mom be so stupid?

"So what can you do to help me?" Mom asks.

"You actually have three options, Kara. Under Proposition 36, you do qualify for treatment, provided that you've never been convicted for the sale or manufacture of drugs," I hear the lawyer explain.

"I haven't," Mom responds.

"Then there's the Diversion program. You would be required to enter a plea of guilty to the drug charge, but you wouldn't be sentenced. Instead, you'd be required to take classes and be tested randomly. If you complete the Diversion program successfully, the case is dismissed."

I want to shout, *Mom, do that one. You won't have to go into rehab,* but I keep quiet. She'd kill me if she knew I was eavesdropping.

"What's the last option?"

"I don't think you want this one, Kara. It's drug court, a special court given the responsibility of handling cases involving drug-addicted offenders through a supervision and treatment program. A period of incarceration is sometimes required, but the case is dismissed when the program is successfully completed."

"You're right, Marvin. I'm not interested in that one. I don't want to be incarcerated. I want to try the first one—Proposition 36, I think you called it."

"You're making a wise decision, Kara."

"I hope so. And I want you to know that I hated having to settle out of court with that witch. One million dollars plus her medical expenses is outrageous. I hope you'll make sure this case goes better."

Now I know why this Ava person suddenly dropped the charges after getting a beat down.

"It's better than serving time in jail, Kara. Besides, Ava was planning to sue you for much more than that. You busted her lip, broke her nose *and* her arm."

"She deserved it."

"Kara, do you think your brother will be willing to be a character witness for you?"

After a brief pause, she responds, "I haven't spoken to him in a long time, but I'll give Reed a call. I just hope I can count on him."

I don't know what my uncle can do for Mom, but I'm hoping he'll forget about the old grudges and be there for her. The last thing I need is to have Mom locked up too.

Mom has totally lost it.

"You want me to go where?" I question, knuckling away the tears dripping from my chin. When she talked about getting help from Uncle Reed, I really thought she meant she wanted him to speak up for her in court. I had no idea that she was planning to send me away.

She has the nerve to wait until the day before her March first court date to tell me. How wrong is that? I know she's upset and all, but Mom's really bugging if she thinks I'm going to some hick town in Georgia.

"Reed and I spoke last night and he's agreed to let you stay with him if I have to go away," Mom says. "Hopefully it's only going to be for a few months—four or five at the most. This is a temporary arrangement, Divine."

The room is filled with dead silence.

"What about school? What will I do about that?"

"You'll finish this year in Georgia."

I shake my head no. "Mom, I can stay here with Mimi."

She pushes a loose curl away from her face. "Oh really? And what about Mimi's parents? Don't they have any say about this?"

Before I can respond, Mom tells me, "It really doesn't matter because you're going to Georgia. I don't want you involved in this media circus going on right now. You see how they're camped outside the gates. I don't want to put you through this."

"Mom, don't do this to me. Please. What about Stella? Why can't I just stay here with her? She usually takes care of me when you travel. Why not this time?"

"Honey, you can barely stand Stella. You complain every time I leave you with her. Besides, she's a newlywed. Reed's on a plane on his way here. When you meet him, you're going to love your uncle. He's a big teddy bear."

Tossing my curls over my shoulders, I state, "I have enough teddy bears. I don't need any more."

Mom glares at me. "I know one thing. You need to watch your tone of voice when you talk to me, Divine. I'm not feeling it today."

Tears roll down my cheeks.

Mom's voice softens. "Look, we don't know what's going to happen when I go to court on Monday, but honey, we have to be prepared. Trust your mama. I know what I'm doing."

"What's so different now? Before it wasn't important for me to get to know him," I snipe. "You just started talking to him yourself. Why didn't you just pick that diversion program Mr. Goldbloom told you about? You could've taken classes and stayed home with me."

"Watch your mouth, young lady," Mom warns. "You need to stay out of grown folks' business. Stop all that eavesdropping."

"If you have to go to rehab, I'd rather stay here with Stella or go stay with Mimi," I insist. "I don't want to go anywhere with your brother."

Mom's tone suddenly changes. She's in Mom mode now. "*I'm not asking.* I've made up my mind. Staying with Reed is what's best for you, Divine."

I wipe away the tears falling down my face. "But I don't even know them."

"Well then, the way I see it, this is the perfect chance to get to know your uncle and his family."

"It's not fair!" I yell before stomping off to my room.

I feel like I'm being punished and I haven't done anything wrong. Waves of anger wash over me to the point that I refuse to speak to Mom or Stella. I stay in my room with the door locked, listening to music.

Three and a half hours later, my uncle arrives.

Curious, I creep down the hallway and stand at the top of the stairs to steal a peek at Pastor Reed Matthews. He's a tad darker than Mom's tawny complexion but they both share the same almond-shaped eyes, high cheekbones and perfect lips. Only his face is round, matching the shape of his body.

It's not long before I'm summoned downstairs to meet the life-size teddy bear.

I go downstairs but I have no intention of being friendly. Maybe if Uncle Reed finds me rude and temperamental, he'll change his mind about taking me back to Georgia with him. Then I can just stay here in California with Mimi.

Mom is all I have left; Jerome is still sitting in jail awaiting *his* trial.

I don't have much to say throughout dinner, so I sit quietly, listening to the boring conversation between Mom and her brother.

"Reed, thank you so much for coming out here. I really appreciate this. I've missed you terribly."

"I've missed you too." He reaches for his glass and takes a sip of water. "How you holding up?"

Mom shrugs. "Okay, I guess. It's my baby over there that I'm worried about, though."

His gaze travels to me. "Are you always so quiet?"

Mom breaks into a short laugh. "Not at all. I have to be honest with you. She's not exactly thrilled about the possibility of having to stay with you for a few months."

"Mom . . ." I can't believe she just called me out like that. She is so in betrayer mode. What did I do to her?

"Well, Divine's never been around us. I can certainly understand her feelings."

I don't need him defending me. It's not going to make me like him any better. Uncle Reed's not getting any cool points from me.

"I'm real sorry about that," Mom confesses. "Jerome didn't want—"

"I know," Reed interjects. "Speaking of Jerome . . . how are things looking for him?"

"Badly. He's told so many lies . . . to me . . . to his lawyers . . ." Mom shakes her head. "They won't even let him out on bail."

They sit for a moment, listening to the silence.

Mom changes the subject. "Do you have any pictures of Phoebe and the kids?"

Uncle Reed's face brightens with his smile. "I sure do."

While they're talking about his children, I continue moving my food around on my plate. I don't have much of an appetite right now. I'm way too upset.

Mom hands me the pictures. "These are your cousins."

I scan the photos briefly before handing them back to her without a word. I'm not interested.

"Alyssa is the same age as you are and Chance is sixteen," Reed announces. "He's a freshman in high school."

I nod but don't respond. I could care less.

Mom glares at me. "If you're done playing around with your food, you can go on upstairs."

I push away from the table.

"Are you all packed?"

Glancing back over my shoulder, I respond, "I'm still working on it." I'm not packing until I actually have to—I'm still holding on to my hope that the judge will let Mom off with a slap on the wrist.

Mom holds out her arms as I'm about to walk past her. "Give me a hug, sweetie."

I do as I'm told.

"Give your uncle one too."

Reed stands up and embraces me. "I'll see you in the morning, Divine."

Whatever.

"This is not going to be easy for her," I hear Mom say when she thinks I'm out of hearing range. "My baby is a major drama queen, Reed, and she can be quite a handful. But I know that spending time with you right now is the best thing for her."

"Kara, you know I'll treat Divine just like I treat my own children."

"I know you will. This is what I'm counting on."

Oh, yeah. Well, Uncle Reed is crazy if he thinks he can handle me. When I get done with his stupid self, he and his family will be sending me back to California. I'm not going to make this easy on Mom or Uncle Reed. If I have to go down Misery Lane, then I'm taking them with me. We all will just be a bunch of unhappy people until I get my way. And I'm getting my way. I'll make sure of it.

chapter 4

The judge sentences Mom to eight months in a rehabilitation center and me to eight months of some serious depression.

This is not the way it played out all those times in my mind. I drop my head into my hands; it's a moment before I can even bring myself to speak.

This is so unfair. Maybe Mom should've offered the judge a million dollars.

"Divine, sweetie, everything is gonna be fine," Mom tells me. "It's not as bad as it sounds."

Who are you trying to kid? I want to ask her.

Mom takes my hand in hers. "Honey, this is the only alternative for me other than doing jail time. When I complete the program, the charges against me will be dropped. I chose rehab because I need help to stop the drugs. To be honest, I might not do it otherwise."

"Eight months is forever, Mom."

"No, it's not. I don't know if I'll be able to call you for a while, but I'll write to you every week."

"Why couldn't he just let you come home? I can't stand him."

"I committed a crime, Divine, and I have to pay for it. It's not the judge's fault. Remember how I'm always telling you that you have to take responsibility for your actions? Well, this is what I have to do."

I try to hold back my tears but they come anyway, rolling down my face.

Mom hugs me. "I've gotta go but I'll see you soon. Before you even know it the eight months will have come and gone."

I don't believe her.

Next, she hugs Uncle Reed. "Thanks so much for taking care of my baby and for being here with me. I love you."

"I love you too. Kara, take care and do what they say. We all want you to come home as soon as you can."

"I will," she promises.

Mom gives me one more look and blows me a kiss before she is taken away. Part of her agreement is that she has to leave from court and head straight to the Wisteria Recovery Center in Santa Barbara for "structured residential treatment," as the judge put it.

"Honey . . . you okay?" Stella inquires.

"Jerome's in jail and my mom's just been sentenced to a treatment center for eight months. What do *you* think?" I snap.

"Divine, we know that this is upsetting for you but it's no cause to be disrespectful," Uncle Reed chastises.

I open my mouth to respond but don't when I notice the stern expression on Uncle Reed's face. He doesn't strike me as the type of man who would tolerate a smart comeback from a fourteen-year-old.

I feel a twisting sensation deep in my belly—some strong emotion struggling to break through the wall I've erected around it. I'm furious with both my parents. They've betrayed me and I will never forgive them. I'm all alone in the world now and I hate this feeling.

I spend the fifty-minute car ride home fantasizing.

In my fantasy, my mom comes to Georgia looking for me but I'm nowhere to be found. Uncle Reed has to tell her that I disappeared shortly after she left for rehab. He's upset and very thin from all those months of searching for me. While everyone is looking for me, I'm in France living it up.

When they find me, my mom is so happy to see me that she doesn't get mad at me for running off. She totally understands and is very cool about it. She tells Uncle Reed off and kicks him out of our lives for good.

I release a long sigh. If only fantasies were real.

Stella offers to help me pack when we get back to the house.

"I can do it," I tell her. She offers to have Miss Eula prepare something for me, but I refuse. I'm mad with Stella too. She's supposed to be Mom's best friend. Why didn't she look out for her better?

Uncle Reed knocks on my bedroom door an hour later. Sticking his head inside, he asks, "Can I come in?"

I nod. What else can I do? It's practically his house now.

"You have much more to pack?"

"I'm almost done."

He sits down on the edge of my bed. "Divine, I know how uncomfortable you must feel about this situation. I just want you to know that we're your family and we care about you. Always have."

"If you care so much for me, you could just let me stay here with Stella," I suggest. "This way I wouldn't have to leave my school. Mom may not have told you this, but I don't do well with change." I'm hoping deep down that there's an understanding bone somewhere in his body. I give him sad eyes, pouty lips—everything.

"Your mother thinks it's best that you live with family. I've known Stella for years and she's a good person. But, Divine— we're your family and we want you with us."

All that work wasted. Uncle Reed isn't buying it. I lift my chin in defiance. "I'm not trying to be rude, but the truth is that I don't want to go home with you."

His expression never changes. "I'm afraid it's not your decision, sweetheart. But look at it this way . . . your mother will be in rehab for less than a year. Eight months isn't that long. When she's released, I'll bring you back here. You only have to deal with us for a few short months."

Sighing in resignation, I give him a sidelong glance. "Do you have any dogs or farm animals running around?"

Uncle Reed laughs. "We live in a small town but not on farmland. We've got paved streets, stoplights and even fast-food restaurants."

Smiling, I respond, "Do you have a mall?"

"There are a couple of shopping centers in the area. Not big malls by any means, but we're not that far away from Atlanta. Your aunt and your cousin love to go there and shop."

We talk for another hour before he goes downstairs, leaving me alone with my thoughts.

Although he seems like a real nice man, I'm still anxious over giving up my pampered lifestyle for a much simpler one.

Tuesday morning, we leave the house shortly after four A.M. to head to the Los Angeles Airport. I stare out the window, wiping away my tears. I pray for a flat tire, a fender bender—anything that'll delay our getting to the airport in time to catch our flight.

We actually arrive an hour and fifteen minutes early. Resigned to my fate, I sit and watch the clock, each tick bringing me closer to my departure.

Despite the early morning departure, I'm wide awake. And I'm even more awake when I realize we'll be sitting side by side in *coach*.

Uncle Reed studies his Bible throughout most of the flight after making several failed attempts to hold a conversation with me. Of course, I just can't be bothered. My neck aches from holding myself rigid in my seat. I refuse to allow my body to come in contact with my uncle's. The seats are way too small . . . I really hate flying coach. Mom knows this but she's going for the gold in trying to ruin my life.

My stomach growls, prompting Uncle Reed to ask, "Hungry?"

"I'm all right."

I refuse anything to eat or drink because the very thought of food makes me queasy. Plus, I've decided to protest my mom's decision to send me to Georgia by starving myself.

Delta Flight 1608 out of LAX touches down in Atlanta at half past four.

"We'll stop and grab a sandwich somewhere when we get to the car," Uncle Reed says after we claim our luggage and head out to the parking deck.

"I'm okay. I'm not hungry," I lie.

Half an hour later, we're driving away from the airport, heading to parts unknown. I console myself with another fantasy. In this one, I pass out from lack of food. The courts grant Mom an emergency leave to come home to me—her very ill daughter. Once we're reunited, Mom promises to never leave me again. She's broken a few shopping dates in the past, but never a real promise.

Mom will be so sorry that I almost died, she'll do whatever she can to make it up to me—including buying me my very own mall.

I'm enjoying my fantasy until I notice the sign that Temple is only a few miles down the road.

Reality sets in.

I sit a moment in the car, eyeing the scene before me. A tall woman and two teenagers are standing in the yard of a modest ranch-style house that is so small it could probably fit inside my mom's twelve-thousand-square-foot mansion five times. They have to be my Aunt Phoebe and my cousins, Chance and Alyssa.

We're barely out of Uncle Reed's black Cadillac before he begins the introductions.

Before he can finish, Aunt Phoebe throws her arms around me, nearly choking me to death in a bear hug. Her big hair blinds me and she's smearing lipstick on my face. "Hey, Divine. Welcome."

I can't believe how tall she is. She's got to be at least six feet tall.

My female cousin is next. "I'm Alyssa. It's real nice to finally meet you."

"You too," I mumble, eyeing her braces. I guess invisible braces haven't made it down South yet. I'm amazed that she and I bear such a strong resemblance to each other, especially since I've always thought I looked more like Jerome. Maybe I need glasses.

Chance holds out his hand to me. "Hey, Divine."

I shake his hand. "Nice meeting you." Chance is the spitting image of his mother. He has her new-penny coloring, her dimpled cheeks and her height. Aunt Phoebe is at least two inches taller than Uncle Reed, so he's got to be at least five eight or nine.

"Well, let's not keep the child outside like this," Uncle Reed comments. "It's chilly. Y'all can all get to know each other inside the house."

I hesitate a moment before following my relatives inside, looking around and checking out the neighborhood, if you could call it that. I'm in the middle of nowhere.

"What's the name of this town again?" I ask Alyssa, trying to be sarcastic.

"Temple, Georgia," she announces.

"You say it like it's something to be proud of."

Her expression changes and her smile disappears. "This is my home. Why shouldn't I be proud? C'mon, I'll show you where you gon' be sleeping."

Following her into the house, I slide the straps of my Louis Vuitton backpack off my shoulders. I eye the photos on the wall as we make our way to who knows where. They're probably going to put me in a cellar.

Family pictures. Hmmph. The only family photos of us are hidden in my parents' bedroom and in stacks of photo albums that nobody ever bothers to open.

My eyes travel the rooms as we walk through the house. Modestly decorated, the living room looks like it could grace the cover of *Country Living* magazine. The dining room is more formal, with dark, gleaming cherry-wood furniture. All the walls are a boring eggshell color. No imagination.

"We're here," Alyssa announces proudly. She steps aside to let me enter a bedroom that looks like it's been drenched in Pepto-Bismol. Ugh.

I love flowers but not all over the bed. The floral décor carries over to the wallpaper border, the curtains and even the rug.

Ugh. I hate pink with a passion. I hate twin beds more. The last time I slept in a twin bed, I was a toddler.

My chest constricts and I'm struggling to breathe. Spying the window, I rush toward it, opening it.

"What's the matter?" Alyssa wants to know.

"I can't breathe . . ." I manage between sucking in deep gulps of air. "This room . . . it's the size of my closet." With my head out the window, my breathing returns to normal.

I turn around to find Alyssa standing with her arms crossed over her chest, watching me with an amused expression on her face.

"Feel better now?"

I nod. I prepare to close the window, but Alyssa stops me by saying, "You might wanna just leave it open. You and I are sharing this *closet*."

"Why?" I want to know. "I'm not afraid to sleep by myself."

"This is *my* bedroom and while you're staying here with us, you're gonna need somewhere to sleep."

"Why don't you and your brother share?" I suggest. The idea works for me.

"Like I just said, this is my bedroom."

"I'm not used to sleeping in a room with another person. I'm sorry but I can't do it."

Alyssa points to the door. "Well, you can always sleep outside in the hall, 'cause we don't have another bedroom."

I sigh in resignation. "Where do I put my clothes?"

This time, she points across the room to a mirrored sliding door. "In there."

My mouth drops open in shock. "Is this all of it?" I question after taking a peek inside.

"Yeah."

"You can't be serious. I can't hang all of my clothes in there," I complain. "There's not enough room."

"Just put what'll fit and take the rest to the garage for now. Daddy's gon' buy something for you to hang your clothes in." Alyssa drops down on the edge of her bed, watching me. "Look, cuz . . . let's get something straight right now. You're not in Hollywood anymore . . . *okay*? You're living in Temple, Georgia, and down here we live like regular people."

I want to cry. Then, to further my distress, my stomach decides to protest once more, a solid reminder that I haven't eaten.

"Dinner should be ready soon," Alyssa tells me. Great. She's got the hearing of a dog.

"I'm a vegan," I announce, lying through my teeth. I'm not going to make this easy on them.

"What in the world is that?"

I'm not exactly sure myself, so I tell her, "I don't eat meat."

"Oh. Here we call people like you vegetarian."

"I'm not a vegetarian. I'm a *vee-gan*."

"Whatever . . ."

No she didn't just dismiss me with a wave of her hand!

"We have some celery and I think some carrots in the refrigerator. I can fix you a plate if you want me to."

"No thanks."

Shrugging, Alyssa leaves the room while I take a seat on the edge of the cot I'm supposed to sleep in, pondering my future.

Thirty minutes later, I'm summoned to the dining room.

After we all sit down, Aunt Phoebe places her hands on the table and I notice that everyone else follows suit—everyone but me.

Uncle Reed looks over at me. "We're getting ready to bless the food."

"Okay," I respond.

Alyssa turns to me saying, "Give me your hand. We hold hands while we bless our meals."

I open my mouth to ask why, but Aunt Phoebe's expression makes me change my mind. Reluctantly, I take my cousin's hand.

Then Uncle Reed closes his eyes and says, "Oh, Heavenly Father, we come before You today to say thank You. Thank You for the meal we're about to eat for the nourishment of our bodies. Thank You for the person whose hands prepared the food. In Jesus' name we pray. Amen."

I release a soft sigh of relief. I thought the man was going to pray forever. It's only food . . .

"Alyssa tells me you're a vegan, so I made you a green salad with a balsamic vinaigrette dressing," Aunt Phoebe chirps. "I'm sorry I don't have any tofu."

Tofu? Why would I want tofu? Yuck. I glance down at the unappealing salad and frown. Everyone else at the table is eating pork chops, mashed potatoes, French-style green beans and homemade biscuits.

"I'm not real hungry." Especially if I have to settle for salad.

"You have to put something in your stomach, Divine. We don't want you getting sick, sweetheart."

I'm starving myself, lady. Just shut up.

I can feel Uncle Reed's eyes on me, so I nibble on the rabbit food while the rest of them throw down on some real food. I make a mental note to find out exactly what a vegan eats.

Mimi calls me later that evening to see how things are going.

"I've been banished to a matchbox," I whine. "Mimi, it's horrible. I don't even have my own room."

Mimi tries consoling me but being the drama queen that I am, I would have none of it. "What do you mean calm down? Girl, if you were snatched out of your mansion and forced to live in some tiny little house in the middle of nowhere, you wouldn't just *calm down* either. You're not hearing me, Mimi. I live with a bunch of strangers I don't know and I'm going to die. Do you hear me? *I can't do this.* And don't you go telling people where I am."

"So what do I tell them?"

I take a minute to think of something that wouldn't make me sound like such a loser. "Tell them I'm vacationing in Europe. Tell them I had to escape all the reporters. Anything but the truth, Mimi."

"Okay. Don't worry. I won't tell a soul."

"I can't believe this is my life," I mutter.

"I feel so bad for you, Dee. This is just wrong. Your being sent away like that."

"I feel like I'm the one being punished."

"I'd run away if I were in your shoes. There's no way I'd just stay there with strangers. Don't you still have one of your mother's credit cards? Just leave and fly back here."

Mimi's well-meaning chatter doesn't help. "Nobody understands," I moan. "Mimi, I have to go. I'll give you a call sometime tomorrow." I hear footsteps behind me and add, "That is, *if* I survive Hick Middle," and hang up.

"It's actually Temple Middle School," Alyssa informs me coolly. "You know, you might want to keep your voice down just a little bit. That way we can't hear you insulting us."

"I wasn't—"

Alyssa cuts me off. "You *were* and I have some advice for you, Hollywood. We didn't ask for this any more than you did. Let's just try to make the best of a bad situation. Okay?"

I fake a yawn.

"You should put your clothes away. If you don't, you'll have no place to sleep."

"My maid usually takes care of stuff like that for me." Smiling, I ask, "You think maybe you could hang them up for me?"

Alyssa flashes me this look of disbelief. "Around here, you're your own maid. Come with me, Hollywood, and I'll show you how it's done."

She's trying to be funny. I roll my eyes and decide I'll be the more mature person and let her comment slide.

She pulls a hanger from the closet and says, "This little thing is called a hanger. You hang your clothes on it."

"*I know what it is,*" I snap. "Only I usually use padded hangers. We'd never use wire in our house."

Alyssa releases an impatient sigh. "Well, Hollywood, we don't have any padded hangers around here. But if you look real hard, you might be able to find a few plastic ones."

"I'll buy some tomorrow," I announce. "I prefer padded hangers." I give her a tiny smile. "If you're nice to me, I might even buy you some. Wire can rust your clothes and from the looks of things, you need all of yours."

"Whatever," Alyssa utters. "I'll leave you to your work. I've got homework to do."

My cell phone rings.

It's Rhyann, my semibest friend. I like Rhyann a lot, but she hasn't elevated to the level of closeness I share with Mimi. I tell Mimi everything. Rhyann only gets to know some things, like newly discovered makeup tips, cool outfits and parties. I don't share much deep personal stuff with her.

"Dee, where are you? Mimi just called and told me that you've been sent to some small town in Georgia."

"I wasn't *sent* anywhere," I correct her. "For the moment, I'm staying in a place called Temple with relatives. I just needed to get away because I'm tired of being hounded by the media."

"Hold on, I'm calling Mimi right now on three-way. We need to help you get out of there. How far are you from Atlanta? I have some cousins there."

Rhyann's just been upgraded to full best friend status. She actually cares about my plight.

I hear Mimi's voice.

"Dee, I hope you aren't mad at me for telling Rhyann where you really are. I'll tell everybody else that you're in Europe."

"I'm not mad," I tell her, but I make a mental note that Mimi is a blabbermouth. When her evaluation comes up, I'm going to have to address this.

Rhyann jumps into the conversation. "Dee, what can we do to get you back home?"

"Mother says you can still come live with us," Mimi announces.

"My uncle is not going to let me go back to Los Angeles without Mom's permission." I realize my slipup too late.

Rhyann doesn't seem to notice. "Girl, I know what you need to do. You need to write your mom and tell her just how horrible things are for you there," she suggests. "Your mom will probably agree to anything if you make her feel guilty for sending you to live with complete strangers."

"Yeah," Mimi agrees.

Rhyann's definitely my new best friend. Especially since it's pretty clear that Mimi has told her everything. "I like it. I'll write the first one tonight and send it off to her tomorrow. I'll even make sure the paper's all stained with my tears."

"I bet it'll work," Mimi contributes. "My parents hate to see me cry. It gets them every time."

"It don't work on my Aunt Selma," Rhyann confesses. "That woman don't care about nothing. I could die and she wouldn't care. But I'm sure it'll work on your mom. She looks like the sensitive type."

Rhyann's mother died in a car accident three years ago and she and her brothers and sisters were sent to live with her aunt. Rhyann's the only person I know who has no idea who her father is.

We plot my escape until Rhyann's aunt makes her get off the telephone.

After my shower, I plop down on the narrow cot in my prison cell to write my letter.

Dear Mom,

I'm here in Temple, GA, where you wanted me to be and I have to tell you—it's horrible. I am in the middle of nowhere and sharing a cramped little room with my cousin. You can't imagine how small the rooms are in this house. I have to sleep by the window because I can barely breathe.

Mom, you didn't raise me in such conditions, so how am I supposed to survive? It's not my fault that I've led a good life. I know you might think this is the right decision but please reconsider. I am not used to such SMALL rooms and it's really affecting my health. I need space. I need to be able to BREATHE.

I hope you're doing well. I miss you so much. As you look around the room you're staying in right now, think about what I'm going through. This is not the life you wanted for me.

Mimi's parents are still okay with me living with them. Just call and talk to them please.

I love you forever,
Divine

P.S. I practically sleep in a crib and my clothes are hanging in the garage.

I read over the letter once more, and then again to make sure I don't have any misspelled words. I sprinkle water on the paper to make sure it looks really tearstained. I want Mom to see just how sad and miserable I am.

If she doesn't change her mind after reading this letter . . . I might as well jump off a bridge.

Hmmm . . . I wonder if maybe I should include that in my letter.

No way. Knowing my mom, she'll send me off to some therapist—or worse, have me hospitalized. That's what she did to Jerome when he once threatened to commit suicide.

Jerome says that made him look weak and ruined his acting career. He always played the tough guy in action-adventure movies, so to be placed in a mental ward. . . . Man, he was really angry with her. He's still angry with her for that because he brings it up a lot when they're arguing.

The image of Jerome being taken off to a padded cell brings a tiny smile to my face. Then the reality of his situation brings tears to my eyes.

chapter 5

"*What* is that horrible sound?" I mumble, pulling the covers over my head to shut out a high-pitched screeching.

"A rooster," Alyssa mumbles sleepily.

I shoot up in bed. *"A what?"*

Alyssa repeats her words. "Don't tell me you've never seen one before."

"No, I haven't. Girl, you *really* live in the country."

"Your mama was born and raised just down the road, Miss Hollywood, so that makes you just as country as the rest of us."

Rolling my eyes at Alyssa's back, I lay down and bury my face beneath the covers once more.

I'm pulled out of sleep a second time when Aunt Phoebe blows into the room an hour later.

"Good morning," she greets in that piercing voice of hers. Her deep Southern accent is going to drive me insane. "Get up, girls. Y'all need to get ready for school. We gon' have to leave a lil earlier than usual so that we can get Divine registered."

Groaning, Alyssa crawls out of bed. "C'mon, Hollywood. Time to get up."

"Alyssa Leann Matthews, don't you call your cousin that," Aunt Phoebe admonishes. "You don't want to hurt her feelings."

"It's okay," I interject. "I know she's just teasing me. Right, *Country*?"

She gives me a tight smile while Aunt Phoebe looks from me to her. After a moment, Aunt Phoebe says, "Okay, get moving," and heads to the door. "Breakfast is almost ready. Divine, I just fixed a bowl of fruit for you. I'll be going to the grocery store this afternoon and I'll pick up some stuff for you. If you would, make me a list of your favorite foods."

Aunt Phoebe is barely out of the door before I run across the hall to the bathroom. I'm not taking a shower after *these* people.

The bathroom is amazingly clean, for which I'm thankful. I'm very particular about where I bathe.

When I come out twenty minutes later, Alyssa takes one look at me and snaps, "Did you leave any hot water for the rest of us? And you need to hang up your towel when you're done with it."

I simply ignore her. She is so beneath me.

I'm dressed by the time Alyssa comes back into the bedroom, wrapped in a towel.

She takes a long look at me and asks, "Girl, where do you think you going? We ain't going to no party. Just to school."

I glance down at my rhinestone tank top and ruffled silk peasant skirt. My outfit probably cost more than all the furniture in the house. "What's wrong with my outfit?"

"Don't you own some jeans and a plain ol' shirt? You don' need all that glittery stuff. Makes me itch just looking at you. All the attention gon' be on you, anyway, Hollywood, because you new to the area. You don't have to work so hard. I already know how much you like to be in the limelight. I see the way you act on television whenever a camera is around."

"I like what I have on," I snap. "I'm wearing this." I play with the bangles dangling on my arm. "Even though I'm being forced to live in this hick town, I'm not giving up on style and good fashion sense."

"Whatever, Hollywood." Alyssa gives me this strange look, then chuckles before slipping on a pair of faded denim jeans, a white T-shirt and an Old Navy sweatshirt. "Oh, it's really cold outside in the mornings, so I hope you have something a little heavier than that jacket you had on yesterday."

"I'm wearing my leather coat. The one that matches these brown leather boots I have on."

Alyssa makes a goofy face and claps her hands. "Good for you," she squeals. "I'm sure you'll look quite fashionable. Too bad there won't be anybody around to snap pictures of you."

"That's like . . . so mature," I reply. I hear Aunt Phoebe calling us. "We're being summoned."

"I'm ready. Let's go."

When I strut into the dining room, my aunt and uncle survey me from head to toe but don't comment. I take a seat across from Alyssa without saying a word.

Everyone prepares for one of Uncle Reed's never-ending

prayers. Holding Uncle Reed's hand in my left and Chance's hand in my right, I sit with my eyes closed, using this time to figure out what I'm going to wear tomorrow.

My mouth waters at the sight of stacks of bacon cooked just right. Not too hard and not too soft. Aunt Phoebe is torturing me with her big, fluffy-looking biscuits. It's the one thing my mom always cooked and I loved her biscuits. Mom always used her mother's recipe and I'm pretty sure Aunt Phoebe does too.

I reach for one, but then stop myself. I'm supposed to be a vegan. I've got to find out what a vegan is.

Alyssa isn't helping when she pushes the plate of biscuits toward me. "Have one. Mama makes the best biscuits in the world. They're so light and fluffy . . ."

My plans to starve myself and pretend being a vegan are forced to the side as I grab not one, but two biscuits.

I ignore Alyssa's laughter as I pile gobs of butter on the warm bread.

"I guess your vegan days are over," she remarks.

"I love biscuits. Mom makes them just like this." I sink my teeth into the light, fluffy bread. "This is sooo good."

"It's your grandmother's recipe," Uncle Reed announces. "She only gave the recipe to your mother and my wife."

I say, "Mom says she'll give it to me on my wedding day."

He chuckles. "That's what Mama did. She gave it to Kara and Phoebe on their wedding days along with a few other recipes."

"Mom only makes biscuits. We have a cook to prepare the other foods."

"I love to cook," Aunt Phoebe announces.

"I do too," Alyssa contributes, as if I care.

"I don't," I make clear. "I intend to hire a chef when I'm grown."

Uncle Reed changes the subject. "Divine, we want you to know that we're so glad to have you with us. We want you to feel welcome in our house. You're family and whatever we have is yours."

"Thank you, Uncle Reed." The only problem with that is that I don't *want* anything they have. They're poor from the looks of it. Maybe this is about money.

"Since you're part of this family and will be living here, we have rules that we expect you to follow—same as Chance and Alyssa. We also expect you to help out around the house."

I look over at Uncle Reed. "Help out? In what way?"

"We all have chores, Divine," Chance contributes. "Dad gives us an allowance."

I relax. "Oh. Well, I don't need an allowance. I'm rich."

Uncle Reed meets my gaze. "I don't care how *rich* you think you are, young lady. You *will* help out around here. Is that clear? Now, your mama has arranged for a monthly stipend to help with your expenses, including your allowance."

"Stipend." I know that word. It was my daily word sometime last week. I have a word emailed to me each morning along with the definition and pronunciation key. I'm trying to enlarge my vocabulary so it's my goal to learn a new word every day. Stipend means a fixed or regular payment.

I swallow my despair. My nightmare is just beginning.

The kids at school openly gawk at me as I follow my aunt and Alyssa into the office at Temple Middle School.

"They're just starstruck," I tell Alyssa. "In a few days, this should all die down."

"Whatever," she responds nonchalantly.

A couple of people even break out cameras to take pictures of me. I make sure they capture my best side.

"You sure love the camera, Hollywood," Alyssa comments.

"Don't hate," I say. "I'm famous and people like taking pictures of famous people. I might as well warn you—now that I'm staying at your house, you're probably going to have more friends than you can count."

Alyssa shrugs off my words. "I already have more friends than I can count."

I check my watch and release a long sigh. It's only five A.M. in Los Angeles. I desperately need to talk to Mimi. My life totally sucks right now.

Half an hour later, I'm officially a student at Temple Middle School and on my way to my first class. Biology—something I can't stand. I'd rather drink a bottle of blood than study biology.

Well, maybe not blood.

I'm introduced to the class, then I'm told to find a seat anywhere. How about on a plane back to L.A.? That'll work for me.

The boy sitting across from me inquires, "Hey, you Kara Matthews' daughter?"

I nod.

"Your mom is hot!"

"Thanks," I reply. Then I wonder, *What about me? Don't you think I'm hot too?*

I look around and notice there are a lot of cute boys in this hick school. For the short time I plan to be here, maybe it won't be so bad.

I spend my first day in biology smiling at the boy beside me with the pretty eyes. On the other side, some chick is sitting there rolling her eyes at me. I discover pretty quickly that the females in this school aren't friendly at all. I can't help it that I'm cute and rich.

"I don't know why everybody actin' like she so special," I overhear someone say as I'm heading to my next class. "Her daddy is a murderer. He killed that girl."

"I bet he killed her because he didn't want the truth coming out about that baby," someone else contributes.

Fuming, I turn around to face the two girls and demand, "How can you be so sure? Were you there?"

My questions are met with silence.

"Were you there?" I ask a second time.

Students stop in their tracks and gather around us, probably hoping for the thrill that comes with watching a fight. Kids are so immature.

"No, I wasn't there," the tallest of the two responds after a moment. "I didn't have to be there to know that he's guilty. Your daddy don't do nothing but stay in trouble. He goes to jail all the time."

"*He's a celebrity,* duh. People are always targeting him for something. Besides, you shouldn't believe everything you read in gossip magazines. Like, read a novel—it's more interesting." I can't resist adding, "That's if you can read at all."

"What did you say?" She inches closer to me.

I'm supposed to be scared now but I'm not about to back down from this Amazon woman. "I didn't stutter."

Alyssa suddenly breaks through the crowd like Superwoman. "What's going on? Divine, you okay?"

"I'm fine." I don't need protecting. I guess she thinks I'm too cute to fight. *Not.*

My cousin turns to the Amazon. "May, what's the problem?"

"Nothing. Me and Cozetta was just having a discussion about your uncle being guilty of murder. I guess your little cousin can't handle the truth."

"The *truth* will come out," I vow. I'm so ready to knock May's buckteeth right out of her mouth. Little does she know that I have my green belt in tae kwon do.

"May, my cousin's been through enough with what's going on. Just leave her alone."

"I'm not bothering her—in fact, I wasn't even talking to her. Me and Cozetta was talking. She the one getting all up in our faces."

"Yeah, I was up in your face." My eyes never leave hers. "I wanted to know if you or your friend witnessed Shelly's murder. Because if you did, then I'm sure the D.A. would love to talk to the two of you." I pull out my cell phone.

The one named Cozetta decides to jump in. "Girl, you don't know who you messing with. May will take you out."

"I don't think so. Don't let the designer clothes and the man-icured nails fool you," I warn. "I may be beautiful, but I *will* fight." I then add a few choice words for flavor.

Alyssa grabs my arm. "C'mon, Divine. You need to get to class and put away that phone. Cell phones aren't allowed at school."

I act like I'm about to lunge at Cozetta, knowing that my cousin will stop me. She doesn't let me down.

"Divine, c'mon. Let's go. Oh, and you don't need to be say-ing words like that. Mama always says that ladies don't cuss."

Whatever. I allow Alyssa to lead me through the crowd, sat-isfied that I now have a reputation for being a fighter. I hope I don't have to worry about any more confrontations.

"I hope she's not a friend of yours." I want to know where Alyssa's loyalties lie.

My cousin shakes her head. "Nope. I've known her all my life though. You have to ignore her. May just likes to gossip. She always trying to bully people. Cozetta's all talk. She can't fight a lick—she'll just push May to do it for her."

"I don't like to fight but I will, so she better leave Jerome's name out of her mouth. And mine. I didn't come down here for all this drama."

Alyssa laughs out loud like I just told her something really funny. "Says the drama queen. Girl, you're all *about* the drama. C'mon, admit it."

"Not when it comes to Jerome or my mom."

"Why do you call your dad by his first name?"

"Because that's what he wants me to do."

"I wouldn't dream of calling my daddy Reed. He'd kill me."

I shrug. "Like it's a big deal. It's his name." I point to Room 231. "This is my class. See you later."

"Meet me outside this class afterward. We have the same lunchtime. I'll show you where the cafeteria is located."

"Great," I mutter under my breath.

A couple of girls whisper and snicker as I walk into the classroom.

The horsefaced teacher, Miss Wilson, accepts the paperwork I give her and tells me to find an empty seat. I consider giving her the number of a Beverly Hills plastic surgeon who could do wonders to help her. I'm not surprised she's such a mean woman. At least that's all I heard about her in my last class. With a face like that, who wouldn't be mean?

I do as she instructs, finding a seat toward the back of the class. History is one of my favorite classes, so I decide to hold off on a nap until after lunch.

When Miss Wilson announces that the class has been studying the events that led up to the bombing of Pearl Harbor, I have to try and contain my excitement.

Ever since visiting Pearl Harbor during our last trip to Hawaii, I've been hungry for more information, specifically on the USS *Arizona*.

"I've been there," I announce. "To Pearl Harbor. I go to Hawaii every year with my mom—"

"That's great," Miss Wilson quickly interjects. "Then this project the class is about to do should be a bit of a breeze for you. All of you will have to select one of the naval ships that was docked in the harbor during the attack and write a report on it."

At this, the entire class groans.

I'm thrilled. I already know that my report will be on the USS *Arizona*.

When the bell rings forty minutes later, I'm almost disappointed. I could spend all day in a history class.

I meet my cousin for lunch.

"Alyssa, just so you know . . . I don't need you coming to my aid," I tell her after we find an empty table in the cafeteria. "I can take care of myself."

Spreading mustard and ketchup on her hamburger, Alyssa gives a slight shrug. "I can see that."

"Then why did you interfere?"

"Because the last thing you need is to get on Mr. McPhearson's bad side."

"Who's he?" I bite into my apple. I'd settled for fruit because the hamburgers looked dry, the pizza half-cooked and the other foods unidentifiable.

"Our principal," Alyssa states. "And he loves sending kids home. Suspension is his middle name, so you better watch yourself."

"I didn't start it."

"It doesn't matter, Divine. If you're caught fighting, you'll be suspended for at least three days."

"I'm not just going to stand around and let somebody trash me or my parents. Hmmph. I'll gladly take the suspension."

"I know . . . I feel the same way, but you got to try and ignore people."

"I don't expect you to understand, Alyssa. People are always in my family's business. I get tired of it. Why don't they just worry about their own lives and stay out of ours?"

"That's the price you pay for fame."

I toss my half-eaten apple. "Like I said, you wouldn't understand." My eyes travel the length of the cafeteria. "This is your life."

"And now it's yours."

By the time school ends, I've picked up five phone numbers. Once I get home, I'll do an evaluation on each boy and decide who will be the lucky guy to hang out with me.

"Those your class notes?" Alyssa inquires when she walks up to me.

"Real funny." Waving the little scraps of paper at her, I say, "These are phone numbers."

"Boys or girls?"

"Boys," I respond. "I don't go around collecting phone numbers from girls. Ugh."

We head to the nearest exit doors.

"Did you at least talk to another female today?"

I shake my head no. "Why should I?"

Alyssa gives me this puzzled look, like she can't figure me out. "Don't you want any friends?"

"I have friends. I don't need any more."

"Yeah, but they're in California."

"I have friends all over the world, Alyssa."

"But you don't have any in Temple."

"No, I don't," I admit. "But I have you, and for the short time I'm going to be here you'll have to do." I stop walking. "Where's your mom? I don't see her car."

"That's because we walk home."

"You're kidding me, right?"

"Nope. C'mon, let's go. Chance will be waiting for us on the next block."

"I don't walk anywhere," I huff. This girl is totally out of her mind. I pull out my cell phone and tell Alyssa, "I'm calling a taxi."

"Divine, we only live ten blocks away. It's not that far."

I dial 411. "I need the number for a taxi service in Temple, Georgia. Could you connect me please? Hey, what's your address?" I ask Alyssa.

"2811 Brent Avenue. See you later, Hollywood."

"You sure you don't just want to ride with me to the house?" I yell out to her.

"Girl, I'll be home long before that cab even shows up."

chapter 6

$\mathcal{A}$lyssa's sitting at the breakfast counter eating a bag of potato chips when I arrive home forty minutes later. She takes one look at me and bursts into laughter. "So, how long did it take the cab?"

I ignore her.

"How was your first day at school?" Aunt Phoebe inquires when she walks into the kitchen.

"Horrible," I mutter. "I'm supposed to be in honors classes, but they put me with idiots. Everybody is so slow here. The stuff they're studying here, I had when I was in sixth grade."

Aunt Phoebe gives me this hard look before saying, "Divine, sweetheart, I don't know if you should be so quick to judge. You've only been to school one day."

"She's not gonna make many friends," Alyssa contributes. "I can tell you that right now."

"I'm not looking for friends in Temple. I already have plenty of friends." I flick a piece of lint off my jacket. "Friends that are in the same league as me."

"Girl, just 'cause your mama got money don't mean a thing," Alyssa snaps. "In fact, a lot of children with celebrity parents are crazy, the way I see it."

I can't believe she's saying this to me. Who does she think she is? "You need to stop reading supermarket gossip magazines."

Aunt Phoebe holds up her hand. "Okay. That's quite enough. Alyssa, apologize to your cousin."

"Mama, I'm tired of Divine's constant complaining and her thinking she's so much better than us. Her daddy's in jail for murder and her mom is in rehab for drugs. And she thinks we're the ones with problems? Hmmph. I don't think so."

Tears stinging the back of my eyes, I run out of the house. I can't stand Alyssa.

I call Mimi. "Commiserate" is my word for today. It means to feel or express sorrow or pity for; sympathize with. I need someone to commiserate with.

"I hate it here," I cry as soon as my friend answers her phone. "I want to come home."

Mimi attempts to calm me down by telling me about her crush on some new boy in school.

"Divine, he's sooo cute," she gushes, making me sick to my stomach. "We were lab partners today and I could tell by the way he was looking at me he's interested, Divine. Can you believe it? He's . . ."

Tuning her out, I wonder how she can talk about boys at a time like this. My life is over and here she is talking about some guy who probably isn't even aware that she's alive.

When I can't bear to listen to any more of Mimi's ramblings, I interrupt and say, "Look, this is supposed to be about me right now. What I need is for you to listen to me for a change. I'm having some real problems right now. Okay?"

I abruptly end the call. I don't even want to hear her stupid voice right now. Mimi tries to call me back but I don't answer. I don't intend to talk to her for at least two days. That'll teach her.

Alyssa and I avoid each other for the rest of the evening since we're not talking to each other. I make sure to use all of the hot water before I go to bed.

I don't just get mad—I get even.

Alyssa is up and dressed by the time I wake up the next morning. She catches on quick.

I glance over at the clock to see if she intentionally let me sleep in. I'm suspicious because it's something I would've done to her.

It's seven o'clock.

I get out of bed without saying a word to her. She packs up her books and leaves the room.

I'm dressed and ready fifteen minutes later. I'm applying the finishing touches to my hair when Alyssa returns with the message, "Daddy wants to see you."

Looking over my shoulder, I question, "For what?"

"Go find out," she snaps.

I follow her out of the bedroom and down the hall.

Uncle Reed is in the kitchen when we walk in.

"Morning, Divine."

"Good morning," I respond.

"I hear you and Alyssa are having a little disagreement. What's the problem?"

"I don't have a problem," I state. "Your daughter is the one with the problem."

Uncle Reed's eyes travel to Alyssa. "What do you have to say on this matter?"

"I do have a big issue with her," she admits. "She's too snobby for me. She thinks she's better than us and I don't like it, sir. She talks about us like a dog to her friends."

"Sweetheart, what have I told you?"

Alyssa sighs. "People talked about Jesus Christ. They did much worse to Him but He died for our sins anyway."

"Words can't kill us, Alyssa."

I stand there with a big grin on my face. That's what she gets for tattling.

Uncle Reed turns to me. "Divine, you've been blessed with parents who could afford to give you everything your heart desires and that's okay. In this house, we strive to give our children the truly important things, like love and security, and we teach them about the love of Christ. We're not concerned about giving them material things."

I'm not sure how to respond to this.

"You don't have to flaunt your wealth in our faces, Divine. My sister—your mother—grew up in a little house just down the road. One smaller than this. Kara's always wanted to give you all the things she didn't have, but in my opinion, that's not always the right thing to do."

I'm wondering what this has to do with me.

"I expect you and Alyssa to treat one another with respect. I don't care how much money you have or don't have—we are family. You can't put a price tag on that."

"Yes, sir," Alyssa inserts.

"Whatever is going on between you two—work it out."

Uncle Reed leaves Alyssa and me alone in the kitchen. She stares at the refrigerator while I concentrate on one of the cabinets.

Chance comes in, putting an end to our staring contest. "Y'all ready to leave?"

"I just need to get my backpack," I respond and rush out of the kitchen.

Alyssa and Chance are standing on the porch whispering when I return. About me, I suspect.

We head out to school.

Chance makes several attempts to start a conversation, but Alyssa won't say a word. When she spots a couple of girls ahead of us, she takes off running to catch up with them, leaving us behind.

"What's going on between y'all?" he asks.

"It's not a big deal."

"My school's right down here. You know the way to Temple Middle?"

"No."

"Then you might wanna catch up with Alyssa, so you won't get lost. See you later."

I'm so screwed.

I walk a little faster to try and keep up with Alyssa. She and her friends are still up ahead. Every now and then, one of them turns around to see if I'm still behind them.

Like where am I going to go?

I almost break into a run trying to keep up with them. *Why is everyone walking so fast?* I wonder. We're not late for school.

I stop on the edge of campus to catch my breath. My heart is beating fast and my chest feels like it's about to burst. I lean against the metal fence and bend over, panting. I'm convinced they're trying to kill me.

Alyssa is suddenly standing over me. "Hey, you okay?"

I'm touched by her concern but I'm still mad with her. "Yeah," I grunt.

She pulls a water bottle out of her backpack. "Here . . . take a few sips."

"Did you drink out of this?" I don't drink behind people, not even my own mom.

"Drink," she orders.

After a moment, I take the bottle, open it and take several sips. "Thanks."

"Get me out of class if you need to," she says. "If you don't feel better. Do you have like a bad heart or asthma?"

"No," I say. "Why?"

"Because of the way you're breathing right now. We'll take it easy going home today. Keep the water with you."

Alyssa walks me to class like I'm some baby.

"I'm okay."

"See you later," she says.

Alyssa checks on me throughout the morning.

During lunch, she apologizes to me. "I'm sorry about this morning."

I finish off my soda.

"I'm also sorry for the mean things I said to you yesterday."

I shrug. "It's true. My parents are locked up. The whole world knows it and for sure won't let me forget about it, so why should you?"

"Because I'm your family. I shouldn't have thrown it in your face like that."

"You only said what you felt about me."

"Divine, before you came, I had all sorts of plans for us. I wanted so much for us to be close, but then you came . . . you came with this attitude."

"I'm going through a lot, Alyssa."

"I know that and I should be more understanding. Let's start over. Okay?"

"Sure."

The two girls from this morning come over to sit at our table. Alyssa introduces me to her best friend Stacy and Penny, who's her cousin on her mother's side.

"I'm glad to meet you both—especially since you tried to help Alyssa kill me this morning."

Confused, they give Alyssa a puzzled look. She laughs and tells them, "Hollywood's talking about our speed-walking. She don't know nothin' 'bout that."

We spend our lunch laughing and talking about our favorite singers, boys and makeup. It really feels good just to be able to laugh. I hadn't realized until now how much I missed times like this. No drama.

"It's our turn to cook dinner," Alyssa announces shortly after we arrive home from school.

My eyes narrow to slits. "What do you mean, *our* turn? I haven't agreed to cooking anything."

"Mama's gonna be at her conference until late, so she wants

us to cook dinner tonight. She told me this morning before she left."

"Why didn't you say something then?"

"I wasn't talking to you."

"I can't cook."

"We kind of figured that, Hollywood. C'mon, I'll show you. You're gonna need to learn so that you'll be able to take care of yourself one of these days."

"I'm rich. I'll always have domestic help."

Alyssa slaps my arm gently. "You need to stop bugging. It's your mama that's rich. Not you."

"I'm rich by association, if we have to be technical." I lean against the kitchen counter with my arms folded across my chest. "So what are *you* cooking?"

"*We're* cooking a very simple meal. Spaghetti, a salad and garlic bread."

"I can make a salad," I volunteer. "Do you have black olives, mushrooms and feta cheese?"

Alyssa pulls a pack of ground beef from the refrigerator. "We have tomato, lettuce and cucumber."

"That's it?"

She nods.

"We need to go to the store. I'll show you how to make a real salad."

"Don't make it too fancy. I don't want to have to dress for dinner. We're just down-home folks."

"You're so not funny. Let's go so we can get back. I've got lots of homework to do."

"So do I. On top of that, I have to do a report for history. It's not due for another week but I need to get started on the research."

We leave the house and walk to the Super Food Store on Sage Street.

"I have a history report too. I have to write about one of the naval ships that was at—"

"Pearl Harbor," Alyssa finishes for me. "Same here. Oooh, I hate history."

"I love it. I can help you with your report. I have pictures and everything from my visit to Pearl Harbor. I'm doing the USS *Arizona*. You should do the USS *West Virginia*."

She gives me this weird look. "Why?"

"That's the ship Dorie Miller was on. He was the ship's cook and he saved a lot of people. He fired a machine gun at the Japanese planes until he was ordered to abandon the ship. He was a hero."

"This is important why? I'm sure he wasn't the only hero back then."

"Like, he was an African-American soldier, Alyssa. During that time, African-American soldiers weren't allowed to shoot guns. They worked in the kitchen. Have you ever seen the movie *Pearl Harbor*?"

"Yeah, I saw part of it. I fell asleep."

"Alyssa, we're going to watch it again. Do you remember seeing Cuba Gooding, Jr., in it?"

"Yeah. He's so cute."

"Well, he played Dorie Miller. Dorie Miller received a Navy Cross and the Purple Heart."

"Okay, I'll do my report on him and the ship he was on. Which one was it?"

"The *West Virginia*."

Inside the store, I ask, "What do you have for the spaghetti sauce?"

"Ground beef, stewed tomatoes and tomato sauce."

I pull out my cell phone and call Stella.

"What does Miss Eula put in her spaghetti sauce?" I ask when she answers.

"Who's Miss Eula?" Alyssa asks when I get off the phone.

"She's our cook." I take her by the hand and lead her over to the meat department. "We need to pick up some beef sausages, onion, garlic and . . ."

"Beef sausages? For what?"

"To put in the spaghetti sauce. Girl, it's good. Trust me."

"I'm okay with everything else. But sausages? I don't know about that." Alyssa pauses a moment before adding, "Hey, I thought you said you were a vegan or vegetarian—whatever?"

"I lied. I'd planned to starve myself until I became so ill, the judge would've let my mom come home early."

Alyssa burst into a peal of laughter. "Girl, that's crazy."

"You're with your parents, Alyssa. I want to be with my mom. Maybe even Jerome when he's not doing stupid stuff. He can be such a loser sometimes."

chapter 7

Leaning back in his chair, Uncle Reed wipes his mouth with a napkin. "You girls sho' did an outstanding job with the meal tonight."

"I like the sauce with the sausage in it," Chance compliments. "Y'all should always make it like this."

Alyssa looks over at me, smiling. "It was Hollywood's idea to put in the sausage. I thought she was crazy at first, but it's good. She made the salad."

"Everything's good." Uncle Reed pushes away from the table. "I had two big helpings. Now I feel like a stuffed pig."

Okay, Uncle Reed just grossed me out.

When Chance stands up and announces, "I'ma get me some more," Alyssa grabs his arm.

"Save some for Mama. I know you—you'll try to eat all of it."

"I'm just gon' get a lil bit, girl."

Uncle Reed chuckles. "Yeah, y'all did good. Make sure to leave your mama a plate on the stove when y'all clean up the kitchen."

I almost choke on a piece of garlic bread. *"Clean the kitchen?"* I look over at Alyssa. "What's he talking about?"

"We have to wash dishes and clean up."

I stare at Uncle Reed in disbelief. *Wash dishes?* Is he sniffing glue? I've never washed a dish in my life and I don't intend to start now. "You mean put them in the dishwasher, right?"

Uncle Reed shakes his head. "We don't have one, Divine. Don't worry; a little water won't kill you."

"I'd like to buy a dishwasher for you and Aunt Phoebe. They're cool. You don't have—"

Uncle Reed interrupts me. "Thanks, sweetheart, but we're fine. We don't really need a dishwasher."

"Anybody with dirty dishes needs a dishwasher," I counter. "Besides, Alyssa and I cooked dinner. Why do we have to clean up the kitchen too?"

"The person that cooks dinner has to clean up afterward."

"That sucks."

Uncle Reed's crazy, I decide. Been in the backwoods way too long. I decide to take another approach. "What if I buy a dish-washer for me to use, then? That way when it's my turn to do the dishes, I'll have one."

Chance and Alyssa double up in laughter.

Uncle Reed doesn't crack a smile, however. "Divine, there won't be a dishwasher coming into this house. Those things make people lazy, as far as I'm concerned. Besides, by the time you finish rinsing off dishes to put in the dishwasher, you could've already washed them."

I never looked at it that way. Probably because I never had to do dishes at home.

Alyssa places an arm around me. "C'mon, Hollywood. I'll wash and you dry. Okay?"

I groan.

After the kitchen is spotless, I call Mimi.

"Girl, you're not going to believe what I had to do earlier. Clean the kitchen . . . Ugh . . . talk about disgusting."

"You're kidding. Right?"

"I wish I were." I glance down at my fingers. "I really need a manicure."

"Ooh Divine, this must be so horrible for you. I'm going to have Mother call Kara and convince her to let you come stay with us. They wouldn't even let you use the dishwasher! I can't believe it."

"They don't have one." I glance over my shoulder to see if anyone was listening to my conversation from the back door. "Can you believe it? Talk about living in the eighteen hundreds."

"I'm so sorry, Divine. Hopefully Mother will be able to talk some sense into your mom. You need to be with us."

"I hope so too. I never thought I'd say this, but I even miss Stony Hills Prep. Mr. Whitcomb worked my nerves, but I kind of miss him. This is so crazy, huh?"

"No. It makes perfect sense. This is your life, Dee."

"Has Jordan asked about me?" He's the hottest guy in school back home and I was planning on him being my boyfriend.

"Yeah. He asks about you all the time."

I feel this tingly feeling in my stomach. "Really? What does he say?"

"He wants to know when you're coming home and stuff like that. I think Jordan really likes you."

This news makes me smile. "Tell him to call me or send me an email. Mimi, don't forget."

Mimi and I talk for another ten minutes. We hang up with my wishing I were back home.

"You okay?" Alyssa inquires. "You look a little sad."

"I'm okay." I notice the biology textbook she's carrying and inquire, "You any good in biology?"

"Yeah. I love this stuff."

"If you help me with biology, I'll help you with history."

Alyssa smiles, the metal in her mouth gleaming. "It's a deal."

"The bodies of those soldiers are still there on that ship?" Alyssa asks as she looks at the pictures I took during my visit to the *Arizona* Memorial. I keep them in a photo album I labeled Hawaiian Adventures.

"Yeah."

"It's so sad."

I agree. "They show a film clip of what happened when the Japanese bombed Pearl Harbor when you visit the Memorial. I cried when I saw it."

Alyssa says, "My teacher says that the Japanese planned to stop the Pacific Fleet so that the United States couldn't interfere with their plans to invade Europe."

"They figured they were sending the message for us to mind our own business, but you know we didn't. They messed up big-time. The United States didn't just get mad—we got even. We declared war and dropped not one, but two atomic bombs on Japan."

"You sure know a lot about these ships."

"Have you ever seen them? I actually got to tour a military ship once. I don't remember the name of it, though."

"I can't imagine you on a naval ship, Hollywood."

"It was actually kind of cool. I love history and I really like studying about the wars. I don't know why, but I want to know everything I can about them. Maybe it's because I don't understand war. Like why we're fighting in Iraq now."

"It's because of what happened on 9/11."

"Alyssa, I know that. What I mean is that I don't really understand why we have to fight like this. I don't think wars make sense. I just don't. I guess that's why I'm so interested. I need to try and make sense of this stuff."

"I don't like that people have to die. I have two friends who have fathers in Iraq. It's strange because their daddies don't even know each other and they're both over there fighting."

"Your friends must feel so scared. They don't know if they'll ever see their fathers again."

"I pray for them," Alyssa confesses. "I pray for all the soldiers and their families. And when I hear about one dying, I feel so let down. I feel like God isn't listening to my prayers."

"I feel that way sometimes. I don't pray to God much anymore."

"You should always pray, Divine."

"Why? You just said that you feel God doesn't listen to you."

"I feel that way but that's not saying it's true. I know God hears me. He hears every word."

"Why? Because that's what your dad tells you? How do you know it's true?"

"Because the Bible says so. I believe the Bible. Daddy always says that you should trust God's Word—not man's."

"Let's get back to our research," I suggest, changing the subject. Alyssa was about to do a little preaching and I didn't want to hear it. "Let's find some information on the USS *West Virginia.*"

I tapped the keys on my laptop. "C'mon . . . girl, I hate dial-up Internet service. It's sooo slow." We worked off my laptop because Alyssa's computer is even slower.

"Well, it's all we got to work with."

I found a website that listed stories from some of the soldiers who survived Pearl Harbor. "You should read these, Alyssa. Like this one here."

"Girl, they went through some stuff," she exclaims after reading a couple of the stories from the site. "You think if I email a couple of them, they'd let me interview them for my report?"

"If they're still alive. I guess so." I point to the computer screen. "There's an email address for him. Do it."

While Alyssa is typing an email to the *West Virginia* survivor, I scan through a stack of books we'd picked up from the school library earlier.

I reach for my cell phone and call Stella.

"How are you, Divine?" The sound of her voice brings to mind just how much I miss her. Who'd've ever thought I'd miss Stella?

"I'm fine. Stella, can you do me a favor please? Can you go to my house and get a couple of books to send me? They're the ones I have on the USS *Arizona.* I need them for a school project. Oh, and I need my *Pearl Harbor* DVD."

"I guess things are going well for you, then," she says.

"It's okay," I mutter. "I really need these books and the DVD, so if you can express them, I'll owe you big-time."

She laughs. "You already owe me big-time. You have been saying that for years."

"Have you talked to Mom?"

"No, not yet. I don't think she's allowed to make phone calls right now."

"Oh."

"Divine, she'll call you as soon as she can. Kara loves you, sweetheart."

"I know."

"Give your family my best. I'll pick up those books in a few and overnight them to you. Do you need anything else?"

"No, that'll be it. Bye."

I hang up.

Alyssa rises to her feet. "I just sent the email. I hope he writes me back."

I hand her a book. "This has some good information on the *West Virginia* you might be able to use in your report."

"Hey, thanks, Hollywood."

We spend the rest of the evening going through reference books and the Internet, searching for as much information as we can find. I work hard to keep my focus on my project, but it's hard. My heart is aching because I miss my mom. I miss seeing her face and hearing her voice.

I even miss Jerome with his stupid self. I miss my friends. I want more than anything to go home. I'm never going to fit in around here.

chapter 8

"You've been here for two weeks and you have almost every boy in school's phone number," Alyssa complains.

"Don't hate, cuz. I just want one boyfriend. You can have the rest."

"Two weeks, Divine."

I frown. It *has* only been two weeks. Time isn't moving as rapidly as I'd like. With it being St. Patrick's Day, the students and the school have gone crazy with the green.

The green eggs and ham for breakfast in the cafeteria takes me back to my Dr. Seuss days. Alyssa even looks like a large shamrock with her green pants, matching top, baseball hat and shoes. Who on earth wears green loafers? And she wonders why she's not getting any phone numbers.

Green is such a sucky color to me. My word for yesterday was "nonconformist," which means one who does not conform to, or refuses to be bound by, accepted beliefs, customs or practices.

I'm being a nonconformist by wearing a bright chartreuse dress with black satin detailing. It's about as close as I'll get to green. Since it's still a little chilly outside, I wear a short leather jacket over it and black leather boots. I make fashion—I don't follow it.

At lunch, I abandon Alyssa, Stacy and Penny for a boy named Rusty Collins. He's so hot!

"Divine, you are so fine. Fine as wine . . . simply Divine . . ."

I giggle. "What do you know about wine?"

"Girl, I'm not gon' be able to get you off my mind."

"Rusty, I hope you can come up with some better lines than that. I need to have Bow Wow give you a call."

His eyes get as big as saucers. "You *know* Bow Wow?"

"Yeah," I lie. "He's a friend of mine."

"Who else you know?" He gestures to some boys sitting nearby. "Hey y'all . . . she knows Bow Wow."

I'm loving the attention, so I list practically every hip-hop artist alive, lying through my teeth. My word for today is "salivate." Rusty is definitely salivating at the idea of my knowing so many celebrities.

When the bell rings, Alyssa catches me by the exit doors. "Be careful with him, Divine. Rusty is a player."

I brush off her advice. "Alyssa, you don't have to worry. I know how to deal with people like that."

After school, my cousin the leprechaun and I walk home. I'm not looking forward to this evening because it's Thursday, which means they'll be having their stupid family game night.

What a joke!

I hide in the bedroom as soon as we get home. I'm not interested in playing stupid games. Aunt Phoebe's cooking tonight, so I get started on my homework.

I finish right before dinner. Aunt Phoebe screeches that it's time to eat just as I'm putting away my books.

I bump into Chance in the hallway. "Hey Divine, wanna play Scrabble with us after we get done eating?" he asks.

"Excuse me?"

"Scrabble," Alyssa repeats from behind us. "You do know how to play Scrabble, don't you?"

"I don't play games. Those are for children."

"Mama and Daddy play all the time with us," Chance says. "You should play with us. It's fun."

"No thanks. I think I'll try and catch up on my email."

We sit down to dinner. This time Aunt Phoebe gives the blessing. I love it when she prays because she's quick and to the point.

"Father God, we just bless Your name, Jesus. Father, we thank You for the food we're about to eat for the nourishment of our bodies. In Jesus' name we pray. Amen."

My stomach growls, bringing laughter from both Alyssa and Chance.

"That's so mature," I utter. "Like your stomach has never growled before."

"Doesn't it go against the Hollywood Diva code?" Alyssa chuckled.

"You're stupid."

"Now we'll be having none of that," Aunt Phoebe stated.

I roll my eyes at Alyssa before turning my attention to my plate.

Aunt Phoebe makes the best fried chicken I've ever tasted. It's even better than Miss Eula's. I devour a drumstick and a wing before finally pushing away from the table. "I'm going to have to do a hundred sit-ups after this meal."

"For what?" Aunt Phoebe asks. "You hardly ate a thing. You had a spoonful of mashed potatoes and I don't know if you could taste the broccoli—you didn't even have a good spoonful on your plate."

"She put away two pieces of chicken though," Chance contributes. Like anybody's even talking to him.

Uncle Reed looks up and smiles at me. "The chicken was delicious. I had two pieces myself."

I smile back.

After everyone is done eating, Alyssa and I help Aunt Phoebe clean up the kitchen.

"You sure you don't want to play Scrabble with us?" Alyssa questions when we're done. "It's a lot of fun."

"I'll pass. I really have a lot of email I need to catch up on. The Internet is either too slow or I get kicked off."

As I'm about to leave the kitchen, Uncle Reed asks, "Where you going, Divine? Don't you want to play a round of Scrabble?"

"No, sir. I'm going to get on my computer. Oh—is it okay for me to order broadband Internet service? You just have dial-up."

"Ooh, Daddy, can we get broadband?" Alyssa echoes. "We won't tie up the telephone line if we have that. And we can all be online at the same time instead of having to wait until one person finishes."

"I'll look into it. Will it work for all the computers in the house? Or do I have to have a separate account for each computer? That can add up."

"No, sir. You only need one account. I already have a wireless adapter on my laptop. It doesn't have to be plugged in to anything. If it's okay with you, I can set up a wireless connection for the entire house."

"You know how to do that?" Uncle Reed asks.

I nod. "Yes, sir. Stella taught me. We set up the network at home."

"Let me know what we need and the cost involved."

"I'll get it to you in about an hour. Thanks, Uncle Reed," I say as I head for the bedroom.

I return to the dining room with all the information on equipment and pricing—I even include the cost of broadband service.

They take a break from their game. "Hmmm, this isn't bad at all. Divine, you did a good job with this." Uncle Reed hands the document over to my aunt. "Look at this and tell me what you think."

Aunt Phoebe is impressed with my research and tells me so. "I think we should do it. Seems like we all can benefit from having a wireless network."

Uncle Reed turns to me and says, "We'll go this weekend and get everything we need. Phoebe will call tomorrow and order the broadband service. That's what it's called?"

"Yes, sir."

Chance and Alyssa jump up in their excitement. "Thank you, thank you," they cry in unison.

I look at them like they've lost their last minds. It's only a wireless network. You would think I discovered a million dollars by the way they're carrying on.

Alyssa comes around the table to where I'm standing and gives me a big hug.

"Thanks so much."

I didn't do this for them. I did it for me. I'm tired of having to wait to use the Internet or it taking two days just to download a song to my iPod.

I'm heading to the bedroom when I hear Aunt Phoebe call out, "Divine, I almost forgot. You have a letter from your mother. It came today."

She goes to get it and returns a few minutes later. "Here you are."

"Thanks, Aunt Phoebe. I've been waiting for this." *Yes!* I'm so on my way back to Los Angeles. But my elation rapidly deflates when I read her letter. She is not going to change her mind. My tears didn't sway her at all.

I stomp my foot in frustration. Maybe I should've included the part about my dying in the letter.

I lay on the bed and call Rusty to distract me from Mom's letter.

While I'm on the phone talking to Rusty, I can hear Alyssa and everyone laughing and talking. It sounds like they're having a lot of fun.

They are still out there laughing and talking when Rusty and I get off the telephone two hours later. Don't they ever tire of this game?

Jerome playing Scrabble with me and Mom . . . that would never happen in a million years. What's so special about family game night anyway? Scrabble can't be that much fun.

chapter 9

I never get up before ten on Sundays, so I'm shocked when Alyssa jumps out of bed shortly after eight A.M. for church.

I don't know what to wear to church. I check out Alyssa and see she's wearing a navy suit that makes her look much older than her fourteen years. The skirt falls just below her knees. The high-collared blouse looks like it's choking her. I wouldn't be caught dead in something so boring.

"Why aren't you dressed?"

"I don't know what to put on," I respond. "I don't really have 'church' *clothes.*"

"You can wear one of my dresses."

"No, thank you." When she gives me this wounded look, I

say, "I'm not trying to be mean, but Alyssa, you and I have very different tastes when it comes to clothes."

"You can wear a pair of slacks and just a blouse or a nice sweater," my cousin suggests.

Despite Alyssa's suggestions, I'm still undecided.

Chance knocks on the bedroom door, saying, "We're leaving in about fifteen minutes. Y'all need to hurry up and get ready."

Alyssa looks over at me with this look of panic. "Just put something on. C'mon, Divine. We gotta go. Mama don't like being late for church."

I pull out three pairs of pants and an armful of tops.

"What about this?" I ask, holding up a white sweater and a pair of navy pants.

Alyssa nods. "That'll look fine."

I toss it on the bed. "I don't want to wear that. It's boring."

"It's church, Hollywood. C'mon . . . just pick something and put it on."

Alyssa breathes a sigh of relief when I'm finally dressed. I don't have time left to curl my hair so I simply pull it back in a ponytail. I can do my makeup in the car on the way to the church.

Ten minutes later we're at the church. Aunt Phoebe parks her car beside Uncle Reed's Cadillac. I stay inside to finish applying my makeup.

"You don't need too much of that," Aunt Phoebe tells me. "You're pretty enough without it. I don't know why you girls want to grow up so fast. Enjoy being a child for a while."

Whatever.

Uncle Reed looks so different in his pastoral getup. He looks exactly the way I imagine a holy man would. If he suddenly started growing wings, I wouldn't be a bit surprised.

My cousins walk up to the choir stand and sit down, leaving me alone in the second pew. Aunt Phoebe's talking to a group of ladies dressed in outfits similar to hers. Bright-colored suits with outrageous hats to match.

I glance down at my own clothes: a pair of black Eisbär Lujan pants and a black Ella Moss top with sequins going down the middle of it. I look like I'm going to a party while everybody else is dressed so saintly.

I'm not going to worry about it, though. I won't be here long enough to have to buy a bunch of boring Sunday clothes.

Aunt Phoebe takes a seat beside me.

I can't believe she's wearing that huge purple hat with fur all over it. And she's wearing a furry boa to match.

My attention is drawn from Aunt Phoebe's interpretation of a hairy grape to the choir. Alyssa's the lead vocalist. Her voice is beautiful. Her solo moves me to tears, although I'm not sure why. Maybe it's because she reminds me of Mom right now.

After the choir finishes, Uncle Reed walks to the podium and starts preaching.

"The sixth chapter of Matthew tells us that if we forgive others the wrongs they have done to us, our Father in heaven will also forgive us. But if we do not forgive others, then our Father will not forgive the wrongs we have done."

I twist uncomfortably in my seat. Not because Uncle Reed's words hold any particular meaning for me. I'm just bored to tears. I'd rather be somewhere enjoying brunch at some crazy expensive restaurant while waiting for the boutique stores to open.

Uncle Reed talks a lot about forgiveness, I notice. That, and if you don't come to Jesus you're going to spend eternity with Satan. The way I see it, it can't be too bad down there because so many people are doing wrong.

Being a Christian sounds boring to me. I don't want to go live with Satan, but I do want to have fun.

A thought occurs to me. Maybe Uncle Reed is only referring to adults. If that's the case, then I don't have to worry about it until I'm at least eighteen. I release a sigh of relief.

Uncle Reed mops his brow with a white handkerchief.

"So why forgive? I'll give you three reasons. The most important reason is because God has forgiven you. You can only really forgive when you have known God's forgiveness. Another reason is because of the alternative. An unforgiving heart can mess up the dynamic of your whole life. The third reason is because God wants us to forgive. He understands our pain and our heartbreak, but He still wants us to move into maturity and forgiveness. Imagine that you're holding all that hurt in your hands." He pauses for a moment. "Now just let it drop. Give it to the Lord."

I briefly consider Uncle Reed's words. I try to imagine all my anger and my hurt in the palm of my hand. I try to imagine it falling away.

I still feel the same. Maybe God's too busy catching other people's hurts right now. I make a mental note to try again later.

Uncle Reed finally ends the service. I stay seated, waiting for Alyssa to come out of the choir stand.

"I didn't know you could sing like that," I tell her as we're walking out to the car. "You have a nice voice, Alyssa."

She gives me a hug. "Thanks, Hollywood. I appreciate that. I love to sing."

"You should let Mom hear you sing. She could—"

Uncle Reed cuts me off by saying, "Alyssa's gonna focus on her studies. She's going to college and she don't have time for no foolishness."

Alyssa sighs softly, then climbs into the car.

"Uncle Reed doesn't want you to be a singer?" I ask when we're alone in the bedroom. She sits down on the edge of her bed to remove her shoes.

"No. He don't want me to do anything but go to college."

I drop down on my bed. "Why?"

"I think it's because of your mom."

"Oh."

"Daddy doesn't think Aunt Kara's a bad person, Divine. He just thinks she got caught up with the wrong people."

"Like Jerome," I reply.

Alyssa shrugs. "It's not like I only want to be a singer. I want to go to college first so that I'll have something to fall back on."

"I'm going to college and I plan to be a model too. I met Hilton, that hot guy modeling for Calvin Klein. He says I'll make a beautiful high-fashion model."

"You have to be tall to be a model."

"Not anymore. At least *I* won't. I have connections—I'm Kara Matthews' daughter."

"Don't you want to get something on your own?"

"I don't care how I do it. I just want to model. It's my dream."

"Well, I don't want anything just handed to me."

"That's your dad talking," I tell her.

Alyssa shakes her head, disagreeing with me. "I'm dead serious, Hollywood. I don't want to make it in the world hanging on somebody else's name."

"I can't help that my mother is Kara Matthews. I can't do anything about that. I won't ever have to struggle or work for anything. That's just the way it is."

"Then you'll never learn anything," Alyssa shoots back. "I almost feel sorry for you."

"Don't. I'm fine with my life."

"You should lose that attitude you have, though. You're not great or anything just because Aunt Kara is your mother. Do you think these people around here like you because of you? No. They only talk to you because they want to meet celebrities. Rusty's going around telling everybody how you're gonna give his demo tape to Nelly."

"I don't even know Nelly."

"Well, for some reason he thinks you do. He said that you told him Nelly and you are tight."

Shrugging, I respond, "I might have said that, but I never told him I was giving his tape to anyone."

"Why would you lie about knowing Nelly?"

"Alyssa, I don't know. I guess I wanted to impress him."

"See . . . Divine, you shouldn't have to impress anyone. You ought to want people to like you for you."

"I know."

"Stop bragging about your life, Hollywood. Because from where I'm sitting, it really isn't that great."

I consider her words. "But people already know who I am and they want to know about Mom, Jerome . . . Hollywood. I can't do anything about it now."

"All I'm saying is that you need to take it down a notch. You don't want rumors flying around all over school. Rusty is a big liar and he'll make up all kinds of stuff. Be careful around him."

"I'm never talking to him again."

"Good. He's a loser anyway." Alyssa brushes her hair back into a ponytail, then turns around to face me. "You really think Aunt Kara will like my singing?"

"I know she will."

chapter 10

After school on Monday I notice I have four calls from Mimi. She didn't leave any messages so I call her as soon as we leave the campus.

I get her voice mail. "Mimi, it's me. Call me back."

I wonder out loud, "I don't know why she called me four times. Something must've happened."

"Maybe she broke a nail," Alyssa teases.

I laugh. "You're probably right."

My cell phone rings almost two hours later while I'm doing my homework.

"Dee, I need to tell you something," Mimi begins as soon as I answer. "Now, I don't want you to be upset. Like, it's just so unfair."

"What is it?"

"Your dad is going to jail. He made some kind of deal with the district attorney's office. Anyway, it's all over the news so you'll hear about it soon. I just wanted to warn you. Gotta go but I'll give you a call later."

I'm speechless. A deal? What kind of a deal? Does this mean he's guilty?

"Something wrong?"

I look up to see Alyssa standing in the bedroom doorway. "My dad just made some kind of deal. He's going to jail."

She takes a seat beside me. "Was that him on the phone?"

I shake my head. "No. That's why Mimi was calling. She just told me."

"I'm sorry."

I'm too stunned to respond.

Alyssa turns on the small television in our room, then takes a seat beside me.

". . . Jerome Hardison pleads guilty to the charge of involuntary manslaughter . . ."

"It doesn't take them long," I comment when my father's face is flashed all over the screen. I've watched enough *Law & Order* to know that involuntary manslaughter is when there isn't any intent to kill, but it ends up happening anyway.

He pleaded guilty. This means he must have confessed to killing Shelly. My eyes fill with tears. Why didn't he bother to tell me first?

Alyssa hugs me. "I'm so sorry, Hollywood."

"It has nothing to do with me. This is Jerome's mess. He has to clean it up."

"I'm sure it still bothers you though. I know it would bother me."

"Alyssa, I don't really want to talk about this or stupid Jerome anymore. Let's change the subject. Okay?"

"Whatever you want. Why don't I get Mama? Maybe she can help you feel better."

"Actually, if you don't mind, I think I'll just take a bath and go to bed."

"I'll go up front and watch TV with my parents so I don't disturb you. Call me if you need anything, or you just want to talk. Divine, I'ma say a prayer for Uncle Jerome. For all of you."

I nod. "I hope God will hear you this time."

"He will."

I allow my tears to flow when I'm in the bathtub. How could Jerome do this to me? How could he kill somebody? My life is so over.

The next morning, Aunt Phoebe tells me, "I want you to hold your head up high, sweetheart. You have nothing to be ashamed of—you remember that."

"My stomach hurts. Maybe I should just stay home."

"You're gonna be fine."

She's just as heartless as my mom.

"I don't want to go to school today."

"Divine Matthews, now I know you're not gon' just hide from the rest of the world because of what's going on with your daddy. You got nothing to be ashamed of. If anybody should be ashamed, it's your daddy. For putting you and your mama through this."

I agree with her totally. But I still don't want to face the students at school. I don't want to face the world.

Aunt Phoebe gives me another pep talk and prays over me right before we leave for school. By the time she's finished, I'm motivated and feel ready to take on the world.

May's bucktoothed face is the first thing I see as soon as we step on campus.

"Told you he was guilty," she shouts. "Your daddy killed that girl!"

"If you don't shut up, you may be joining her."

"Did y'all just hear her say she was gonna kill me? She just threatened me. Wait 'til I tell Mr. McPhearson."

Alyssa steps in May's path. "Don't you go telling lies, May. *You started this.*"

"You gon' threaten my life too?" May steps around Alyssa. "Y'all both 'bout to be suspended."

"Don't worry, you're not going to be suspended," I tell Alyssa. "I'll make sure of it."

"I'm not worried. May is wrong and she knows it. On top of that, she's a big liar and Mr. McPhearson knows how she is. She stays in his office."

"Keep talking . . . just keep running yo' mouths. See what's gon' happen."

I glance at my cousin. "Sounds like a threat, don't you think, Alyssa?"

"Sounds like one to me."

Before May knows what's about to happen, I punch her as hard as I can in the face.

She takes the punch like a man, then returns the favor, striking me in the eye. I'm in way too much pain to even think straight, much less attempt tae kwon do moves.

I can't see a thing but I hear scuffling. Somewhere, I hear someone shout, "Kick her butt, Alyssa."

I can't have Alyssa getting all the credit, so I dive in, not sure of who I'm hitting. I just keep punching and punching.

A strong pair of hands practically lift me into the air.

"That's enough," a deep voice booms.

I'm almost grateful that I'm being pulled away. My eye is killing me. The bruise is going to be ugly. But I won't be the only one walking around black-and-blue. I'm almost sure I left a few marks on May.

chapter 11

*A*unt Phoebe and Uncle Reed arrive at the school in record time. The assistant principal called them not more than ten minutes ago.

Alyssa gives them a short summary of what went down while I sit holding an ice pack to my face.

Mr. McPhearson gives me and Alyssa detention for the next week. He's sympathetic to my plight and sends us home for the day.

After a lecture on fighting, Aunt Phoebe tells me, "Divine, we really wish there was something we could do to take this pain and heartache from you."

"I'm fine."

"Despite what you've heard on the news, until you can speak

with your father, you shouldn't jump to conclusions," Uncle Reed advises.

"I'm not thinking about Jerome."

"You're angry right now."

I look at Uncle Reed and shake my head in denial. "I'm not angry. He's a killer and I hate him."

"'Hate' is such a strong word. I don't believe you hate him. Sweetheart, I know this is hurting you. Your father is accused of a heinous crime. He—"

I cut him off by saying, "He's a killer and I don't want anything to do with him. Uncle Reed, I'm okay. I've accepted it."

Standing up, I say, "If you don't mind, I'd like to go lie down. My eye really hurts."

"Let your Aunt Phoebe look at it."

"The school nurse says I'll be okay. Just have to walk around with a black eye for a while." I chuckle. "No amount of concealer is going to hide this."

Aunt Phoebe checks me out and gives me Tylenol and a fresh ice pack. Alyssa is walking around with a bruise on her cheek but other than that, she seems fine.

"We're here for you if you need to talk, sweetie," Aunt Phoebe says before leaving me alone in the bedroom. She's really trying hard to make me feel better, but nothing will help. My life is so over.

Alyssa sits at her desk to study. She has a big math test tomorrow. Mine is the day after, but I'm not in the mood to study anything.

I just want my mom.

I can't help but wonder what she'd say about my fighting. Especially after the way she acted with that news reporter.

Jerome would be thrilled that I was fighting for him. What was I thinking? He doesn't deserve this. I have a black eye because of him.

I'm suddenly filled with renewed anger. Before I know it, I toss my pillow to the floor. "I hate you, Jerome," I scream as loudly as I can. "*I hate you.* Jerome, I hate you for doing this to me."

Alyssa runs out of the room.

I don't care. I can't stop myself. I scream and scream and scream. When I can't scream anymore, the tears come harder and harder.

I hurt so badly. The pain in my heart just spreads throughout my whole body.

Somewhere through the fog of my brain, I realize that Aunt Phoebe is holding me tight. I can hear her heartbeat, the same way I used to listen to Mom's. Only this isn't Mom.

I break into another round of tears. Aunt Phoebe holds me, talking softly, or she might be praying. I don't know for sure.

"I want my mom," I manage between sobs.

"I know, sugar. I know. Reed's gonna see if you can talk to her. Okay? It's gonna be all right. Everything is gonna be just fine. You'll see."

When no more tears come, I get up and go wash my face, embarrassed by my actions. I'm uncomfortable now that Aunt Phoebe, Uncle Reed and Alyssa have all witnessed my tantrum.

She and Alyssa are still in the room when I return.

"Sugar, why don't you try to get some rest for a little while? Alyssa, you go study in our room."

I climb back into my bed.

Aunt Phoebe stands in the doorway until I close my eyes.

I don't open them until three hours later. I can't believe I slept so long.

I get out of bed and leave the room. Alyssa's still in her parents' room studying. Chance is home and in his room. I find Aunt Phoebe in the kitchen preparing dinner.

She glances over her shoulder when I pull out a stool from the breakfast bar.

"Hey, sugar. You feeling any better?"

"A little."

"Feel like eating? I made fried chicken, corn on the cob and some collards for dinner, but if you're not real hungry, I can make you some soup."

I love Aunt Phoebe's fried chicken and her collards, so I say, "I'll just have a wing or drumstick and some greens. Not a lot, though."

I take a seat at the breakfast counter while she fixes my plate. "Thanks."

"You're quite welcome, Divine."

"Aunt Phoebe . . ." I begin. I'm still ashamed of my actions earlier. "Thanks for being there for me. I guess I needed . . ."

"You have been through a lot in a short period of time, Divine. It's a lot for a fourteen-year-old girl to go through."

"I'm sorry for throwing a tantrum like that."

"Honey, you don't have to apologize. You can't keep all that anger bottled up. You have to cut loose every now and then. I do it all the time."

My eyes open wide in surprise. I can't picture Aunt Phoebe throwing a tantrum. "You do?"

"Sure I do."

During dinner, Aunt Phoebe and Uncle Reed share stories about my mom.

"Your mama, Stella and me—we were known as the party girls."

"Really? Stella and Mom, I can believe, but you . . ."

"That's because you didn't know me back then. It's before I got saved."

"So what did you all do?"

"We just loved to party. We never did drugs or anything like that. Didn't need to—we were on a natural high. High on life, that is. We partied a lot. Your uncle and I broke up one time because of that."

Alyssa glances over at her father. "Why, Daddy?"

He takes a napkin and wipes his mouth before responding. "I didn't want a party girl. I wanted a wife."

"That's just what he told me too. He said if I was gonna be his wife, then I needed to slow down. Start acting like a wife would."

"What did you say to him, Mama?"

"I told him if he wanted me to start acting like I was a wife, then he needed to put a ring on my finger, quick-like." Aunt Phoebe picks up her drumstick. "We got married three months later."

"Where was Mom then?" I want to know.

"She left for Spelman that August. We got married in June. We didn't go on a honeymoon—instead, Reed used that money for your mama's college. I didn't mind at all. She's the first one out of the Matthews family to go and we were so proud of her. Kara's a smart girl. Always been."

"Education should always come first," Uncle Reed blurts. "I don't ever want y'all to forget it. Get your education first."

"Mom tells me that all the time," I feel a need to add. "She always says she's not going to settle for less from me."

"I'm glad to hear that, Divine. You just make sure you listen to your mother. She knows firsthand what . . ." His voice dies as the expression on Aunt Phoebe's face changes.

The air in the room suddenly seems filled with tension.

"Divine, did I ever tell you about the time Kara and I tried to form a singing group? Girl, it was the funniest thing . . ." Aunt Phoebe goes into her story, while I watch Uncle Reed. I drop my eyes when he looks over at me.

I wonder if he's ever going to forgive Mom for dropping out of college. He's always preaching forgiveness, but I don't think he's doing any of it. One day, when I'm feeling brave, I intend to ask him. I feel betrayed by everyone in my life—I don't want to think of him as a hypocrite too.

"Your mom's on the phone," Alyssa yells to me from the bedroom.

"Mom, why didn't you call me on my cell?" I ask her. "Why haven't you called me in all this time? I've been going crazy."

"I couldn't. They have some pretty strict rules around here. Honey, I can only talk for fifteen minutes so I don't want to waste any of it. First off, I want you to know how much I love you and I miss you like crazy."

"I miss you too." My eyes fill with tears. My life is horrible and I just want to see my mom.

"How you doing, baby?"

I decide not to tell her about the fight I had or my black eye. "I've had better times in my life. Did you hear about Jerome?"

"Yeah, I heard, but I don't want to talk about that. Right now, my only concern is you. Divine, I know this hasn't been easy on you. Hon, I really need you to understand that I did what I felt was best for you. You know that, don't you?" Mom sounds like she's about to cry.

"I'm okay, Mom. I had a totally bad day yesterday and I just wanted to talk to you. Aunt Phoebe and I had a long talk so I feel better. I still want to see you, though."

"I'm doing everything I can to get home to you. I go to the meetings and I participate. As much as I miss you, I'm glad to be here right now. Who knows what would've happened if I was home."

I know she's referring to Jerome and his pleading guilty to involuntary manslaughter. I recall Uncle Reed's words about handing hurt and anger over to God—I just can't seem to let it go entirely.

"Your father is going to prison for ten years," Mom says quietly.

"I know. It was all over the news." A tear slips down my face.

"I'm so sorry I'm not there with you. If I were a good mother, I—"

I wipe my eyes and say, "Mom, it's okay. You're doing what you can to come home. I'll be okay. Uncle Reed and Aunt Phoebe are taking good care of me. You don't have to worry about me. Really, you don't."

"I'm proud of you, baby. You're being so mature about everything. I'm writing you a letter. You'll get it in a few days. I love you."

"I love you too."

The phone call ends, leaving me with my heart aching. I really miss my mom.

* * *

responsibility for what happened too. C'mon, let's see if we can salvage some of this stuff."

Chance stops me before I leave the room. "Hey, Divine, I'm sorry. I'll replace whatever can't be fixed. I'll get a job or something."

"One of those shirts cost more than everything . . ." My voice dies at the look on my aunt's face. "You don't have to do that, Chance. I shouldn't have asked you to do my laundry in the first place. Besides, I have loads of clothes still packed away in the garage."

Chuckling, Alyssa leaves the laundry room.

I follow her out into the hall. "Why didn't you tell me that Chance couldn't wash clothes?"

"Why didn't you ask him before just handing over your stuff?"

Alyssa has a point but I refuse to acknowledge it out loud.

"Besides, I don't think you can do much better than him."

Frowning, I ask, "What are you talking about? I can wash clothes. It's not like it's hard."

"If you knew anything about doing laundry, then you would've had them all separated before giving them to Chance. Some of your stuff is dry clean only. You have to read the little labels inside the clothes, Divine. I know for a fact a lot of your stuff is dry clean only, especially those silk skirts, so you'll have to throw them away."

"You could've helped me, Alyssa."

"I would have if you knew how to ask. You walk around acting like you're so together—you don't know a thing about living in the real world."

"I'm doing the best I can," I say quietly.

"You're so spoiled, Divine. Sometimes it just gets on my nerves," Alyssa confesses. "Then when you look like you do now, I feel horrible."

"I know you think I'm this person who brags all the time and is spoiled beyond words . . . and I am. But Alyssa, I can't change overnight. I'm trying to be . . ." Tears fill my eyes. "I don't even know who I am anymore. I just don't fit in around here and I never will."

Alyssa surprises me by giving me a hug. "You're not a bad person, Divine. That's not what I'm saying. The truth is that . . . maybe I'm a little jealous. You get all this attention and . . . I mean, I love my life, but there's this part of me that wants to be like you. I want people to see me sometimes. I mean *really* see me."

"Sometimes I want to be invisible," I confess. "I feel like I'm always on parade and I want to be a normal kid." Wiping my eyes, I add, "A normal kid with a rich mom, of course."

"C'mon, Hollywood. Mama's waiting on you. I'll help you with your laundry this time. You're on your own next Friday."

"Alyssa, I want you to know that you are not only my cousin. You're almost one of my best friends. You still have a ways to go, but I'm liking you."

"I love you too, Hollywood."

chapter 12

"*If* I have to put my hand there, I'm going to die." I point to the toilet. "This is so gross. Alyssa, you're used to manual labor. You clean it."

"I hope you know you're not winning any cool points with me." Alyssa holds a stick with a sponge on the end of it, pointing it in my direction. "You use it just like me and Chance. You use it, you clean it."

"Alyssa, you c-can't just expect me to know how to clean something like *that*. I've never even had to clean my own room. I certainly don't do bathrooms."

"It's easy. I'll show you how to do it."

"No. My nails. It takes a lot of effort to keep them looking this good. You don't have any nails. You clean the toilet and I'll clean everything else."

Alyssa isn't buying it. "You don't have to worry about your precious fake nails. You can wear plastic gloves."

"They should put a nail shop somewhere in Temple. I hate having to go all the way to Carrollton just to get my hair and nails done."

"You can go to Fancy Nails in Villa Rica or Tango Nails," Alyssa responds. "We just always go to Carrollton."

"I feel sick," I say and put a hand to my mouth. "This is so gross."

Alyssa laughs. I can't believe she's standing here laughing at me.

"You are such a drama queen. You know, you should try acting instead of modeling."

"Shut up!" I brush past her to leave the bathroom.

Her hands clamp down on my shoulders. "I don't think so. You're cleaning this bathroom today. I've let you talk me into doing your chore the last time it was your turn. Not today. You're doing your own work. You only have to do it—what?— once a month? It's not gon' kill you, girl."

I can't stand Alyssa. "If I pass out in here, you're going to be so sorry."

"Whatever. Just hurry up. If you're not done by the time I finish mopping the kitchen, I'm leaving you. We're supposed to meet Penny and Stacy at the Carrollton mall in one hour." She holds up a finger as if I'm stupid. "One hour."

Resigned to my fate, I turn around to face the task ahead. I hate doing housework. I'm definitely getting a maid when I grow up.

My nose wrinkled up, I spray some bathroom cleaner into the toilet. *Ugh.* I hate this so much.

I'm almost done when Alyssa returns.

"I see you survived."

I roll my eyes at her in response.

"Think you'll be ready to go in ten minutes? Mama's got to be at the church by twelve."

"I'll be ready. I hope they have a nail shop in that mall."

"They do." Alyssa pulls a clean towel out of the linen closet. "I'ma need to take a shower."

"I'll be out in a minute." I pick up the broom and my cleaning supplies. I'm totally feeling Cinderella at this point.

That night I'm still on the phone with Rhyann when the clock strikes midnight.

"What you doin' on the phone, young lady?" Aunt Phoebe demands. "You know what time it is?"

"Hold on, Rhyann." I turn to Aunt Phoebe and say, "Did you need something?"

"I need you to get off that phone and take yo'self to bed," she huffs.

"I'm not through talking to my friend. She's telling me about all the things I'm missing back home."

"She can call you tomorrow."

"Aunt Phoebe, I'm on my cell phone. It's not costing you a penny."

She snatches the phone out of my hand. "Honey, Divine's gonna have to call you another time. And just so you know, she can't take or make calls after eleven." Aunt Phoebe clicks off.

"Why did you do that?" I shout. "You can't tell me when I

can have phone calls. My mom's accountant pays the bill for my cell phone."

"Divine, you are in my house and while you're under my roof, you follow my rules. Is that clear?"

Uncle Reed comes out of his office. "What's going on?"

"I was talking to a friend of mine on *my* cell phone and *she* comes in here bugging." I'm sure Uncle Reed will get his wife straightened out in no time.

"Divine, do you know how late it is?" he asks me, instead of getting on Aunt Phoebe like he's supposed to be doing. Don't tell me he's afraid of her!

"It's a little after midnight. Why?"

"It's too late for you to be talking to anyone on the phone."

"Uncle Reed, my friends are in California, on California time." Duh. "We're three hours ahead of them."

"You'll need to make your calls to them earlier."

"I don't get it. It's my phone . . . what's the problem?"

"You have a curfew. You can't go out after a certain time and you can't use the phone after a certain time," Aunt Phoebe explains.

"I don't know why you're picking on me. If you don't want me here, just say so."

"Stop being so dramatic," Aunt Phoebe tells me. As if. "Divine, we have rules. We've told you that. You are only fourteen years old. We have church tomorrow and you don't like getting up. You need to get your rest."

I sigh in frustration. "Why do people keep saying that? I'm not a little baby and I'm so tired of people treating me like one."

"Maybe you should try acting your age," Aunt Phoebe suggests.

"What do you mean by that?"

"What I mean is that you should stop trying to act so grown-up. Enjoy being a teenager."

"You're the one with all the rules," I argue.

Sitting beside me, Uncle Reed takes me by the hand. "Divine, honey, we're not trying to keep you from having fun. But we have to have rules—it's for your own good. We are the adults and we have years of experience behind us. We're just trying to protect you and teach you to be responsible."

"What are you protecting me from by not letting me talk on the phone after eleven?"

"We're teaching you to follow rules. We're teaching you to be responsible and we're protecting you from staying up so late that you're not going to make it through my sermon tomorrow."

I chuckle. "Yeah, I'd hate to miss that."

Aunt Phoebe sits down on the other side of me. "You know, you're always talking about beauty. I'm sure you know from those beauty magazines you always reading how important it is to get lots of rest."

"You didn't have to embarrass me when I was on the phone with my friend."

"I'm sorry for that. It wasn't my intention, but I didn't like your little attitude. You really need to work on that, Divine. It's more than outward appearances that make you beautiful. You have to be beautiful on the inside too."

"Aunt Phoebe, I'm sorry. I just didn't think it was such a big deal."

"Breaking rules are a big deal to me," she tells me.

"Can I at least make calls until twelve? We're three hours ahead of my friends."

"I think eleven is fair enough." Aunt Phoebe pats my hand. "Why don't you go on to bed? And I don't expect you to have any trouble getting up."

I can't stand her.

I open my email and jump up for joy.

"What's got you so excited, Hollywood?"

"Madison sent me an ecard. Come read it. He's so sweet."

Alyssa leans over me, reading. "Girl, that boy really likes you."

"I like him too. I'm going to send him one back."

"Maybe I should send Stephen one."

"No. You can't do that. You can't copy off me and Madison. Besides, Stephen probably knows that I got one and he'll know that you're copying us."

"Maybe I should check and see if he sent me one. He sends me emails all the time." She laughs. "Mostly stupid ones."

Alyssa goes to her computer to check her email while I search for the perfect ecard to send to Madison. I send Mom one just in case she's able to get on the Internet and check her email.

I notice Jerome's name on Yahoo under the Entertainment section and click on the link. Why are they still talking about him and Shelly? I wish they would just drop it. Enough already.

I just want to put this out of my mind. It's bad enough I'm still walking around with a bruise under my eye. I'm amazed that Madison even wanted to talk to me. When I asked him about it, he said that he likes a girl who can handle her own. I like that he treats me like a normal person. He isn't threatened by my celebrity status.

I glance over my shoulder to see what Alyssa's doing. Her face is almost glued to the computer monitor. "You must be talking to Stephen."

"Yeah, I'm talking to my baby."

I leave her alone to IM back and forth with Stephen. I'm about to shut down my computer when I see that Madison's just signed on. I send him an IM thanking him for the card.

He responds and we IM back and forth over the course of an hour.

Alyssa and I both have to get off the computers when Uncle Reed calls out for us.

It's payday. Time to collect our humiliating allowances. I usually spend this much on one lunch alone. Life is totally unfair.

chapter 13

Thank the Lord for spring break. We're out of school for a week and I'm so ready for a vacation.

Normally, we go away on a trip every year, but with Jerome in jail and Mom in rehab, I won't be going anywhere. It's not all bad, though.

Penny and Stacy are here at the house, spending the day with me and Alyssa, and we're discussing one of my favorite subjects: boys.

Stacy calls out to me. "Hey, Divine. Has Madison tried to kiss you yet?"

"Don't talk so loud," Alyssa cautions. "I don't want Mama hearing us."

"Well, has he?" she asks.

"Stacy, what goes on between me and Madison is my business." Wearing a big smile, I add, "I don't kiss and tell . . ."

"Girl, you know you ain't kissed nobody so don't even try to lie."

I stick my tongue out at Alyssa. "Have you kissed Stephen?"

"No and I'm not going to. He's not my boyfriend. We're just talking."

"Divine, I don't know what you're doing to Madison, but that boy don't do nothing but talk about you. Every time he comes over to the house to see my brother, he's always bringing your name up. Girl, he's got a serious crush on you," Stacy says.

Penny nods in agreement. "He's always asking me about you. He keeps telling me to bring you by his house when you come over. I told him I'm not gon' get on Aunt Phoebe's bad side. I ain't crazy."

I perk up. "Really?"

"Yeah," responds Stacy. "He really likes you."

"Why? Is it because of me or is it because my mom is Kara Matthews?"

Penny gave me a look of disbelief. "Hmmph, all the girls crazy about him. From middle school on up. You should hear them talking about Madison Hartford."

"Then why doesn't he have a girlfriend already?" I want to know.

"He did but they broke up right before school started. He used to be with Marlene Pemberton. But she didn't know how to act, so he dropped her. Now he wants you to be his boo," Penny replies.

We burst into a round of laughter.

"How come none of you trying to get with him?" I ask. "If he's such a great guy, why don't you want to be with him? I mean, he is *fine.*"

"My boo Kennar is Madison's cousin," Penny announces. "You do know they related, right? They look like brothers."

"I see them together all the time but I didn't know they were cousins." I glance over at Stacy. "You sure you don't want him? You know how females get when a girl comes from another city. I know I used to get fired up when a new girl came to school and ended up with the dude I was trying to hook up with."

"Divine, if you weren't so cool, we'd probably be that way with you; but you all right."

"Thanks, Stacy. You and Penny are all right with me. Even my old crazy cousin here—I like all of you."

Alyssa begins jumping and down. "Hollywood likes me. She really likes me. I'm so honored."

"Like ugh. Don't ever do that again."

Stacy chuckles. "*Like* your cousin has some Valley Girl in her."

"*Like* yeah, she does," Penny agrees. "It can *like* get on your nerves."

I'm laughing so hard, I almost pee on myself. "You guys are *like* so fired. I need to go to the bathroom."

When I return to the family room a few minutes later, Alyssa is going through a stack of DVDs. "What are you looking for?"

"*Pearl Harbor.* Penny and I want to watch it. Especially since you think it's so great."

I pick up a box of tissues from the breakfast counter and toss it to Alyssa.

"Why'd you give this to me?"

"Because you're going to need it."

We make ourselves comfortable on the floor with these huge floor cushions Aunt Phoebe keeps in one corner of the family room.

I look around and realize that my life is no longer filled with luxury and star-studded parties. But I'm okay with it. I've discovered something I don't think I've ever really had before: simplicity. The property, condition or quality of being simple or uncombined. Absence of luxury or showiness; plainness.

I've been in Temple for a little over two months now. I'm proud of my accomplishments. I can cook some, but I still hate washing dishes and won't unless I'm wearing rubber gloves—I hate the way my hands feel after they come out of the dirty water. Thanks to Aunt Phoebe, I can do a decent job with my laundry. I still feel nauseous when it's my turn to clean the bathroom. I have a feeling that'll never change.

Uncle Reed and Aunt Phoebe moved a large armoire into the bedroom where Alyssa's desk used to be so that I can hang my clothes in there. My cousin is thrilled to get her closet back. Her desk and computer are now in the family room, but Uncle Reed's thinking about getting her a laptop.

Mom and I write each other weekly and I look forward to her letters. Jerome's called a couple of times. Our conversations are short. He still thinks Uncle Reed is brainwashing me. I don't write him because I don't have anything to say.

Today, Sunday, I think I'll wear the simple black suit that I purchased last Thursday when we went to Phipps Plaza in the Buckhead area of Atlanta. I love that shopping center, and especially the Elie Tahari store. I wanted to buy this stretch velvet cropped jacket, but Aunt Phoebe almost fainted at the price. She thinks five hundred dollars is way too much to spend on a jacket. She'd probably go into a coma if she ever went shopping with Mom.

Alyssa sticks her head inside the bedroom. "You ready yet, Hollywood?"

"Yeah. I'm ready. Just putting on my shoes."

Ten minutes later, we're walking out of the house.

Aunt Phoebe makes Chance's day by allowing him to drive us to church. I pray for the first time in a real long time. I've never been with him and Uncle Reed when he was getting driving lessons, but from what Alyssa says, I hope to see my next birthday.

We make it to the church safe and sound. I jump out of the car, giving thanks to God.

"Drama queen," Alyssa mutters with a laugh.

I find a seat in church in the fourth row. Uncle Reed doesn't want us to sit any farther back—he thinks we should be right up front, in his face. Chance is in the back talking with some of his friends and Alyssa walks off to take something to Uncle Reed's office.

Aunt Phoebe turns around and gestures for me to sit with her.

Groaning softly, I get up and move.

Alyssa joins us a few minutes before service begins. The combined adult choir is singing today and I'm glad. I love listening to them. The youth choir is very good, especially my cousins, but I really enjoy the senior choir.

Right before Uncle Reed gets up to preach, the choir sings a selection that has become a favorite of mine. Before I realize it,

I'm standing up, clapping and singing right along with them.

Next comes the sermon. Uncle Reed sure likes talking about forgiveness, because he's talking about it again this Sunday. I always feel like he's talking directly to me.

He's kind of long-winded, but I'm beginning to like listening to him. Uncle Reed can be so funny at times. He can tell a joke without it coming out corny. I'm glad, because I'd die of humiliation otherwise.

As soon as we get home, I'm going to ask him if he's forgiven Mom.

On the way home, Aunt Phoebe tells me, "Divine, you have such a beautiful voice. I've heard you sing some around the house, but not like today. You must have been really feeling the spirit."

"Alyssa's voice is much better than mine. She can *really* sing."

"Honey, so can you," Aunt Phoebe assures me. "Why don't you join the choir? Alyssa and Chance love singing up there."

I shake my head. "I don't know . . ."

"Your mama used to sing right up there. She would sit in the front row. Had a voice just like an angel—that's what people always used to say about her. Now *she* could sing."

"She still can."

"Yeah, she can," Aunt Phoebe agrees. "But Divine, I wish you could've heard her back then. Maybe it's because it was church music, but listening to Kara sing was ministry to me. Ooh, she used to just minister to my soul with her singing."

I've never heard anyone say something like this about Mom's singing. A part of me wishes I could have heard her way back then. Before Jerome.

"You know, you sound a lot like Kara. When I heard you

singing today during service, it felt like I was listening to your mama."

"I don't think so."

"*You do.* You sound just like her. I'm going to ask your uncle if he still has some of those tapes of your mama singing. You should listen to them."

"I hope he does. I'd like to hear them."

When I tell Uncle Reed that I want to hear some of my mom's church songs, he pulls out a stack of cassette tapes from a dusty box that he keeps out in the garage.

"I'd forgotten I had these," he says. "People at church used to tell me that your mama sounded like an angel."

"That's what Aunt Phoebe says."

"The songs used to sound like they came from her heart, Divine. When Kara was singing, it was like she was standing before the Lord and she was giving Him her all. Y'all listen to them love songs on the radio . . . they make you all emotional and you lose your mind . . . you think the boy's singing to you."

I laugh.

"I know how you do," Uncle Reed says pointedly, raising his eyebrows. "Well, that's what Kara did with her singing. She was singing love songs to God."

"People don't appreciate Mom like they used to," I say. "Everybody's into hip-hop right now."

"It's not so much the song as the heart behind it, Divine. I think when you put your heart into something—you can't fail."

I consider his words. "Uncle Reed, can I ask you something?"

"Sure. What is it?"

"Will you ever forgive Mom for dropping out of school and marrying Jerome?"

"I forgave your mama a long time ago, sweetheart."

"Sometimes I feel like you're still mad at her."

"I'm not angry with Kara. I'm disappointed in some of the choices she's made but that's because I love my sister. As you know, I'm ten years older than your mama. I wanted a baby sister; I prayed for her, for five years. My mother lost three babies trying to give me a little sister."

"I didn't know that."

"When Kara was born, she was given the name Carol Jean Matthews. The nurse at the hospital couldn't hear very well. That's how she got the name Kara."

"Really?"

Uncle Reed nods. "I promised the Lord that I would protect my baby sister, and I took those words to heart. I only wanted the best for her. She grew up to be a beautiful young woman. Man, she could sing . . . bring tears to your eyes. I knew she wanted to sing but I urged her to go to college. I felt like she'd gain some maturity. If she still wanted to sing after she got her degree . . . well, I thought she'd be ready for it."

"But she met Jerome."

He nods. "I never liked your father, Divine. I knew he'd suck the life out of Kara and I didn't want that to happen." Uncle Reed looks at me. "Divine, it's not your mother I have to forgive. I have to forgive your father."

"So do I," I confess. "Uncle Reed, I'm so angry with him. There are times I want to really, really hate him. Then sometimes I think maybe I love him. I don't know *what* I feel for him. It's not like he ever acted like a real dad. Except to boss me around."

"You love him, Divine. No matter what, Jerome is your father. He's family. I preached today on forgiveness—I need to follow my own teaching."

"How do you forgive somebody who's hurt you so much?" I wonder aloud.

"Like I said this morning in church, prayer makes the process easier. Divine, we already know God's will for us. He wants His people to live in love and unity, and forgiveness toward one another is essential for that to happen. Do you understand what I'm telling you?"

"Yes, sir." I'm sure what Uncle Reed is saying is true, but actually doing it—forgiving—isn't easy. "I've tried and I'm still trying to forgive Jerome," I tell him. "I just can't seem to do it."

"Divine, forgiving is not simply a mind game. Just because we say we forgive, our souls are not washed of the hurt. We are not free of the pain and heartache until we stop reacting angrily. Our having this discussion right now tells me that God is showing me my deficiency in the area of forgiveness. He is teaching me about forgiveness. Class is still in session, even for me."

I begin to worry that he's about to start preaching a second sermon.

"We can forgive Jerome together," he tells me. "How does that sound?"

"What do we have to do?"

"We can pray together."

I look around the garage. "Right now? In here?"

"Now is as good a time as any," Uncle Reed responds. "So is the place."

He takes my hand and we bow our heads. I'm still a stranger to prayer, so I'm relieved when he finally says "Amen."

I give Uncle Reed a gentle jab in the arm. "I still feel the same. You think we need to pray some more? I don't think it worked."

He laughs. "It's not always instantaneous. Just give all that anger and disappointment you feel to the Lord. Give it to Him and leave it there."

"Yes, sir." Maybe I should give prayer another chance.

Uncle Reed leaves me standing in the garage. I guess he senses I have something more to say to God, which I do. I look up and say, "Okay, God. You can have Jerome. You're probably the only one who can handle him. And please don't give him back until he knows how to act right. Amen."

chapter 14

I listen to the tapes of my mom singing over and over again. Aunt Phoebe's right. Mom sounds totally different when she's singing church music. It's almost like she was much happier back then. So now I have to wonder if she was ever really happy with us. With *me*.

Alyssa and I have to practice our song for this coming Sunday. I'm so not into this. I don't know why I let her and Aunt Phoebe talk me into singing.

I cut off the tape when Alyssa enters the bedroom.

"You listening to your mama again?"

"Yeah. So?"

"Hey, I like listening to her too. Not a big deal to me. What's wrong with you? Why you bugging?"

I get off the bed and stand up. "Alyssa, I don't think I can do this. I'm not a singer."

"Girl, with a voice like yours, I'm surprised you're even thinking about modeling. You should get a record deal. You know you can get one of them with no problem. Especially since you don't mind using your mama's connections."

Alyssa's clearly been sniffing glue, I decide. "Whatever. I'm not going to let you fill my head up with lies. Then I get up there on Sunday and choke." Shaking my head, I add, "I don't think so."

"Divine, you really have a beautiful voice. You can sing. *We* can sing. Do like your mama. Close your eyes and act like you singing for Jesus."

"That's supposed to make me relax? Jesus is . . . you know . . . *Jesus.* I don't want to mess up in front of Him."

"But you won't. If you're singing from your heart, Divine, Jesus will love it."

"You think so?" I ask. "And what about the church? They'll be sitting out there cracking up."

"Divine, stop bugging." Alyssa turns on her CD player. "C'mon. Let's try it. We're gonna sound so good . . ."

I'm still skeptical. "I hope so. If I get up there and choke, I know I'll die from the embarrassment. I'll never open my mouth to sing another word. I mean it."

Sunday, April twenty-fourth, my singing debut in church. Madison wanted to come but I couldn't have him here, watching me. It would make me nervous.

Alyssa and I walk over to the microphone. It's time for our song.

Everyone's clapping and we haven't sung our first note. I pray we don't have them running out of the church with their hands covering their ears.

I sing well when I'm not under pressure. Mom asked me to do a solo with her two years ago and I couldn't. I froze up. Now I'm standing in front of a church filled with about two hundred people.

I've lost my mind.

The music starts. I close my eyes and think about Jesus sitting on a throne. The only image of Him I have to go by is the painting in my uncle's house. The image in my head is so real; I can actually feel the warmth of His smile.

I feel the words of the song in my throat and open my mouth to sing. I'm no longer aware of Alyssa, who's standing beside me, or of the church congregation. It's just me and Jesus.

After I've sung my last note, I open my eyes and the entire church is standing on its feet, clapping.

Alyssa takes my hand. "Girl, you *sang* that song! Amen!"

Uncle Reed comes over to hug me and Alyssa. "Praise God," he says over and over. "Thank you, Jesus."

We take our seats.

When service is over, Alyssa and I are nearly run over by the congregation.

"Y'all sure tore up that song this morning," one lady tells us. She reaches over and pinches my cheek. "You sound just like that mother of yours."

"See, I told you so," Alyssa whispers. "You're a star, Hollywood, and you didn't even know it. You were so busy trying to walk in your mama's light. Now you got your own."

"You want to know what's funny, Alyssa? It doesn't even matter to me anymore."

* * *

I'm more than ready for the weekend after having to study for two major tests. Both tests were on Friday. Alyssa and I came home yesterday tired but thrilled that we have two days of freedom.

I usually don't like to get up until nine on Saturdays but this morning I was up at seven-thirty. I needed to write Mom a letter. All the studying I had to do put me behind.

"We're going to see a movie," Alyssa announces around noon. "Wanna come with us?"

I glance up from my computer. "Who's going?"

"Me and Chance."

"Sure." I finish typing my email to Madison and click "Send." After shutting down the laptop, I go to the bathroom to freshen up.

"Okay, I'm ready."

Chance is driving us to the theater. I have to admit that he's not a bad driver at all. Much better than me or Alyssa. I think Uncle Reed's given up on us. He never volunteers to take us for driving lessons anymore.

At the movie theater, Alyssa and I whisper back and forth about Madison and Stephen while Chance is buying our tickets.

I notice this girl standing at the edge of the counter watching us.

Chance looks over at her and waves.

Since he seems to know her I inquire, "Who is that?"

"She's just a friend. Her name is Trina."

"Uh-huh." In a low voice, I whisper, "I know what's up. You think you're so slick."

He feigns innocence. "What?"

Alyssa turns around. "What's up?"

"Your brother has a date."

"No, I don't."

Alyssa follows my gaze. She turns back to Chance, saying, "Oh, this is why you wanted to come to the movies."

"It's not like that," he tries to convince us.

"Ooooh," Alyssa teases. "You know you're not supposed to be having dates. You know if Daddy finds out . . ."

"I ain't on no date," Chance argues. "I wouldn't bring y'all if I was gonna meet a girl out here."

I don't believe him and from the look on Alyssa's face, she doesn't either.

"C'mon, y'all. Let's just go see the movie. Y'all some nosy females."

"You can say whatever you want. But I know the truth. By the way, it looks like your *friend* is planning to see the same movie," I tease.

"I ain't got nothing to do with what movie Trina sees. I see a lot of people I know here today. Y'all really need to stop trying to be in my business."

Alyssa and I burst into laughter. Chance looks so guilty. We're convinced something's up since Trina keeps watching Chance's every move.

"Divine and I are going to sit up high," Alyssa tells her brother. "I know how you like to sit to the front."

"What's really going on?" I whisper.

"I wanna see if Trina comes in and sits with Chance," she whispers back.

We don't have to wait long. Trina comes in and appears to

be looking for someone. Chance raises his hand to get her attention. He turns around to see if we're watching.

Of course we are and we let him know it.

When Trina follows his gaze, I wave to her. She smiles and waves back.

"I knew it," Alyssa whispers. "They planned this—I know it because this is something I'd do."

"You? Not you."

"I'm human. And Daddy's really strict about dating. Chance and I can't date until we're seventeen."

"I'm glad he's not my dad."

"So you'd rather have Jerome then?"

I glare at her. "It's not like I have much choice, do I?"

"Right now you live with us, though. Just be glad your mama will be home in a few months."

"Hmmph. Even if she wasn't, I don't have to follow Uncle Reed's rules when it comes to dating. Mom wouldn't even go for that."

Chance has to buy us something to eat after the movie to ensure our keeping his little secret. I wanted to hold out for dessert, but Alyssa thought hamburgers were enough.

When we get back to the house, I see mail hanging out of the mailbox. I climb out of the car and run down the driveway.

"I'm getting the mail."

Even in the light coming from the porch, I recognize my mother's handwriting. I begin jumping up and down.

"Did you win the lottery?"

"I got a letter from my mom," I tell Alyssa.

"You've been looking for one all week. I'm glad it finally came."

"Me too."

Alyssa knows I like to be alone when I read my letters, so she doesn't follow me into the bedroom.

In her letter Mom writes about the treatment center—the eight acres of grassy meadows and beautiful vegetation. She gets off on this kind of stuff.

She tells me how they are able to enjoy a gym membership at a local health club and that she works out three days a week. Like she really needs to work out. She's already so skinny.

When I read about her oceanfront activities, sailing and surfing, I think, *This doesn't sound like rehab. It sounds like she's on vacation.* They even take trips to Catalina Island for retreats.

My mood changes when I get to the portion of her four-page letter that says she might be able to come home a little earlier because she's doing so well with her treatment. I'm proud of Mom and make a mental note to tell her so when I write her back. I mail off the letter I wrote to her this morning, telling her about my singing in church, how I'm doing in school and about my telephone and Internet relationship with Madison.

If only there was hope for Jerome. I'm still plagued with the question of why he pleaded guilty. In my imagination, I see him being tortured into confessing to a murder he didn't commit. Or I wonder whether he's lying to save me and Mom because the real killer is threatening to harm us if he didn't confess.

I'm not sure if I'll ever find out the truth.

My chance to discover the truth behind Jerome's guilty plea arrives hours later, when Aunt Phoebe announces, "Honey, you have a phone call. It's your daddy."

"Jerome?"

She nods. "He wants to speak with you. Hurry up. He's only got about twenty minutes to talk."

I rush to her, taking the telephone out of her hand. "Hello."

"Baby girl." Jerome sounds tired. "How you doing?"

"I'm fine."

"I would've called you on your phone but we're not allowed to call cell phone numbers."

My response is dead silence.

"I called the house earlier and spoke to Stella. When she told me you were living with Reed, I was surprised. Yo' mama knows that if I was home I'd've never allowed that to happen."

"Well, you're not home," I state. "So it really doesn't matter. Anyway, why you calling me?"

" 'Cause I wanna talk to you. You my daughter."

"When did you remember that? You've only been in jail since February fourteenth."

"I know I let you down, baby girl. Honestly, I didn't know what to say to you." He pauses a moment before continuing. "I'm sure you heard what happened."

"Yeah. Who hasn't heard, Jerome?"

"The district attorney told me that if I pleaded guilty on the involuntary manslaughter charge I wouldn't have to spend as much time in prison. Ten years is a long time but it's better than what I was facing if I'd been convicted on a murder charge."

"Did you do it?"

"Divine, I'ma tell you the truth. It was an accident. I swear on my life, baby girl. I never meant . . . I went to see Shelly that night. I needed to see her. You know . . . to straighten things out. We started arguing as soon as I got there. I wanted her to drop the paternity suit against me. But she wanted me to leave yo' mama and marry her. Anyway, when I refused, she took my gun and threatened to shoot me. I was only trying to take it from her . . ."

Jerome starts crying, which totally surprises me. I've never seen him cry—not even on film.

I try to think of something to say. "Jerome, I . . . I'm sorry."

"Baby girl, I promise I'ma make this up to you when I come home. I *will* make this right between us."

"Jerome, I need to ask you a question. The baby . . . do you have a son?"

It's a moment before he finally answers me.

"Yeah. The child is mine. I'ma do right by him too. Divine, I want you to get to know your brother. Be there for him."

My word for today is "astonish," which means to fill with sudden wonder or amazement. I can truly say I'm totally astonished by his admission. This means he cheated on Mom. He cheated on me.

His voice brings me out of my musings. "You talk to yo' mama lately?"

"I got a letter from her today. She's doing well and might be able to come home a little earlier. Jerome, does she already know about the baby?"

"I wrote her a letter a couple of weeks ago and told her everything, but I haven't heard a word from her since then."

"Mom's hurt." Silently, I add, *I'm hurt. Our hearts are broken.*

"Yo' mama's mad and she got every right to be. I haven't been a good husband to her. I'ma make some changes, though. I promise. Divine, I'm real sorry." He pauses for a moment, then says, "My time's almost up. Don't you let Reed turn you against me. I know he don't like me, but it don't matter. I'm

Kara's husband and your father. He's probably listening to us now. Right, Reed?"

His words make me defensive for some reason. I think of the prayer Uncle Reed and I prayed. "He's not like that, Jerome," I say.

"He thinks he's better than me. Don't you, Reed?"

"He's not on the phone." Jail's making Jerome crazy.

"When you talk to yo' mama, tell her that I love her and just wait for me. Tell her don't do nothing stupid."

"I think I'll let you tell her that yourself. I'm not getting in the middle. Good-bye, Jerome."

I slam the phone down hard. If it's broken, I'll just buy Uncle Reed and Aunt Phoebe a new one.

Still reeling from shock, I drop down on the sofa in the family room. Jerome shot and killed Shelly. A woman is dead because of him.

I'm not sure if I believe him about it being an accident now. I don't want to speak ill of the dead—I heard Mom say that a few times in the past—but Shelly was a day actor at best. She appeared in a couple of soaps. Jerome never would've left Mom for a struggling wannabe actress. He enjoyed living off Mom's success. I guess I did too.

I pick up one of the huge photo albums that my aunt and uncle like to keep on the coffee table. There are loads of pictures of Mom in this one.

I crack up over a photo of my mom with all these curls. There's a light in her eyes that I don't recall seeing, which makes me question once again if Mom was ever really happy being with me and Jerome.

That question plagues me for the rest of the evening.

chapter 15

*M*adison walks me home. Well, at least as far as the block before Uncle Reed's house. He tries to hold my hand, but I'm too worried about getting caught. I never know when Aunt Phoebe's going to be home or if Uncle Reed or his church members will be driving by.

Today it's just me and him because Alyssa had a doctor's appointment and Aunt Phoebe picked her up early. Chance had to stay after school for rehearsal of the upcoming play. I could have gone with Aunt Phoebe and Alyssa but I didn't want to miss out on this time with Madison. This is the only time we can see each other alone.

"Why don't you talk to your mom and see if she can talk to your uncle about me coming by to see you?" Madison asks.

"My mom wouldn't go for it, Madison. She's as bad as they are when it comes to boys. They're just real strict."

"I can wait," he promises.

He's got the prettiest teeth I've ever seen on a boy. I need to get the number of his dentist. Madison's big, bright smile makes my heart beat faster and makes me feel so tingly inside. I wonder if I'm in love with him. I do know I'm crazy about him.

I like the way he looks at me, the way he smells and the way he dresses. Mostly, I like the way I can't just wrap him around my little finger. He's older by two years and more mature. I'm tired of dumb boys. Like that dumb Jordan. He's hanging with Natalia and he knows how much I hate her. How could he do this to me? I couldn't believe it when Mimi told me, so I emailed him directly asking him about it. He had the nerve to tell me that he was with Natalia because he'd heard that I was messing around with some boy in Georgia.

Madison and I near the corner where we have to part. I'm not ready to leave him but it's completely out of my hands, thanks to parents who don't know how to let their children grow up.

"I guess I'll see you tomorrow," he says.

"Call me tonight, okay?"

"You know I will. I got to talk to my boo."

He called me his boo! It's official! I'm his boo!

Madison takes his hand and gently lifts my chin. My knees are knocking so hard that I can barely stand. It's going to happen . . .

His lips touch mine. Madison kisses me.

My first kiss. I float the rest of the way home. I can't wait to tell Alyssa.

I'm so glad she's home when I get there. I shut the bedroom door. "Guess what?"

"What?"

"Madison kissed me."

"Really?" Alyssa hugs me. "I'm so happy for you."

"I'm happy for me," I say. "Girl, I saw fireworks."

She cracks up with laughter. "You're stupid."

"I know it sounds corny but it's true. I saw fireworks when we kissed. Just wait until Stephen kisses you. You'll see."

Lowering her voice, Alyssa tells me, "We already kissed."

"And you didn't tell me?" I'm so hurt. I thought Alyssa would've told me something so important. "Do Stacy and Penny know? Did you tell them?" If she did, I'm about to get really fired up.

She shakes her head. "No. I don't go around telling my business. I was gonna tell you—I just didn't want you thinking I was fast."

"I wouldn't think that about you. I know better than that."

Alyssa hugs me again. "We're growing up, girl."

"Don't say that too loud. We don't need Uncle Reed or Aunt Phoebe hearing about this. They'd lose their minds or lock us up forever."

"You wrong." Laughing, Alyssa tosses a pillow at me.

Alyssa and I get up early to finish our chores so that we can go with Aunt Phoebe to Phipps Plaza for the Memorial Day sales.

I already know the stores I plan to hit. Elie Tahari, Nordstrom, Saks Fifth Avenue, Jimmy Choo, and Juicy Couture. All favorites of mine. Aunt Phoebe loves Parisian.

I watch a girl nearby with her father and my conversation with Jerome comes back to mind. I still can't believe how he reacted to my staying with Uncle Reed. I'm living with a preacher. My own father has taken someone's life.

"It must be nice to have a father who's normal," I say to Alyssa while we're strolling through Saks. "Uncle Reed is kind of a nerd, but you're lucky."

She shrugs. "Daddy's okay. He's nice and all but sometimes I think he's too strict. And he spends a lot of time at the church."

"That's much better than chasing women," I point out.

"What's going on, Divine?"

"All those stories about Jerome and Shelly are true," I blurt out. "Even the one about the baby. Jerome has a son. He admitted it. He even said that killing Shelly was an accident. I just don't know if I believe him about that."

Alyssa gives me a sympathetic look that makes me feel worse. "I was hoping that it wasn't true. For your sake."

"Me too. I'm totally grossed out."

"I guess I would be too." Alyssa loops her arm through mine. "It's gonna be okay, though. You'll be fine."

"He wasn't always very nice to my mom. Or to me. I've never told anybody this. Not even Mimi."

"I kind of figured that. Just from the things I heard on TV and read in the magazines. I'm surprised Aunt Kara stayed with him. I always thought she would leave."

I shake my head no. "She just talked about it. I don't think Mom could leave Jerome because she loves him too much." I stop walking when I spy a pair of 7 For All Mankind jeans. Holding them against my hips, I say, "I don't ever want to love like that. It's crazy. Now, I'd buy these jeans here."

"I want to have a relationship like my parents. Mama met Daddy when she was nine years old. He's her only love."

"Wow. That's nice. I like that too. No drama." I look for a top to go with the jeans.

Alyssa tries on a denim jacket. "I'm sure they had plenty of drama but their love was strong enough to overcome it."

I straighten her collar. "You need to stop reading all those romance novels."

"Why?"

"You're beginning to sound like one."

"Maybe you *should* read them. Then you'll never give up on love." She looks at herself in a nearby mirror. "This is definitely not me." Alyssa takes off the jacket and puts it back on the hanger.

I take it from her. "You need to get it. It looks good on you and it's not even expensive. It's marked down to seventy dollars."

"That may not be expensive to you, but to me it's still a lot of money. For a jean jacket?"

"I'll get it for you. You looked hot in it." We move to the next sale rack. "I'm really surprised Aunt Phoebe lets you read romance novels." I glance over my shoulder to see if she's anywhere nearby. I don't see her so I speak freely. "They're full of sex. Stella reads them all the time and Mom almost lost her mind when I borrowed one."

"My novels are Christian romances. They don't have any sex in them at all. They hardly have kissing."

"I didn't know there were romances like that. Hmmmm."

"You should read some of mine. They're good."

"We'll see." I point straight ahead. "This dress is so cute."

Alyssa checks the price tag and her mouth drops open. "Girl, did you see how much this dress costs? Eight hundred and fifteen dollars."

"It's a Blumarine. Believe me, eight hundred dollars for a dress like this isn't bad. You should see some of the couture pieces Mom's bought me. You're talking thousands of dollars."

"No way I'ma spend that kind of money on one outfit."

"If you're rich you will. It won't matter to you."

Alyssa shakes her head. "I could do so much more with money like that, Divine."

"Like what?"

"Help feed the homeless or help abused women's shelters. You could take that money and buy clothes for them."

"You would do something like that?"

Alyssa nods. "The Bible tells us that we're to help one another."

"A lot of the homeless can work. They're just too lazy to do it."

"Not all the time," Alyssa counters. "Have you ever been to a shelter?"

"Yeah. Mama and I went to Florida a couple of years ago to help out when they were hit by a hurricane. We gave money."

"I remember. It was all over the news. It was just before your mom's new movie came out."

"So what are you trying to say?"

"I'm sure her visiting shelters during that time helped her box office."

"It wasn't just about the publicity. I'm sure my mom really wanted to be there." But deep down I'm wondering if Alyssa's right and if I really know my parents at all.

* * *

Yesterday was the last day of school. *Yes.*

Today Alyssa and I are going to the pool at a local recreational center to show off our new swimsuits. We're planning to meet Stacy and Penny there.

Alyssa is still pouting over the fact that she couldn't buy a bikini. Aunt Phoebe's as bad as Mom when it comes to stuff like this.

Mom's a bit of a hypocrite in my opinion, though. She wears some really skimpy clothing when she's performing and on film. She calls them her work uniforms. True, she doesn't dress like that when she's home with me, but still . . . they are scandalous.

Alyssa turns around slowly. "Tell me the truth, Divine. How do I look in this swimsuit?"

"Hot."

"I hope you're talking about the weather," Aunt Phoebe says when she enters the bedroom. "'Cause if you're not, then my child might need to wear a T-shirt and shorts in the pool."

"She was talkin' 'bout the weather, Mama."

Aunt Phoebe laughs. "You think I'ma fool, don't you? C'mon, girls, let's head out. I need to go up to the church this afternoon."

She drops us off at the recreational center with instructions to meet her at four P.M. sharp. "Be out front when I come."

"We will," we say in unison.

I hear my name and turn around. "What are they doing here?" I ask Alyssa.

"I told Stephen I was coming to the pool. I guess he told Madison."

"Girl, you are as bad as your brother."

"Like you wouldn't have invited Madison. I heard you hint-ing to him last night on the phone."

I laugh, but deep down I'm feeling a little guilty. Uncle Reed and Aunt Phoebe trust us and we're betraying that trust. I know what that feels like.

My guilt increases the longer we're at the pool. When I can't take it anymore, I pull Alyssa to the side.

"I know you're going to hate me, but I think we should leave."

"Why? We just got here."

"Because I feel bad, Alyssa. We're betraying your parents' trust in us. We're no better than Jerome."

Alyssa steals a peek across her shoulder to where Madison and Stephen are sitting. "You sure you want to leave? It's not like we're doing anything bad. We're just hanging out. Penny and Stacy are here too."

"I don't feel right about this, Alyssa. I just don't. I'm sorry, but I've been going through some weird stuff lately. Maybe I'm about to die or something. I just want to get right." I give a light chuckle. "Funny, huh?"

"No. I get that way sometimes. And you're right, Divine. We should go home."

We tell the others that I'm not feeling well and leave. Since we have to walk home, I'm relieved the recreational center is only three blocks away.

We call Aunt Phoebe to let her know that we're home. When she wants to know why we left the pool so early, Alyssa looks over at me before saying, "Divine just wanted to come home. We're gonna make some sandwiches and watch a couple of movies, I guess."

Uncle Reed and Aunt Phoebe come home shortly after three. They find us in the family room watching TV.

"I can't believe y'all just up and decided to come home early from the rec. I know how much y'all love the pool."

Alyssa's eyes travel to mine.

"I just felt like being in the house today. I didn't really want to mess up my hair. I don't have another appointment for two weeks," I reply. How's that for quick thinking?

"You know, when I was leaving the rec, I saw Madison and Stephen." Aunt Phoebe looks from me to Alyssa. "Now, I was thinkin' that maybe y'all had this all planned. You know . . . to meet at the pool. But then when you called and said you were back home, I got to thinkin'."

"We didn't bring them back here," I tell her. "We walked to the house alone."

"Calm down, sugar. I know that."

"How?"

"I went over to the rec and the boys were still there," Uncle Reed announces. "This is what I believe happened today. I think you or Alyssa or the two of you planned to meet up with those boys at the pool, but then your conscience started to bother you."

My heart starts beating faster. We are so busted.

"You two can relax. We're proud of you for taking the out that God generously provided. You listened to the Holy Spirit and came home."

Aunt Phoebe took over. "Girls, I know what it's like to be young. I know you've developed these feelings and you want boyfriends. You want to experience dating, but you're both just not ready yet. You're too young."

Here we go . . . Mom mode.

"Give yourself time. There will always be boys. The world's not gonna run out. Just slow it down. We trust you both and we want to keep that trust. Do you understand what I'm saying to you?"

"Yes ma'am," we respond in unison.

When they leave the room, Alyssa and I collapse to the floor in relief.

"Thank you, Holy Spirit," I whisper. That was close.

chapter 16

On the thirtieth of June, I get a call from Mimi, who tells me that she's coming to Atlanta.

I scream with excitement. I run out of the laundry room and down the hall to the bedroom, looking for Alyssa. She's changing the sheets on her bed.

"Mimi's going to be in Atlanta tomorrow and she's coming to see me on Saturday. I can't wait for you to meet her."

"That's great," Alyssa says. "I know how much you must miss her. After all the things you've told me about her, I can't wait to meet this Mimi."

"You're going to love her. I just know it."

"I don't know about that. I can't believe there's two of you in this world."

"You're so not funny. Seriously though. You're going to like her, Alyssa. Mimi talks too much sometimes, but other than that she's a lot of fun to be around."

"Are her parents coming out here with her? I love all of her daddy's movies."

"I don't think so. She just mentioned that they planned to order a car for her."

"Wow, the lives of the rich and famous . . ."

"One day when you're all done with college, you're going to be just as rich and famous, Alyssa."

She laughs. "Only in my dreams."

I could hardly sleep last night. I'm so excited about seeing Mimi again. It's only been since March but it feels like ages. We're going to have the best time ever.

Mimi calls from the plane to give me an update and then again when she lands in Atlanta.

"Why don't you order a car and come here tonight?" she asks me. "You can stay in our suite."

"Uncle Reed's not going to let me do that."

"Divine," Mimi whines. "Father's getting some dumb award tonight, so I have to stay around here for that. I'm so bored. Just ask your uncle, please."

"I already know he's going to say no."

We talk until it's time for her to get ready for the awards banquet. I call Madison as soon as I hang up with her.

"I thought you said your girl was in town."

"She is. She's in Atlanta at an awards banquet, but she's coming out here tomorrow."

"Will I get to meet her?"

"I don't know. We'll have to see."

Madison and I talk for a little over an hour, then my phone starts to die. "I'll have to call you later," I tell him. "I have to recharge my phone. Alyssa's on the house phone with Stephen so I probably won't get to use that one."

We say our good-byes and hang up.

While I'm waiting for Alyssa to get off the phone, I pick up one of her romance novels and start to read. Soon my eyes feel heavy.

When I open them up, the sun is rising. I glance over at the clock. It's seven forty-five in the morning.

I sit up in bed.

"You must have been tired," Alyssa says from beneath her covers. "I came in the room at ten-fifteen and you were knocked out. You didn't even hear your cell phone—girl, it was blowing up. I thought I was gonna have to toss it in the toilet."

I pick up my phone and check the caller ID. "It was Mimi. I need to call her back."

She picks up on the second ring. Her voice is muffled like she's still in bed. "Hullo."

"Sorry for calling you so early. I went to sleep around ten and didn't wake up until a few minutes ago. Are you still coming out here today?"

"My car is coming to pick me up at ten."

"Great. I'll be looking to see you between eleven and noon."

Alyssa shoots up in bed. "Mimi's coming?"

I nod.

She jumps out of bed. "Divine, we need to clean up. I want the house to be straight."

* * *

Mimi arrives a few minutes after twelve.

I make the introductions. "Uncle Reed, this is my friend Mimi. And this is my Aunt Phoebe."

I'm looking around for Alyssa so much that it doesn't register when Mimi says, "It's so nice to meet you, Phoebe. You too, Reed. Divine totally—"

Aunt Phoebe interrupts her. "Young lady, please address me as Miss Phoebe or Mrs. Matthews and my husband as Pastor Matthews. You are Divine's friend, not ours."

Mimi sends me a weird look before saying, "Okay. Sure."

"What was that about?" she asks in a whisper when my aunt and uncle leave the room. "What did I do to her?"

"It's the way things are done down here," I explain. "They're big on respect."

Mimi's eyes travel the room. She takes a peek down the hallway. "Dee, tell me this is not where you've been living all this time?"

"Excuse me?"

"Oooh. Girl, I know your mother hasn't seen this. There's totally no way she would let you stay here."

"Mom grew up in this town, Mimi."

"My mother grew up in a small town outside of Birmingham, Alabama. She doesn't even like going back to visit much less let me stay there for longer than an hour. Like, you practically live on a farm. I saw some cows and goats just down the road."

Her comments are totally putting me in a bad mood. "Mimi, it's not that bad here."

"They've brainwashed you. We've got to get you out of here."

Mimi is my best friend but if she doesn't drop this, I'm going to demote her to semi-friend.

"Omigod, who's that girl staring me down?" Mimi asks. "Is that your cousin?"

I glance over my shoulder. "Yeah, that's Alyssa. I want you to meet her."

"*For what*? We don't have a thing in common."

"Be nice, Mimi." I gesture for Alyssa to join us.

Smiling, she walks over and extends her hand to Mimi. "I've heard so much about you from Divine. I feel like I already know you."

"Well, you don't," Mimi retorts and ignores Alyssa.

I'm so embarrassed. "This is my cousin. The one I've told you about."

"Dee, let's go. I'm starving. The car's outside. Father told the driver to take us anywhere we want to go."

"You have fun, Divine. I'll see you when you get back." Alyssa walks out of the room. I can tell she's upset and I don't blame her.

I turn to my soon-to-be-former friend. "Mimi, I don't appreciate your being rude to my cousin. She didn't do anything to you."

"I didn't like the way she was staring at me. Is she gay?"

I look at Mimi as if she's insane. "No. Just very nice. Something you should learn to be."

Flinging her weave over her shoulders, Mimi demands, "What did you say to me?"

"You heard me loud and clear, Mimi. You're rude and you think you're so much better than other people. I hate to break it to you, but you're such a snob."

"Oh and like you're not," Mimi shoots back. "You're just as much of a snob as I am. If not more. You're the one who's always bragging about your house, your cars and who you know. Like you're the only one with parents who are stars."

I couldn't deny any of that so I say, "I don't go around being nasty to people just because I can. *You do.*"

"Look Dee, I came all the way here to see you, not argue. I'm sorry your country cousin got her feelings hurt but I'm not here to visit her."

"I think it'll be better if you leave, Mimi. I'm not going to have you being rude to Alyssa. And don't ever refer to her as being *country* again. If you do, you can consider our friendship over."

"What's gotten into you, Dee? Why are you treating me this way?"

"Give me a call when you develop manners. You come to my aunt and uncle's house and you insult their house and their children. That's so not cool. You never heard me talk about *your* relatives—and you know yourself some of them are straight-up crazy."

"So what do you want me to do? Apologize?"

I shake my head. "I want you to leave, Mimi. Let's just call it a day. I'm sorry you came all the way out here for nothing."

"I don't know what's wrong with you, Dee, but I'm going to have Mother call Kara."

"Whatever . . ."

"These people are not your real family, Dee. They don't even know you."

"See Mimi, that's where you're wrong. They *are* my family." I finally have that normal family I've always wanted. Pointing to the front door, I tell her, "Your car's waiting."

Mimi storms out of the house.

I watch her car pull away and take off down the road. The driver's probably thrilled he didn't have to chauffeur around a couple of teenage girls.

"Where's your friend?" Alyssa asks from behind me.

I turn around to face her. "I sent her back to Atlanta. I'd forgotten how badly Mimi can get on my nerves. I'm so sorry about the way she treated you."

"I'm okay. You don't have to worry about me. I can't stand your friend though."

"That's just the way Mimi is. She's very snobby. I wanted to laugh so bad when Aunt Phoebe set her straight." I give her a brief recap.

"That's Mama," Alyssa says with a short laugh. "She don't play when it comes to stuff like that."

Together, we make our way to the kitchen.

"Divine, I feel bad about you and Mimi fighting. Why don't you give her a call? Don't be mad at her because of me. You've known her a lot longer."

"But you're my family, Alyssa. Nobody insults you but me."

"Same here, Hollywood."

"Do you think we can talk Aunt Phoebe into dropping us off at the mall? We can have lunch and maybe catch a movie."

"Yes. Let's do lunch, dah-ling." Alyssa puckers up her lips. "Smooches."

"Don't ever do that again. *Ever.*"

Alyssa and I do everything we can to get Uncle Reed and Aunt Phoebe to bend their rule when it comes to boys. "Please, Uncle Reed. We're not talking about dating. We just want Madison and Stephen to be able to come by here. Just a couple of days a week."

"I'd settle for just one day a week," Alyssa tells them.

You're not helping our case, I want to shout. "I'm going to be fifteen soon and so is Alyssa. You guys will be here at the house, so I don't get why you want to be so strict. We're not asking to go out somewhere."

"We know what you're asking, Divine, and you have our answer. Phoebe and I both feel that y'all are too young to be seeing boys. Right now you just need to focus on your studies."

"But you're being unfair."

"I'm sorry you feel that way."

Tears sting the back of my eyes. "I can't believe you're treating us like this! We could be sneaky and see them anyway."

"You could certainly try," Aunt Phoebe declares. "But you wouldn't like the consequences. We want to be able to trust you girls. We do trust you. This is not the issue."

"Then what is it?" Alyssa asks. "Other girls our age are already dating. I know a girl who goes to the movies with her boyfriend every weekend and she's only in the sixth grade. Her parents or his parents take them."

"I don't care what someone else does in their household—I have to worry about mine." Aunt Phoebe gets to her feet. "You're not missing anything. Boys will be around through the end of the world. Your chance for education won't. When you get your head filled up with boys, you start messing up."

"But we won't, Mama."

"Honey, you'll say just about anything right now. I understand. Really I do. When you start getting close to these boys and you start messing around . . . you know what I'm talking about. You start kissing and then you get to feeling things. Your body reacts and then before you know it somebody's pregnant."

Alyssa and I exchange glances. *Who wants to be pregnant? I don't.* "I don't even like kids," I say.

"You don't have to like 'em to get 'em, sweetie."

My mouth drops open. "I'm not interested in doing nothing like that, Aunt Phoebe."

"You may not now, but as soon as boys start sniffing around, your feelings will change. I know what goes on."

I sigh in resignation. "Well, thanks for hearing us out." I start out of the room.

Aunt Phoebe calls me back. "Honey, I promise you there will be enough time for boys and dating. Just focus on your education right now."

I nod. Whatever. Thankfully, school is starting in a couple of weeks. We'll get to see Madison and Stephen every single day.

Most of my summer vacations have been spent traveling abroad and to the Caribbean Islands, but not this year. This year, the highlight of my summer will be the upcoming church picnic in mid-July.

With Mom still in rehab and Jerome in prison, I have no choice but to accept my misfortune. In all honesty, it's not been too terrible.

I'm settling into a nice routine, and there have been many times that I've actually enjoyed myself. I guess my aunt and uncle are kind of growing on me. I just wish Aunt Phoebe would let me pick out her clothes. She's already as tall as a tree and she loves wearing those big hats to church. Hats with feathers.

Thinking about Aunt Phoebe's hats had me thinking about church again. Mom and Jerome never talked much in front of me about it. Our cook, Miss Eula, used to talk about church all the time though. She even invited me a couple of times to go with her, but I wasn't interested. I didn't think I could find cute boys there.

I was so wrong. Uncle Reed has lots of cute boys in his church. They won't really say much to me and Alyssa because Aunt Phoebe always gives them this real evil look. She's out to ruin our lives—I'm convinced of it.

But then again, she did let us go to a party this past weekend. It was given by one of the girls from church. I have to admit I was a little surprised that we were allowed to dance and just have a good time.

I overheard a couple of girls talking about going to Bible college after they graduate. They were talking about surrounding themselves with like-minded people. Other Christians, I'm assuming.

They were making being Christian almost sound fashionable. I just might have to give it a little more thought.

"Are you ready to go over to the pool?" Alyssa inquires just as I finish the last of my lemonade.

Throwing away my plastic cup, I respond, "Not yet. I told Aunt Phoebe I would help her serve the kids." I swatted at a fly with my hand.

"Oh. I guess I'll help y'all too."

I glance around the John Tanner State Park where the annual church picnic is being held. Everybody looks like they're having a good time.

I break into a laugh. Uncle Reed is actually out there trying to act like he can play basketball. "Girl, look at your dad," I tell Alyssa.

"Now my daddy knows he gon' be hurtin' tonight."

"Maybe your mom will give him a *special* massage."

Alyssa frowns. "Oooh, don't even say that."

I laugh. "You have a dirty mind. C'mon, Aunt Phoebe's looking over here at us. She's ready to get those plates filled."

The mid-July weather was nice. Not too hot but it was humid, which did nothing for my hair. I was going to have to pull it up in a ponytail. The curls were gone anyway. No wonder Aunt Phoebe laughed when I insisted on getting my hair done before the picnic.

Alyssa and I helped with the children, making sure they had everything they needed. Then we fixed plates for ourselves.

"This is nice," I tell Alyssa. "My first church picnic. I'm having a good time."

"See, Hollywood . . . I told you things wouldn't be so bad here. You just have to have an open mind."

"I still miss Mom. I kind of miss Jerome too. Even though he stayed on my nerves."

"You'll see your mom in about four months. That's not too long."

"It seems like a lifetime to me, Alyssa."

chapter 17

School starts in another week so we're out with Aunt Phoebe doing the last of our shopping.

"One thing I like about here is that I don't have to wear uniforms to school." I pick up a sheer shirt and press it to my body.

Aunt Phoebe takes it from me and puts it back on the clothing rack. "Definitely not for you."

Alyssa reaches for a pair of jeans. "Oooh, I love these."

"They're jeans," I tell her. "You already have like a million pairs of them. Try something different for a change."

"But I don't have any like these."

Alyssa is hopeless when it comes to fashion. I'm doing everything I can to help her but she just doesn't get it.

"Divine, you should get a pair of these for yourself. You look real cute in jeans."

"Really?"

Alyssa nods. "Nobody really dresses up for school here. Get some jeans—they don't have to be plain. Get the cute ones with the cool pattern."

I stand there considering her suggestion. "Hmmmm, maybe I should." Alyssa's right. Kids don't dress up for school and I don't really want to stand out that much. Well, it's not like I can help it. I'm an original.

Alyssa and I head to the dressing room to try on clothes. I'm so excited about going to high school. Madison and I will finally be in the same school. We'll get to see each other and hopefully have lunch together.

I end up purchasing three pairs of rhinestone-studded jeans. I'm too much of a fashion diva to just settle on plain denim. It's just not me.

"I knew you couldn't do it," Alyssa tells me as we're walking out of the department store. "You just got to be cute."

"It's in my blood. I have to be fashionable. I admit it, I'm a diva."

Aunt Phoebe laughs. "You are your mother's child."

We get home in time for Chance and Alyssa to go to choir rehearsal. They are still trying to talk me into joining the choir but I'm not ready. I'm still not real comfortable with my singing.

After cleaning the kitchen for Aunt Phoebe, I retreat to the bedroom to write Mom. She's still got three months to go before she can leave rehab. I miss her so much that I cry each time I write her.

No more splashing water to make the paper look tearstained. These are for real.

Jerome's written me three letters so far and I refuse to open them. I just can't read them right now. I'm not sure why. Uncle Reed tries to get me to share my feelings, but I'm not interested.

Jerome's a loser. Big-time.

I go online after I finish my letter to Mom. Rhyann IMs me as soon as I sign in, wanting to know if I'm still mad at Mimi. I'm pretty sure Mimi's put her up to asking me. I haven't spoken to her since July and don't know if I ever will again.

I type that I'm not mad but I have no words for Mimi right now.

She responds, saying that Mimi is so hurt.

And? How does she think she made my cousin feel? I type in that I have to sign off and close the little window before Rhyann has a chance to respond. I don't want to discuss Mimi.

My cell phone rings and I know without picking it up that it's Mimi. She calls at least twice a day.

Hellooo . . . take a hint. I'm not talking to you, loser.

Suddenly Uncle Reed's words on forgiveness rush to my mind. I need to forgive Mimi for the way she acted with Alyssa. It's the right thing to do.

I'm still mad at her, but I have to be the bigger person. I reach for the phone and key in Mimi's number. She answers almost immediately, like she was just waiting on my call.

"Dee, I'm so glad you finally called me back. I'm so sorry."

"I'm sorry too."

We talk for at least twenty minutes and while I'm glad to be on speaking terms with Mimi again, I can tell that our friendship has changed. Maybe it's because *I've* changed. I'm not the same girl who left Pacific Palisades back in March. Thankfully, I'm still cute. Some things just never change.

August twenty-second is my first day as an official high school student. I'm a freshman.

Alyssa and I have history and math class together. Madison and I have lunch together, so I'm able to spend time with him daily. I don't see him much between classes, so the time we have is special.

I still have a bunch of girls hatin' on me but I just ignore them. I can't help that I'm beautiful. Life is what it is.

After school, I wait out front for Chance and Alyssa to come. Since Chance is seventeen now, he and Trina are officially dating. He's even bringing her over to the house on Sunday for dinner.

I'm looking forward to turning sixteen so that Madison and I can date. Okay, I need to slow it down. I'm not going to even be in Georgia by that time. I'm leaving in a couple of months. As soon as Mom gets out of rehab.

I suddenly feel a touch of sadness. I'm going to miss Alyssa, Uncle Reed, Aunt Phoebe and Chance. Madison, Stacy and Penny. Everyone . . .

I don't want to think about it right now because it depresses me. I just need to enjoy the next couple of months as much as I can. I'll create wonderful memories that I can cherish forever. And I'll do like Aunt Phoebe and take lots of pictures.

I'm so caught up in my thoughts that I don't realize Alyssa is right behind me. I scream when she taps me on the shoulder.

"What's wrong with you?"

"You scared me. Don't sneak up behind me like that." I start walking. "Where's Chance?"

"He's got football practice."

"That's right. I forgot."

"The first game is Friday. We're playing Villa Rica High. They beat us last year but I hope we win this time."

"You like football?"

"I do since Chance is playing."

"I've never been to a high school football game. I've been to a couple of NFL games though."

"Those are probably much better than the high school ones."

I shrug. "I don't like football, so I don't really watch the games."

Alyssa laughs. "Who goes to a football game to actually watch the game?"

A week later, Aunt Phoebe hands me a letter from Jerome when I arrive home from school.

"Thanks," I mumble and head off to the bedroom. *Why is this loser still writing me?* I wonder. *Can't he take a hint?* I toss it into the box where all the others are.

"Hey, is it safe for me to come in now?" Alyssa asks. "You look like you were ready to kill somebody when Mama gave you that letter."

"I got another stupid letter from Jerome. I'm not even going to open it right now."

"Aren't you at least curious about what he has to say?"

I shake my head. "Jerome lived with me forever and didn't bother talking to me. Why is he so interested in me now?"

"Maybe he really feels bad about that. He's in jail so I'm sure he has a lot of time on his hands right now. Time to think."

"Well, it's too late."

"Mama has Bible Study tonight, so we have to cook. She took out some chicken."

"Let's do barbecue chicken. I cut out a recipe out of *Ebony* magazine. I think we have most of the ingredients already. We bought the stuff but decided to fry the chicken last time. Remember?"

Alyssa laughs at the memory. "We messed up that chicken. Chance had to run out and buy some KFC—and then you tried to convince Mama and Daddy that we cooked it."

"Anyway, let's do barbecue this time around."

I look back at the box of letters I've collected. Maybe Alyssa's right. Jerome's not going anywhere for a long time, so I figure I have plenty of time to read his letters.

Uncle Reed pulls me into his office after dinner. "I notice you're still not reading your letters from your daddy."

"I'm not ready."

He nods. "I see."

"I'm not doing it because I'm angry, Uncle Reed."

He studies my face as if he doesn't believe me. "Then why won't you read the letters?"

"I guess I don't want to give him a chance to hurt me again," I confess. "I've had enough. Enough to last a whole lifetime."

"Jerome can't hurt you, Divine. I believe in his own way that he loves you."

"He cheated on me and Mama. He had an affair with Shelly. They have a baby." Okay, I'm a little bit angry still.

"He made a mistake, Divine."

"He keeps saying that he's going to make it up to me. How?"

"I don't know. But what I do know is that you'll never find out if you don't read his letters. He can't make it right if you won't give him a chance."

"Why do you care so much, Uncle Reed? It's not like you like Jerome."

"Because I can look in your eyes and see how unhappy this makes you. Even though you don't want to admit it, you love your father."

Maybe Uncle Reed knows me better than I know myself.

"What are you two over there plotting?" Aunt Phoebe asks when she enters the family room. "You've had your heads together all afternoon. What's going on?"

Alyssa nudges me. "Ask her," she whispers.

"You ask her. She's your mom."

"*Somebody* ask me," Aunt Phoebe says.

I forgot she's got the hearing of a dog. Mom used to call it mother's ears.

My cousin is sitting on the sofa waiting for me to speak up. "Chicken . . ." I hiss.

Aunt Phoebe's watching us both. "C'mon, out with it. What do you two want?"

"There's a dance on Friday, after the football game. And we were wondering if we could go."

"Sure."

We jump up for joy until she adds, "I'll be going with you. I'm sure the school's gon' need some chaperones."

"Our teachers chaperone the school dances," I rush out. "You don't need to do it." The last thing we need is for Aunt Phoebe to be at the dance with us. We'd look like losers for sure.

I'd die from the humiliation alone. Besides, we were planning to hang with Madison and Stephen. They're our dates—only we don't dare tell Aunt Phoebe.

"Now why is it you don't want me to come?"

"Mama, it's not cool. All the kids at school will laugh at us. Please don't do this. You can take us and pick us up."

She laughs. "Oh, I can, huh? You girls think I was born yesterday, don't you? I know you planning to meet those boys at the dance. Y'all ain't as slick as you think you are. I'ma let you go, but only because Chance will be there. He knows to keep an eye on you. Both of you."

I jump up and rush to Aunt Phoebe, hugging her. This time my hair is all in her face and her cheek is shiny from my lip gloss.

"Thanks."

"Now listen to me. You and Alyssa are going to the dance with Chance. You two stay where he can see you. I don't want to hear about you and those boys sneaking off somewhere. I got spies all over that school, so I will find out."

Her words unnerve me.

"And y'all better make sure you keep your lips to yourselves. I'm not a fool."

My first high school dance is everything I thought it would be. Madison and I stay out on the floor showing off our moves. I'm a good dancer, if I say so myself. I've worked out with some of the most talented choreographers in the country.

We have a curfew and have to be home by midnight. The dance doesn't end until one, but Aunt Phoebe wasn't about to let us stay out that late. Even Chance has to be home the same time as us, which totally makes him mad because he's older.

"Trina's curfew is midnight too, so what difference does it really make?" I tell Chance when his complaining starts getting on my nerves. "You plan on coming back here without her?"

"Yeah," Trina says. "What's up with that? Why you so upset about leaving at midnight?"

He glowers at me. "See what you started."

"Stop bugging." I take Madison by the hand and we head back out to the dance floor. "Do you see Stephen and Alyssa?"

Madison's eyes scan the dimly lit room. "Naw."

We move to the music. In the back of my mind, I'm getting concerned over where Alyssa could be. She'd better not be getting into trouble. She'll ruin everything for all of us.

Pretty soon, I hear laughter and it sounds like her. I turn around and Alyssa's a few feet away from us dancing with her boyfriend. Madison and I move until we're right beside them.

"Girl, I've been looking for you. Where were you?" I ask.

"We went outside for a few minutes. I was getting over-heated in here."

I brush back a tendril of hair that's come undone from her upswept style. "I bet you were."

She gives me a playful jab. "Shut up, Hollywood."

The evening ends way too soon for me. This is always the case, it seems, whenever I'm with Madison. We have strict orders to be home no later than midnight, so we walk out of the gym twenty minutes before. This gives us plenty of time to say our good-byes and meet Uncle Reed in the school parking lot.

Alyssa and I leave our boyfriends in the front of the gym. We don't want Uncle Reed seeing them at all. He could have arrived earlier than we anticipated and I just don't want the drama after having such a good time. Chance is a little more daring. He and Trina walk hand in hand toward the parking lot.

"Tonight was fun, wasn't it?" Alyssa asks.

"It was," I confirm. "I had a good time. Did you see Madison out there on the dance floor? My boo can dance. He'd put Usher to shame."

"I don't know about all that, now. He can dance a lil bit . . . but Usher . . . I think Madison might have to work up to that."

I don't realize just how tired I am until we get home and undress for bed. Alyssa's still rambling on about Stephen, but I'm not really listening. All I want to do right now is go to sleep and dream of Madison.

chapter 18

November is finally here!

Mom's getting out of rehab in another week and I can hardly wait. I've missed her so much.

Alyssa and I get along well except for a few arguments here and there. Chance is hardly ever home long enough to get into anything serious with him. He believes he's in love with Trina and when they're not making goo-goo eyes at each other, he's either practicing or playing football.

Madison and I are still talking. Actually, we've kissed a few times. I'm never telling Mom or my aunt and uncle. They'd freak out. Only Alyssa knows and I've sworn her to secrecy. Besides I know that she's been kissing Stephen. I've caught them smooching a couple of times.

Uncle Reed wants me to sing a solo on Sunday but I'm thinking of having a bad headache, cramps—something. I don't think I can do it. Maybe if Mom were here.

Yeah, right. Like that would make it easier. I think she'd probably make me even more nervous.

I steal a peek at the clock on the bedside table. I need to study for a test and stop all this daydreaming.

I pick up my history book and open it to the Civil War. I'm not worried. I've read a lot of books on the subject so I feel confident that I'll pass the test with no problem.

I can hear Alyssa in the hallway with Aunt Phoebe, talking and laughing. I really can't wait to see my mom. I want us to be like my aunt and cousin.

I'm still bothered by those pictures in the photo albums—the ones taken before she met Jerome. The ones where she seems happier than I've ever seen her. I have to know if I make her happy.

But will I even know if she's telling me the truth? I pull out my notebook and jot down all the things I need to talk to her about—and, of course, stuff we need to do.

"Hey, what's the list for?"

I glance up from my notebook. "Stop being so nosy, Alyssa. But since you asked, I'm making a list of all the things I want to do with Mom when she gets out of rehab." Breaking into a smile, I go on. "She called me earlier and said she's getting released this Friday."

Alyssa starts jumping up and down. "*Yes.* I finally get to meet her. I get to meet Aunt Kara."

I frown. "Like, I don't believe you."

"I'm sorry. Hollywood, I'm so happy for you." Alyssa's smile disappears. "I'm a little sad about it too."

"Why?" I ask.

"Because it means you're going to be leaving soon. I'm going to miss you."

I'd been so focused on Mom getting out of rehab and seeing her again, I hadn't given much thought to the fact that this meant I was leaving Temple and everyone here behind.

"We'll still see each other and we can keep in touch, Alyssa."

"It won't be the same, Hollywood."

"Don't start crying on me, girl." I'm sitting here trying to cheer up Alyssa, but deep down, I'm feeling a little sad myself at the thought of leaving.

"There's a car pulling into our driveway," Chance announces.

"Who is it?" Alyssa runs to the window and peeks outside. "Oh my goodness," she yells. "It's Aunt Kara. She's here."

I can't believe I'm hearing her correctly. Mom isn't due here for another three or four days. At least that's what she said in her last phone call.

Alyssa throws open the front door.

I can barely believe my eyes. I run toward her. "Mom, what are you doing here?"

She brushes my hair out of my face. "Well, I thought you'd be glad to see me, sugar."

"I am. It's just that I didn't expect to see you for a couple more days." I look over my shoulder at Aunt Phoebe. "Did you know she was coming today?"

"Nobody knew," Mom replies. "I wanted to surprise you, hon." Mom holds her arms open. "Come give your mama a big hug. I haven't felt your arms around me in a long time."

When I feel the warmth of her embrace, my eyes fill with tears. "You're finally here. I can't believe it."

"Believe it because I'm here, baby. I sure am."

I hold on to her tight because I'm afraid if I let go, she'll vanish and I don't want her to disappear. "Mom, I never thought this day would come. I've missed you so much."

"This day here is what kept me going when it got rough," Mom tells me. "I just kept thinking about seeing you."

Her words bring more tears to my eyes. I wipe them away with the backs of my hands. I don't want her thinking I'm a little baby.

Mom's gaze travels to Alyssa. "Now you know you got to come give your auntie a hug." She welcomes Alyssa with open arms. "Ooh, it's so nice to see you. You're such a beauty. I know my brother and Phoebe keep you under lock and key. Divine tells me you can really sing. I want you to sing something for me. Okay?"

Mom certainly hasn't forgotten her roots. She's home not even five minutes and it's like she's never left, to hear her talk anyway.

Alyssa's grinning so hard her braces are blinding me, but I don't mind. She's really wanted to meet my mom.

Mom gives Chance a big hug and busts me out by telling him that I've told her all about Trina. He doesn't seem to mind, though.

"You didn't tell her about me and Stephen, did you?" Alyssa questions in a low voice.

"No," I whisper back.

Mom's watching us. "What are you two up to? All that whispering back and forth—you up to something."

"Just talking. Alyssa's very excited about meeting you."

"Uh-huh."

I get the feeling Mom doesn't believe me. She lets the matter drop, however.

Uncle Reed and Aunt Phoebe take Alyssa and Chance to see a movie to give us some time to catch up.

"You look like you're fitting in here well."

I nod. "Things are going okay."

"Alyssa and Chance seem like sweethearts. Y'all getting along real good?"

"Yes ma'am," I respond without thinking.

Mom looks surprised. "Wow, Reed's whipped you into shape, huh?"

"I'm just showing you respect."

"Oh, I like it. Keep it up."

Mom looks beautiful and she's put on some weight. Now she doesn't have that anorexic look about her. "You look good, Mom."

"I gained a few pounds."

"It doesn't look bad on you."

"I like the new me. I feel good; I'm happier."

"Are you really?" I question. I think about the pictures in the photo album on the table and reach to pick it up. Now seems like the perfect time to ask her the one question that's been burning in my heart for weeks now.

"What's the matter, honey?"

"Aunt Phoebe has all these pictures of you when you were younger. I saw you with an Afro."

Mom laughs. "I remember those days."

"In the pictures you look happy. Really happy. Like I've never seen you look."

Her smile disappears as she takes the album and opens it.

"This was before you met Jerome."

She nods. "Yeah. It was. Right before I left for college."

I point to a photograph. "See how happy you look right here. Look at your eyes."

Mom looks at me. "My little girl is growing up. Divine, I have some very fond memories of my youth. They were very happy times for me."

"What happened?"

She plays with my ponytail. "Life happened, sugar. You won't really understand until you're much older."

"Mom, do I make you happy?"

"Divine, of course you do," she assures me. "Honey, you are my best work ever. You are my life."

"Mom, I love you and I want . . . I want you to be happy. It's my prayer."

"I am happy. Now that I'm here with you, life just doesn't get any better than this."

When the rest of the family returns home two and a half hours later, we hold a meeting to decide on dinner. Mom is dying for a home-cooked meal, so my dreams of eating out at some fabulous restaurant in Atlanta are quickly extinguished.

I'm thrilled to have Mom back, but I'm a little depressed over the fact that I'll be leaving soon. There's a part of me that would like to stay in Temple.

I like the school and I like my friends. I really like Madison and of course, I've grown to love Alyssa and Chance.

I finally have a sense of normalcy and I really don't want to give that up.

I'm confused.

Mom's voice brings me out of my fog. "What's got your mind working so hard over there?"

"It's nothing," I respond. "What are we going to do about food? I'm starved."

"Daddy's gonna do a fish fry," Chance tells me.

I can live with that. I love fish.

I'm amazed at how easily Mom sheds her celebrity skin to become this down-home kind of person. She's no longer Kara—she's Carol Jean.

She and Uncle Reed are in the kitchen talking and frying up trout, whiting and catfish.

"Aunt Kara's so beautiful."

I agree with Alyssa.

"She's real nice. I thought she'd be a little different. You know, like she's this rich lady, but she's not that way at all."

"You need to see her in Los Angeles. Mom's totally different than the way she's acting now." Rehab certainly changed her. Or maybe it's just being back in Temple. I don't care what the reason is—I'm just glad to have my mom back.

During dinner, I find out that Mom's planning to stay around until Thanksgiving. I'll go back to Stony Hills Prep after the holiday.

For the longest time, going back to California was all I could think about. But now, the thought of leaving Alyssa and everyone behind doesn't make me happy at all.

Thanksgiving Day comes much too quickly for me this year. I'm still having mixed emotions about leaving with Mom. I love her and I want to be with her, but I also want to stay in Temple to finish school.

Mom received a call from her agent yesterday; she's been offered a part in a new movie with Denzel Washington. She's going to have to fly to Hawaii in two weeks. I don't relish the idea of Stella babysitting me. I'm in high school now.

Aunt Phoebe prepares a feast for our meal today. Some of her sisters and their families will be joining us. I'm actually looking forward to a large family dinner like the ones I've seen on television. When it was just me, Mom and Jerome, we usually celebrated with a catered meal or Mom would pay Miss Eula extra to prepare one ahead of time. But it's never been like this.

Madison and I talk long enough to wish each other a happy Thanksgiving. He's having dinner at his grandparents' house. *That's kind of cool,* I think. All my grandparents are dead. I met Jerome's mother once. Right before she died. She was nice and smelled like peppermint.

Our dinner is straight out of a movie. Everyone gets all dressed up and we talk about what we're most thankful for this year.

When it's my turn, I say, "I'm thankful for having this chance to get to know my family. And I'm thankful to be able to share this day with my mom."

She gives me a big kiss right in front of everyone.

Talk about lame.

"I'm thankful for my daughter, Divine, and I'm forever thankful for Reed and Phoebe who never gave up on me." Mom wipes away a tear from her eye. "They came through for me when I needed it the most. I'm thankful for family."

Alyssa and I volunteer to clean the kitchen afterward even though it's a huge job, because we're planning to hit up Aunt

Phoebe and Mom big-time tomorrow when we go shopping. Alyssa wants an iPod. Not like mine, but a mini one. She's afraid her parents will say no if she asks for anything bigger.

Me, I'm going to see if I can convince Mom to buy me a new pair of Jimmy Choos. They have these leather boots that I've been dying to get but Aunt Phoebe wouldn't let me. She still gets heart palpitations when she takes me shopping.

Alyssa hands a stack of plates to me. "I'm so excited for your mom. She's going to play Denzel's ex-wife. I wish I could go with her to Hawaii. Then you could show me Pearl Harbor."

"I won't be going with her this time anyway."

"Why not?"

"School."

"That sucks."

I nod in agreement. "Yep. It really does."

Life is so not fair. And not just for the reason Alyssa thinks either. I don't want to have to choose between my mother and staying here. I can't hurt Mom like this.

When we finish cleaning up, Uncle Reed calls me into his office. I'm not surprised to find Mom and Aunt Phoebe with him. The three of them have become inseparable since Mom left rehab. I'm assuming this is the big good-bye talk, the one where Aunt Phoebe and Uncle Reed tell me how much I've enriched their lives by being here.

"Divine, how do you feel about staying here to finish out the school year?"

Stunned, I glance over at Mom.

She gives me a smile and says, "I've noticed that you haven't seemed real thrilled about going back to California."

"Mom, it's not that I—"

She holds up a hand to stop me. "Divine, honey, it's fine with me if you'd like to stay here until school ends. I know how you feel about me leaving you, but I need to get back to work. Jerome's legal bills and . . . well, I just need to get back to work. Then there's the new album to record. I'm gonna be pretty busy."

"I'd rather stay here then. I really like my school and I'm doing well. I have friends here." I look at Uncle Reed then back at Mom. "Are you sure you don't mind?"

"I'm okay with it, baby. Of course, I want nothing more than to have you come home with me, but I have to be fair to you as well. You've made a nice life for yourself here and I don't want to disrupt that."

"Will you come visit me?"

"Every single chance I get, sweetie. I promise. Besides, my brother and I have a lot of catching up to do."

I can relax now and enjoy what's left of the holiday.

The pressure of having to decide whether to stay or go is gone, leaving me to enjoy my very first real Thanksgiving with family. Aunt Phoebe takes lots of pictures. She's big on capturing those memories. I make a mental note to ask her to order duplicate copies. I'm going to start a photo album of my own. Only this one won't be filled with loads of press shots.

chapter 19

$\mathcal{M}$om flies me home to California the first weekend in December to spend some time with her before she leaves for Hawaii.

Uncle Reed isn't too happy about me missing a day in school, but Mom wouldn't change her mind or my early Friday morning flight.

I arrive in Los Angeles at two P.M. Mom is there waiting for me with flowers and a teddy bear.

"He looks just like Uncle Reed," I tell her.

She checks out the bear. "I hadn't really noticed it before but you're right. It sure does look like him."

"I'm kind of surprised that Leo or Stella didn't meet me."

"I wanted to do it. I want to spend every single moment with you that I can."

Her words make me smile.

We spend the rest of the day in a spa getting polished from head to toe. I come out feeling and looking like a new person.

"I so needed this," I tell Mom. "Aunt Phoebe never does spa dates. She says she can just make some mud at home for free and slap it on her face."

Mom cracks up. "Phoebe's crazy. I love that girl."

"You've known her a long time?"

"A real long time. Seems like she and Reed been together forever. She used to babysit me."

"Really?"

"Uh-huh. Her and Reed would watch me for Mama."

I laugh. "So that's what they were calling it back then?"

"I'ma tell your aunt what you said."

"Like I'm so scared."

"All right . . ." Mom teases. "Wait 'til you get back to Georgia. Remember, I'm not gonna be there."

Mom takes me to the Cheesecake Factory in Beverly Hills for dinner. Afterward, we do a little shopping for Christmas gifts. We're both worn out by the time we get home.

"It's good having you back home, baby. How does it feel to you?"

"Okay. The house seems really huge to me now."

"I guess it does. Reed's house isn't that big."

"When I first got there, I couldn't breathe. I had to sleep with the window open."

"Yeah, you wrote me and said something about not being able to breathe. That was the first letter I received from you, wasn't it?" Mom asks as we walk to the kitchen.

I laugh. "I was trying to make you feel guilty. I sprinkled water all over it."

"I knew it."

"How?"

"I know my little drama queen. I knew you wouldn't go down there without kicking and screaming." Mom pours a glass of water for herself. "Why didn't you ever tell me about the fight you had?"

My mouth drops open in my surprise. "How do you know about that?"

"You weren't the only one sending me letters in Reed's house. He wrote me too. He kept me informed. I know about the laundry and I know that you're not reading the letters from your daddy."

"Uncle Reed has a big mouth."

"He loves you. We all do. Including your daddy."

I yawn. "It's been a long day for me. Do you mind if I go to bed?"

"Honey, you can't run away forever. You're gonna have to talk to him."

"Is this why you brought me out here?" I ask. I have a feeling I already know the answer.

"Yes and no. I want to spend time with you but I think you need to see your daddy. At least this one time."

"I'll think about it." I give my mom a hug and leave the kitchen, taking the back stairs to the second level.

"Where are we going today?" I inquire the next morning when I come down for breakfast. It's my last full day in California.

Miss Eula throws her chubby arms around me, hugging me tight. "I missed you, gal."

She's the only person who can call me "gal" and get away with it.

When I sit down across from Mom at the table, she lays down the newspaper she was reading and says, "I have to take a drug test first, but after that we can go anywhere you like."

"You still have to do that?"

Mom nods. "It's part of my probation. For the next fifteen months, I have to be tested for drugs."

"Do you still drink?"

"Nope. I quit drinking, smoking marijuana, everything when I went into rehab. I'm clean and I intend to stay this way."

Miss Eula makes me an omelet with all of my favorites—onions, bell peppers, mushrooms, ham, bacon and lots of cheese.

"I'm so proud of you, Mom."

She smiles. "I'm pretty proud of me too."

"I thought about what you said last night. About Jerome. When he calls Uncle Reed's house he's always so mean. He thinks Uncle Reed listens in on our conversations. He doesn't and I try to tell Jerome that, but he never listens to me."

"I'll talk to him about it. He's not thrilled that you're living with Reed. He really laid into me about it, but I don't care. I did what I felt was the right thing to do. And to see you so relaxed and happy . . . I know in my heart I made the right decision."

"I guess now *I* have to make the right decision."

"Which is?"

"I need to see Jerome face-to-face. At least once. I want to do it today, before I lose my nerve."

"I'm proud of you, baby. I know this isn't easy for you but you won't have to do it alone. I'm gonna be right there with you."

After Mom's drug test, we drive out to Lancaster, where Jerome is incarcerated. I'm a little surprised Mom decided to drive to the prison without Leo. I would think this is when we need him the most. After all, we're going to be surrounded by a bunch of criminals. I notice a sign that reads "California State Prison" and point. "We're almost there." Mom looks a little tense, I notice. "You okay?" I ask.

She gives a slight nod. "I'm fine, honey. Just fine."

I don't believe her but I keep quiet.

We park the Mercedes and get out. "I'm sorry you have to come see your father in a place like this, Divine. I never wanted this for you."

"It's not your fault."

She surveys my face. "Thanks for coming."

"Let's get this over with," I tell her.

I'm not thrilled at all with being searched. A few of the visitors recognize Mom and so do the guards. There are no perks for celebrities in prison, I note.

Our first visit is no-contact because Jerome got into a fight with another prisoner and this is part of his punishment. The man's in jail and still getting into trouble.

I also learn that Jerome places us on his visitors' list every week. This kind of makes me feel very sad for him.

We sit at a table with this huge glass partition separating us.

I hear Jerome's voice and look around. He walks up to the table and takes a seat.

He picks up the phone on his side and Mom does the same. I can hear him clearly.

"Well, well, well . . . the world must surely be coming to an end. My wife and my daughter here visiting me. To what do I owe this honor?"

"We can leave, Jerome," Mom hisses. "Stop making a scene."

I'm so grossed out by his appearance. Jerome's growing dreadlocks and has a scar on the side of his cheek that makes him look kind of scary to me. I totally can't believe a plate of glass is separating us from Jerome. He gestures for me to pick up the telephone.

"Baby girl, how you been?"

"Fine."

"That's all you got for me? Fine?" His face suddenly transforms into a mask of rage. "What Reed been telling you? I know he trying to turn you against me."

Mom snatches the phone from me and says, "You leave her alone. My brother isn't interested in you, Jerome. Not at all."

Ignoring Mom, he turns his gaze to me. "Did she tell you she wants to end our marriage? She wants to break up our family."

I take the phone from Mom in disbelief. "What did you say?"

He repeats his words.

I glance over at Mom. She never mentioned that she wanted to get a divorce. *When did she decide this?* I wonder.

"Tell her you don't want to see your family torn apart."

Is he kidding? "You're in jail, Jerome. My family isn't together because of *you.*"

"See, I know that Reed is trying to take you from me."

"Uncle Reed isn't the guilty one here," I snap angrily. "You're the one who's sitting behind bars. You took someone's life. You stole a mother from her child, Jerome. You even robbed Mom of a relationship with her mother and her brother. You broke up my family. *You did this.* Not Uncle Reed."

"I'm your father. Don't you sit here talkin' to me like I'm nothin'."

"You've never once acted like a father to me, except to order me around."

Tears form in his eyes. "I did the best I could. I did."

I don't know how to respond, so I hand the phone over to Mom.

"We both messed up," she says. "I can't blame you for everything, but Jerome . . . there comes a time when we have to put ourselves and our feelings aside. We have to do what's right. We gave Divine life and she deserves the best that life can bring her. You and I . . . we got caught up in the madness."

He nods, then gestures for me to take the phone once again.

"Divine, I love you. I want you to know that."

"I know you do, Jerome."

"Yo' mama's right. I messed up. I made a promise to you that I was gonna do right by you. I meant that. If that means you gotta go stay with Reed and his family for a while, I'm okay with it."

Jerome really believes he's running things. He has nothing to do with this. Staying with my uncle is my decision, but if it makes him feel better, whatever.

Jerome wants to talk to Mom. My ears perk up when I hear her say, "This is not the time or place to discuss this, Jerome. Just enjoy your visit with Divine. She's leaving tonight to fly back to Georgia. She has to get back for school."

My eyes travel the room, checking out the crowded visitation area. I see a woman coming our way and blink again. It can't be . . . Yes, it is. It's that reporter Mom beat up. Why is she here?

I look back at Jerome. He looks so busted.

Mom turns around. "I should've known." She rises. "C'mon, Divine. It's time for us to leave."

"Hi, Divine. I'm so glad to finally meet you. Jerome's told me so much about you."

"My daughter has a plane to catch. We have to go." My mother practically pulls me toward the nearest exit.

"Is she seeing Jerome?"

"I don't know and don't care. Ava Johnson can have him."

Once we get into the car I say, "Mom, can I ask you something?"

Mom drives onto the highway. "Sure. What is it, hon?"

"Is Jerome telling the truth? Are you divorcing him?"

"Yeah. I can't deal with his stuff anymore. Divine, I know you don't understand, but just trust me. This is for the best."

"He's the reason you were drinking and taking drugs," I say quietly. "Right?"

Mom tears up. "I'm sorry for what I put you through, baby. I hope that one day you'll forgive me."

For the first time, I can really see just how hard our time apart has been on her.

"I do forgive you, Mom. Uncle Reed and I had a long talk about forgiveness and it's something I have to do."

Wiping at her eyes, Mom says, "My brother is a good man."

I agree with her. "He's real strict about some stuff though."

"Reed used to take care of me when Mama was sick. She was

sick a lot back then. He's always been good to me—he worked hard to pay for my college education. He worked two jobs and took out a loan . . . What do I do? I repay him by dropping out and running behind your daddy."

"Uncle Reed loves you, Mom. He says he's real proud of you too." I reach over and take her hand. "I'm very proud of you."

"Really?"

"Yes ma'am."

She laughs. "I can't get used to you saying that to me."

"Mom, would it bother you if I went to see the baby?"

"What baby?"

"Jerome's son. He lives in Atlanta with his grandmother. At least that's what I read in one of the magazines."

"Is this something you want to do?"

"I don't really know. But how would you feel about it, if I wanted to see him?"

"He's your brother, hon. If you want to see him, it's fine with me."

"I'm not sure his grandmother will even let me near him."

"I could try and call her," Mom offers. "Would you like me to do that?"

I nod. "You sure it won't bother you?"

"I'll be just fine."

"Mom, have you met someone?"

"No, baby. I need to get my life stable before I try to bring another person into it. I want to focus on you and on myself. That's about all I can handle right now."

Over dinner, I tell Mom about Madison. "He's real nice. I think you'd like him."

"Don't you go getting all serious about this boy, Divine.

You're way too young for that. And don't you go being all fast tail either."

"I'm not. We just talk on the phone and sometimes we e-mail back and forth. That's all."

"That better be all."

I hate it when she goes into Mom mode. Some things just never change.

chapter 20

*U*ncle Reed and Aunt Phoebe meet me in the baggage claim area.

"Welcome back."

I hug Aunt Phoebe, then Uncle Reed. "I'm so glad to see you. My plane was an hour late taking off, so I wasn't sure Mom would reach you in time."

"She did," Aunt Phoebe confirms. "We were just about to leave the church when she called us."

After gathering up my luggage, I follow them to the car.

I look around. "Where's Chance and Alyssa? Didn't they come with you?"

"They're at home putting up the Christmas tree. They wanted to have it up by the time you came back."

"That had to be Alyssa's idea," I say. She's the only one going around acting like this is my very first Christmas.

Tired from my flight, I take a short nap during the ride home.

It's around eleven-thirty when we pull up into the driveway. Chance and Alyssa run out of the house to greet me.

Alyssa takes a moment, surveying me from head to toe. "You actually look happy to be back here."

"I am," I confess. "I missed you guys while I was in California. Never thought it was possible but really, I did miss you."

"I missed you too."

"I have so much to tell you," I say as we walk up the steps and onto the porch. "You won't believe who I saw when we were out shopping."

Alyssa follows me into the house. "Who?"

"Omarion."

Alyssa nearly falls to the floor. "No way . . . For real?"

I nod. "Girl, that boy is so fine."

Our conversation comes to a halt when Uncle Reed and Aunt Phoebe walk into the living room.

Pointing to the two large shopping bags near the fireplace, I tell Alyssa, "I took care of my Christmas shopping while I was there. I have presents for all of you."

"You're not the only one." Alyssa turns toward the tree. "We did some shopping too."

I stretch and yawn before saying, "I'll put these presents under the tree. Then I think I'm going straight to bed. I'm tired. I'll tell you all about my trip later."

Alyssa begins to yawn too. "Okay. Glad you're back."

In the bedroom, Alyssa and I finish our conversation while

sitting on her bed. "I can't believe you actually saw Omarion. I mean—I know you see celebrities all the time because Aunt Kara is one, but Omarion . . . wow. That's so cool."

"I don't care that he's famous," I tell her. "He's just so cute. Omarion is fine."

"He sho' is. I love me some Omarion." Alyssa tries to stifle her yawning.

I stand up. "I need to get out of these clothes. I'm so tired."

"I know you have to be. I'm exhausted and I haven't been anywhere." Lying back, Alyssa places a pillow beneath her head.

She's sound asleep before I can slip on my pajamas.

Yawning, I climb into the twin bed. It feels so good to be back.

"I don't know what to get Chance for Christmas," Trina complains while we're walking through the mall in Carrollton. "I need to find something nice for him."

"You'd better hurry," I tell her. "After today, there's only one more shopping day 'til Christmas."

"All the good stuff has probably been taken since I waited so long to get something."

"Get him some cologne," I suggest. "Chance loves to smell good."

Shaking her head, Alyssa says, "Sorry. That's what I bought him."

We head into a nearby department store.

I nudge Alyssa on the arm. "Then you suggest something. He's your brother."

"How much money do you have to spend?" she asks Trina.

"Fifty dollars."

Alyssa gasps. "Girl, don't spend that much on him. I know Chance is my brother but noooo. Just get him a nice sweater or a tie."

"But I want to buy him something nice."

"Mama always tells me that unless you're married to a man, you don't need to act like his wife. She didn't just mean sex. She meant money too."

"I guess Chance didn't spend too much money on me, then."

"I don't know how much money he spent. He didn't buy your gift when we were with him. He went out on his own."

Trina groans. "This is so hard."

"I told you what to get him. A sweater or you can get him a tie."

"What about a game for his Xbox?"

"Too much money."

"They have them on sale sometimes," I offer. "Maybe she can buy him the football one he's been wanting. They have a new one out, so she might be able to get the other one at a good price."

"Let's go see. But if not, this sweater is real nice and he doesn't have one like it. Chance would look good in this."

Trina agrees. "You know what? I think I'll get this. It's really nice."

After Trina pays for her purchase, we head to the food court to grab a bite to eat.

A girl I've never seen before approaches Alyssa. "Hey girl. I haven't seen you in a while."

They embrace before Alyssa turns to me and says, "This is Janine. We went to elementary school together, but then they moved to Douglasville." She introduces me by saying, "This is my cousin, Divine."

I smile. "It's nice to meet you." I'm waiting for her to recognize me—usually everybody does.

She smiles back and says, "Nice meeting you too."

Janine holds out a flyer. "I'm so glad I saw you today. My dad's church is having a concert on Friday. We're having some contemporary gospel artists perform. You and Divine should come. It's going to really bless us. I know some souls are going to be saved during the concert."

I try to keep from staring at her. Janine looks like she's our age but she sounds like Aunt Phoebe. Alyssa glances over at me and says, "Janine is on fire for God. She wants to be an evangelist. She's always speaking at churches on youth day and stuff like that."

"God has done so much for me and my family. I just want other people to know how much He loves us and wants to be a part of our lives."

"That's nice," I utter, not knowing exactly how to respond.

Janine and Alyssa talk a few minutes more and exchange phone numbers before we go our separate ways.

"Alyssa, do you like being a Christian?" I ask when we return home.

"Yeah. Why'd you ask me that?"

"Because I don't know any other Christians. None of my friends in California go to church."

Alyssa is totally amazed by this. "Really?"

Shrugging, I respond, "I don't think so. I know for sure that Mimi and Rhyann don't. Except for like weddings and funerals. That kind of stuff."

"Why you so interested in my walk? You planning to get saved?"

"I don't know. I need to find out more information. I'm not sure what it means to be saved."

"It means that you choose God to be the head of your life and that everything you do and say should bring Him glory. It means that when you die, you go home to heaven and not down there with the devil."

"Jerome always says that there's no place worse than living here on earth."

Alyssa doesn't respond.

"Okay. I know he's crazy," I say.

"I wouldn't really call him crazy. Maybe he just never went to church. He may not know anything about the Lord."

"I don't think he ever did. I know Mom used to say that his parents never saw the inside of a church until the day they died. I wonder if God was mad at them when He saw them."

"*If* He saw them," Alyssa corrects. "If they didn't know Him before, He's not gonna know them on Judgment Day."

"Isn't that taking it a little personal? I thought God was so loving."

"He is. This is the way my mama explains it. God is like our parents. You know, how they love us and even though we mess up sometimes and get into trouble, they punish us, but they never stop loving us."

"Hmmph. I sure hope God's nothing like Jerome. If He is, I'm doomed."

"I really don't think you have to worry about that, Hollywood." Alyssa loops her arm through mine. "Let's go make some brownies. Mama bought all the ingredients we need."

"Ugh. Another cooking lesson."

"You like brownies, don't you?"

"Yeah."

"Then you'll really enjoy these because they were made by your little manicured fingers."

"And what will you be doing?"

"Standing by and giving you moral support. Go Hollywood. Go Hollywood."

I laugh. "I love you too, cousin."

Mom drives up the driveway shortly after one P.M. with less than twenty-four hours to Christmas.

I run out of the house and into her arms. "You're here! I'm so glad you made it."

"I told you I'd be here, didn't I?"

"I know. But I thought you might have to back out because of your shooting schedule or something."

"I made it clear that I had to be home for Christmas and for your birthday. Guess what? Stella and her husband will be here sometime this evening. They're spending Christmas with her mother. They're gonna come by tomorrow. Don't tell Phoebe. I want to surprise her."

"It'll be good to see her."

"She misses you so much."

"I bet."

Mom laughs. "C'mon. Help me get my stuff out of the car."

"Is all this for me?" I question.

"No. I bought presents for everyone. Not just you."

"You can't blame a girl for trying."

My mom is here and we're surrounded by people who really care about us. It couldn't get any more perfect than this. This is going to be the best Christmas ever.

chapter 21

Christmas morning, Alyssa picks up one of the presents I bought her and I can barely contain my excitement. I was so hoping that she picked mine first because she's going to love her gift.

She's wanted a Louis Vuitton purse for a while and now she has one. It's not a big one and I know Uncle Reed will probably faint if he finds out what I paid for it, but Mom says she'll tell him that she okayed it.

Alyssa screams when she sees the box. "Louis Vuitton! *Yes!*"

Uncle Reed nudges Aunt Phoebe and asks, "Is that one of those expensive pocketbooks she's always talking about? The one like Divine carries?"

Aunt Phoebe nods. "Divine, that's very sweet of you, but—"

"She really wanted to buy this for Alyssa," Mom interjects quickly.

Alyssa practically knocks me down when she comes over to hug me. "Thank you so much, Divine. Thank you."

Chance is a big fan of Kobe Bryant, so I got him an autographed jersey and hand-signed framed jersey number display piece.

The boy looks like he's about to cry when he opens my gift. "Divine, you the best. Thanks, cuz."

Alyssa hands me a beautifully wrapped present. "Now my gift ain't nothing like the one you gave me, but it comes from my heart. I know how you like to bling, so I think you'll like it."

I smile when I see my gift, a jeweled case for my iPod. "This will fit perfectly," I tell her. "Alyssa, I love it. Thank you."

Mom and I give our gift to Uncle Reed and Aunt Phoebe.

Uncle Reed's smile lights up the room. "Kara, you and Divine have really touched our hearts. A cruise to the Caribbean. Wow."

"I know how much you've always wanted to go. You wanted to take Phoebe on a cruise for your honeymoon. Well, it's long past time, don't you think? Chance and Alyssa can visit with us in California while you're on your second honeymoon," my mom replies, smiling right back at her brother.

"We appreciate all the nice gifts y'all gave us, but we don't want you thinking you got to spend this kind of money on us."

"It's only money. And I can't think of anyone else I'd rather spend it on," Mom responds. "I love all of you and I'm blessed to be able to lavish you with nice gifts. This is something I want to do. Okay?"

"I don't have a problem with it," Chance announces. "If you want to throw a million my way, won't bother me at all."

"I'm glad you said that, Chance. Reed, I hope this won't upset you but this has been on my mind for a while. I haven't forgotten how hard you worked for me to go to college and how I blew it. I regret not finishing college. I do. But I want to repay you by sending both Chance and Alyssa to the college of their choice. I will pay for everything."

Uncle Reed opens his mouth to speak, but Mom won't let him.

"I'm not taking no for an answer. I'm sitting on all this money, so let me do this for my niece and nephew because they *are* going to college. Divine too."

"I love you, sis. And thank you for your generous offer."

Alyssa jumps up and sings, "I'm going to Spelman . . . I'm going to Spelman . . ."

I laugh.

"You need to be thinking about where you want to go too."

"Mom, I already told you. I'm going to Spelman too."

Uncle Reed looks over at Chance. "Son, any idea where you'd like to go? I know you wanted to go to Morehouse at one time."

"I've been thinking about going to Georgetown University. I really liked the campus when we were there last summer."

Christmas dinner is being hosted by Penny's family. Her mom and Aunt Phoebe look like they can pass for twins. Mom surprises me with a digital camera after I go green with envy over the one she bought Aunt Phoebe.

I'm planning to take lots of pictures today. I want to remember this day forever. Mom is happy and looks stunning.

It's kind of funny watching how everyone treats Mom like she's a fragile piece of glass. She's a star and she's worked hard. I'm not hatin' on her because Mom deserves to be treated special. Especially since Jerome's jailhouse romance with Ava Johnson has been all over the tabloids. I'm not sure just how true the stories are, but Mom doesn't seem too bothered by it. In fact, she seems happier. The sparkle that I noticed in the pictures is back in her eyes.

I wake up in a wonderful mood early in the morning on December twenty-eighth.

I'm fifteen. Happy birthday to me. Happy birthday to meeee.

"Good morning, sweetheart," Aunt Phoebe greets me as I walk into the kitchen. "Happy birthday."

I give her a hug. "Thanks. Where's Uncle Reed?"

"He's in his office. Did you need something?"

"Yes, ma'am. Birthday presents. Lots of them."

She laughs.

"We're not letting you open one present until your mother gets here."

"But it's not *her* birthday," I argue. "And you let Alyssa open hers during breakfast."

"We were all here. Your mother doesn't want you opening anything until she gets here."

"Then why did she leave the presents here?"

Aunt Phoebe gives me a hard look. "How do you know about that? Were you listening to us?"

"Somebody just got busted," Alyssa sings. Laughing, she wraps an arm around me. "Happy birthday, Hollywood. You finally caught up to me."

"Like your birthday was only two months ago."

"Which makes me two months older than you, dah-ling."

Aunt Phoebe laughs. "You two act just like me and my sisters used to do."

"I've always wanted a sister," Alyssa says.

"Well, Divine's as close to one as you're gon' get. My baby days are long over."

"What did I just walk into?" Mom questions as she gives me a hug. "Happy birthday, baby."

"Mom, can I open my presents now that you're here?"

Uncle Reed joins us in the kitchen. "Can we at least have breakfast together?"

I stomp my foot. "Awww, come on. This is driving me nuts. It's my birthday and I want to start the celebration off early."

"You're such a whiner," Mom teases. "A spoiled brat."

"Amen," Uncle Reed and Aunt Phoebe say in unison.

"But I'm cute."

"And humble," Mom mutters while everyone laughs.

Aunt Phoebe makes all of my favorite breakfast foods. She and Mom are in the kitchen laughing and talking like I imagine they used to do when Mom still lived here. I can't get over how she's a totally different person here. She seems more normal or something—I can't really describe it. I'm just glad she's smiling a whole lot more and not faking it like she used to do for the media and on television.

I love all of my presents, even the ones from Alyssa and Chance. My mom gives me one more gift.

"This is from your daddy."

"He's in jail. He doesn't have shopping privileges. You bought this for him, didn't you?"

"No, I didn't. I don't think your father bought this—I believe he made it for you."

I open the present. "It's a tiny wooden teddy bear."

"He made it himself. He's taking some kind of class and he made that just for you."

"Wow. He did a pretty good job too." I'm in shock. Jerome did this for me? What is going on with him? Maybe being in prison is really getting to him.

"You should write him and thank him, hon."

I look up at Mom. "I know."

"He really does love you, Divine. Your daddy . . . he just didn't realize how much until all this stuff happened. Give him a chance, baby."

I don't want to get all emotional on my birthday, so I quickly change the subject. "So when are we having the cake and ice cream?"

Mom glances over at Uncle Reed, who answers, "This evening. Your mother wants to take everyone out to dinner at some fancy place in Atlanta."

Alyssa and I jump for joy. "Can we leave early enough to do some shopping?" I ask. "I don't want to miss the after-Christmas sales."

"I've created a monster," Mom wails.

The next morning, Mom leaves for Hawaii. Before she leaves, she tells me the disappointing news that she wasn't able to get in touch with Shelly's mother.

"It's okay," I tell her. "It's probably too soon anyway. She lost her daughter and I'm sure she probably doesn't want anything to do with me since Jerome is my dad."

"Honey, she can't blame you for what happened."

"She might not want to be reminded of it each time she sees me though. It's enough she has to raise that little boy."

"You're growing up so fast." Mom hugs me. "I'm not giving up on this. If you want to meet your little brother, we're going to try and make that happen. Okay?"

"Let's give it more time."

"Let me know when you're ready," she tells me. "I have to get going, but I love you, baby."

"I love you too. Call me when you arrive in Hawaii."

"I will. Now don't you go around being a fast tail, you hear me? Don't give Phoebe and Reed any problems."

"Mom, you don't want to miss your plane. Bye."

I always get this little tug whenever Mom and I have to part. I guess it's a mother-child thing. Christmas was good. I got lots of tight clothes and bling from Mom. Nice gifts from Aunt Phoebe and Uncle Reed. Even Chance and Alyssa gave me stuff I'd actually use.

I had a good birthday too. Spending it with Mom was the best present.

I always miss her when we're not together, so I'm already looking forward to spring break.

chapter 22

Jerome weighs heavily on my mind. Why did he have to go and give me that little bear? I was so prepared to just hate him for the rest of my life.

I sit down to write him a letter. I give up after about ten minutes. I just can't do it. I don't know what to say to him.

Jerome, how are you? How is prison treating you? Are you really involved with that witch?

I find a card that basically says thank you. I sign my name to it and put it in an envelope. This will have to do for now. I can't fake it. I can't fake how I feel about the man right now.

I pick up the little bracelet that Madison gave me for Christmas, holding it close to my heart. I want to see my boo so badly but I'll have to wait until we go back to school in a few days. I hope he'll be carrying the leather wallet I bought him. Alyssa would die if she knew how much money I spent on that wallet. But since Madison and I are going to be together forever like Aunt Phoebe and Uncle Reed—it's okay.

She bought Stephen some stinky-smelling cologne. I tried to talk her out of it but nooo . . . she had to get that one. Alyssa's nose needs a serious tune-up. The stuff stinks to me.

After I mail Jerome's card, I go back into the bedroom and turn on my computer. Hopefully, I'll catch Madison online and we can IM. He has two sisters and they live on the telephone, so we don't get much talk time. Thankfully, they don't have dial-up because as much as he says they're on the computers at his house—we'd never be able to communicate.

Madison's online. I break out in a big grin. My boo is on-line. He IMs me first.

Hey QT. What r u doing?

I type my response. Zip. How about u?

Chance comes into the room. "Hey Divine. Can you do me a big favor?"

"What?"

"Can you type up my report for me? I need to have it done by the time we go back to school."

"Why can't you do it?" I wish he'd leave. I want to get back to my boo.

"C'mon, Divine. You do a much better job than I do and I need to get an A on this report. Will you do it for me?"

"Only if you do me a favor in return."

He looks suspicious. "What?"

"Take me and Alyssa to the movies next Saturday."

"You want to meet Madison and 'nem there, huh?"

"Yeah. It's not like you don't do it all the time with Trina."

He holds up a hand. "Calm down, girl. Don't be bugging out like that. I didn't say I wouldn't do it. Chill."

I give him a grateful smile. "Bring me the report." When he leaves, I IM Madison, telling him my plan.

Alyssa and I follow Chance out to the car. We're meeting Madison and Stephen at the theater. As usual, I'm feeling guilty, but I really like Madison and I want to see him. Spend some time with him face-to-face. Okay, I miss his lips.

This is Uncle Reed's and Aunt Phoebe's fault. If they'd get rid of that stupid no-boys rule, then we wouldn't have to sneak around like this. If we get caught, that's the argument I intend to use. I doubt it'll get us anywhere, but it's better than nothing.

In the theater, Madison and I sit in the middle row while Chance and Trina are near the top. Stephen and Alyssa are somewhere on the left. I thought we should all sit together but everybody wanted to split up.

Whatever.

My eyes travel the theater, just being nosy, when I notice a couple walking up the aisle. The woman is tall and the man . . . I lean forward for a better look in the dark. I nearly drop my popcorn when I see that it's Aunt Phoebe and Uncle Reed.

Panicked, I glance around to see if Alyssa has noticed the Amazon woman and the teddy bear heading straight for her. Aunt Phoebe's looking around as if she's looking for somebody. Is she here spying on us?

She nears Alyssa but I'm assuming the girl's had enough sense to hide her face from her parents. Aunt Phoebe walks halfway up the aisle, then stops and backs up.

My heart nearly stops. She's found Alyssa all hugged up and kissing Stephen. Aunt Phoebe gestures for Uncle Reed, but it looks like he's spotted Chance and Trina. I cringe when my cousin points in my direction. Ducking down, I try to crawl past Madison but he stops me.

"We're busted, Divine. Come on. Let's just get out of here and face the music."

"That's easy for you to say," I hiss. "You don't have to live with them."

I've never been so humiliated in my entire life. Some of the people in the audience start laughing as we're being escorted out by angry adults.

I already know it's going to be a long night.

"I can't believe y'all," Aunt Phoebe is saying as she paces back and forth in the family room. She's been fussing nonstop from the moment we arrived home. "We hadn't even planned on going anywhere this evening, but God just placed it in our hearts to go to the movies." She points a finger at me and says, "See . . . your sins will surely find you out."

I look around at Chance and Alyssa, who's crying her eyes out. Why is Aunt Phoebe pointing at me? She didn't catch me kissing anybody. Chance looks so scared, I expect him to just pass out in a minute.

Uncle Reed suddenly stands up. "Chance, why would you go along with this?"

"We didn't make him do this," I interject. There's no way I'm taking the blame for this. Chance is the one who started this sneaking around in the first place. I got the idea from him. I don't say this out loud because I'm not going to betray him.

"It wasn't their idea," he says, totally shocking me. Chance is actually going to take the fall for this? I have renewed respect for him. "I wanted to spend some time with Trina before we go back to school and so I offered to take them to the movies."

"Did y'all know he was meeting Trina?" Aunt Phoebe asks. "Is that why y'all met up with those boys?"

Chance nods but Aunt Phoebe says, "I want to hear it from their mouths."

I steal another peek at Alyssa. She wipes her face and responds, "I told Stephen to meet me there."

"How long has this been going on?" Uncle Reed wants to know.

"This is the first time," I say truthfully. "I wanted to see Madison before we went back to school."

Aunt Phoebe turns to Alyssa. "And you, Miss Fast Tail. That boy practically had your face down his throat, you was kissing so hard. I'm very disappointed in you. I've taught you better than that."

Is she saying I wasn't taught better? I'm not sure so I tell her, "I didn't force Alyssa into anything, if that's what you're trying to say."

Aunt Phoebe's head whips around and she looks ready to pounce at any given moment. "I know you're not talking to me in that tone of voice, Divine. I didn't accuse you of anything—although I can't speak for how you were raised in California. I'm very disappointed in all of you. I really am."

"I'm sorry, Mama." Alyssa wipes away another tear. "I won't do it again."

"I'm sorry too," Chance utters. "We didn't mean to let you down."

I look at him like he's crazy. What did he mean by that? We knew what we were doing. We didn't mean to get caught. End of story.

Uncle Reed gives us a stern lecture about trust and responsibility. Then after sentencing us to two weeks without phone and computer privileges—unless it's homework—he sends us to our rooms to pray and seek God's help with the choices we make in life.

Outside Chance's room, I stop him. "Thanks for trying to cover for us."

He shrugs, then goes into his room.

I wonder if they're mad at me, because even Alyssa won't talk to me. I try a couple of times to engage her in conversation, but she basically tells me to just shut up.

I didn't tell her to kiss Stephen or let him almost swallow her head right when her parents were coming down the aisle. If she'd been watching the movie, she could've seen them come in and hide like I was planning to do. We could've waited until they left the theater before coming out. Uncle Reed and Aunt Phoebe always leave as soon as the movie ends.

I get ready for bed, feeling naked without my cell phone. I make a mental note to ask Mom if they have the right to yank my phone from me like this. I don't think so, but with Mom, I can't really tell which way she'll go. Especially if she goes into Mom mode.

I don't know if she's trying to impress my aunt and uncle, but Mom's been acting more like them. What's up with that?

The more I think about losing my phone privileges, the angrier I become. It wasn't like we did anything really bad. They should give us a break.

An uneasy feeling comes over me. What if Madison decides he doesn't want to talk to me anymore? Aunt Phoebe and Uncle Reed weren't exactly friendly toward him when we walked out of the theater.

I'm overreacting, I decide. My boo would never leave me for something like this. He's not like Aunt Phoebe and Uncle Reed—always tripping over nothing.

I just wish my uncle and aunt would realize they can't stand between true love.

We survive our punishment, the worst part being that I couldn't talk to Madison. We still saw each other at school every day, but at home, I only had my dreams of him. The Monday after we got busted by my aunt and uncle, I avoided him out of embarrassment.

I wanted to die right on the spot after being marched out of the theater like that in front of all those people. I don't think I could ever go back there for fear of running into someone who witnessed the whole humiliating ordeal.

I'm still a little uncomfortable around Aunt Phoebe because I feel like she blames me for corrupting her precious daughter.

"Divine, can I talk to you?" she says one day after we come in from school. I follow her into Uncle Reed's office. This is serious.

"Have a seat."

I'd rather stand but I do as she says.

"I want you to know that I love you like my own child. I treat you like I treat my children—don't you agree?"

"Yes ma'am."

"I've noticed that you don't seem very comfortable with me

and I'd like to know why. Have I said or done something to you?"

"It's just that when we all get in trouble, I feel like you're blaming me. I know Alyssa and Chance grew up . . . differently than me, but Mom is just as strict as you and Uncle Reed. She didn't just let me run around like a crazy person."

"I'm not blaming you for the choices they make, sweetie. I'm sorry if I made you feel that way."

My eyes water. "Aunt Phoebe, I know I drive you crazy sometime but I'm not a bad person. I feel like people know how Jerome is and that they think I'm like him. I'm not. I'm nothing like him. I would never do the things that he's done." I angrily wipe away my tears. I can't believe I'm sitting here in front of Aunt Phoebe crying like some stupid baby. This is so not me.

"Honey, I know that." She moves to sit beside me. "Come here, sugar. I know who you are. I know that you are a very smart and beautiful young girl. I also know that you have an acute sense of style."

I look up to see if she's making fun of me. Aunt Phoebe is smiling. "I'm so proud of you. Of *all* of you. I have such high hopes for y'all. I just want you to stop trying to grow up so fast. Enjoy being young while you can. It goes by fast. Believe me. It seems like it took me forever to be eighteen. Then twenty-one and twenty-five. After that, I started having birthdays every other month."

I laugh with her. "Aunt Phoebe, are you going to tell Mom what happened?"

She shakes her head. "I think you should be the one to tell her."

As if.

"If you don't tell her, *I will.*"

"Why can't this just be one of our little secrets?"

"Nope. Your mom needs to know what you're doing. I mean it, Divine. Tell Kara."

"I will. But not right away. I don't want to get yelled at so soon after getting off punishment."

She laughs. "I guess I better get up and start dinner. Your uncle will be pulling up in a minute."

"I need to get started on my homework. I have a test in math and I really need Chance to help me with some of the problems." I frown. "I can't stand math."

I get up and take off to the bedroom while Aunt Phoebe heads to the kitchen.

"What did Mama want with you?" Alyssa questions as soon as I enter the room.

"Nothing. She just wanted to talk. Make sure I'm happy here, I guess."

"Oh."

"You know how I was feeling like she blamed me for the whole movie thing—well, she says she doesn't."

"I told you that."

"I know. I guess I just thought maybe your parents considered me as big a screwup as Jerome."

Alyssa sits up on her bed. "Do you really feel that way about your daddy?"

"Doesn't everybody?"

"It shouldn't matter what anybody else thinks, Hollywood. He's your daddy and you should know him best of all."

"Jerome stays in trouble, Alyssa. You know that. It's been in the newspapers, in magazines and on television. What do they call him? The bad boy of Hollywood. Do you know how much it hurts to hear something like that about your father? I hate it."

"I guess I'd feel the same way if it were me."

"You would. I don't like hearing all these terrible things about Jerome. Or that Mom is a recovering drug addict—that's how they refer to her. I read it in a magazine and on the Internet."

"You're always telling me not to believe that stuff, so why are you bugging? You know your mom and she's fine. You said so yourself. She just needed to get away from your daddy."

I consider Alyssa's words. "You're right. Mom is better than I've seen her in a long time. She'll be back on top in a short time. Jerome . . . well, he'll be in prison a long time. Hopefully when he gets out, he'll be a changed man."

"I think he's trying to do that now."

"Maybe . . . I don't know."

"You still haven't read any of the letters he wrote you?"

I shake my head. "I'm not ready yet."

Alyssa climbs off her bed. "I'm calling Stephen before Chance gets on the phone with Trina. I wanna ask Mama to get a phone line for my room but I'm scared it's too soon. I don't even wanna mention Stephen's name around her."

"I know what you mean. I'm glad I have my cell phone." I turn on my laptop. "If Madison is online, I'll IM him and you can use my cell to talk to Stephen."

"You don't mind?"

"No. It's not like it's going to cost anything. I have free nights and weekends. Talk as long as you want." I see that Madison's online when I sign on. "Okay, he's here." I hold out the telephone to Alyssa. "Call your boo."

chapter 23

I stay so busy with my studies over the next few weeks that February completely sneaks up on me.

I'm surprised to come home and find my mom in the kitchen with Aunt Phoebe.

"When did you get here?" I ask after giving her a hug.

"This morning around eleven. I thought I'd surprise you."

"How long will you be in town?"

"For a week. After that, I leave for Sydney, Australia. I'm shooting a movie there."

I pick an apple out of the fruit bowl and take a bite. I chew slowly, then swallow before asking, "How long will you be in Australia?"

"Eight to twelve weeks. I have some good news. As soon as I

get back, I'm going to find a place to live in Atlanta. Since you're going to finish school down here, I figure I should get a house close by."

"If you buy a house in Atlanta, will I have to go to school there?"

"Do you want to?"

I shake my head. "I really like my school out here. I don't want to change again." The truth is that I don't want to leave Madison.

"Okay. That's fine with me. I just want you to be happy, hon."

Aunt Phoebe gives me this knowing look. She *thinks* she knows why I really don't want to leave. Whatever. I take another bite of my apple. Suddenly it dawns on me. "You're not going to be around for my spring break."

"Actually, I have another surprise for you. I spoke with Reed and Phoebe and they've agreed to let your cousins come to Australia with you for your break. You'll meet Stella in California and she'll fly with y'all to Sydney."

Alyssa joins us just as Mom makes her announcement. We scream and jump up and down in our excitement.

"We're taking y'all in a few minutes to have passport photos done," my aunt tells Alyssa. "As soon as your brother gets home from the library."

Alyssa and I go to our room, making plans for everything we want to do while we're in Sydney. I get on the laptop to search for tourist information while we're waiting for Chance to get home.

"I can't wait to go to Australia," Alyssa says. "This is so cool."

"I have the coolest mom in the world. What do you expect?"

* * *

That Sunday, Uncle Reed's sermon gets straight to the point.

"How much do you love Jesus?" Uncle Reed asks when he walks up to the podium. "This is our topic this morning. Let's pray."

I bow my head along with the rest of the congregation. "Our Father, we pray that the Holy Spirit will purge sin from us. Help us never to give first-class loyalty to second-class things. Father, enable us to see as You see, to judge as You judge, and to choose as You choose. Show us how You can become high on our list of priorities. In Jesus' name we pray. Amen."

I open my eyes and glance over at Mom, who is wiping her eyes. Is she crying?

She looks over at me and smiles. I can see that her eyes are wet.

"What's wrong?" I whisper.

"Nothing," she responds. Mom reaches over and takes my hand in hers. I believe it's her attempt to make me believe that she's okay when she really isn't.

I drift in and out of Uncle Reed's sermon. I'm trying to pay full attention but I can't; I'm nervous about singing.

Like an idiot, I let Mom and Aunt Phoebe talk me into singing a solo at church. My legs are trembling the whole time I'm sitting in the front pew waiting for my moment to arrive. I send up a silent prayer to God: *Please don't let me get up there and embarrass not only myself but my mom.* Mom must sense that I'm nervous because she reaches over and gives my hand a squeeze.

Uncle Reed reads a few lines of Scripture, then calls me up. I glance over at Mom, hoping I don't look as panicked as I'm feeling. This is such a bad idea. I should've just said no when Uncle Reed asked me. I'm such a loser.

I open my mouth to sing. The words bring tears to my eyes and it's not like I'm the person singing. The voice I hear doesn't sound like mine. Soon I realize I'm not the only one singing.

I open my eyes and I see Mom standing beside me. The love I see shining from her eyes is all the urging I need. I sing with my all, the words coming from my soul.

Mom seems caught up in a world of her own. She's looking at me but I'm not sure it's me she's really seeing. Then I remember.

She's singing to Jesus. Together, we block out the rest of the world because this is our gift to the Lord. I'm so happy to be able to share this experience with my mom.

After church, as we're walking out to the car, I ask, "Do you realize that this is the first time we've ever really sung together?"

"You used to sing with me when you were little. You don't remember?"

I shake my head no. "Mom, why did you go up to the front of the church during the invitation?"

"I wanted prayer. I need to get my life right, sweetie. I used to have a close relationship with the Lord but then after I met your daddy—I got away from it. Jerome became my focus. He became my life."

"He stopped you from going to church?"

"Not in the way you think. Hon, I'm not sure you'll understand this yet, but my relationship with God had nothing to do with your daddy. I chose not to attend church. I put everything else first. My career, my man and whatever else. I didn't want to lose your father so instead of being me, I started becoming more like him."

"I think I understand."

"Divine, I love you with all my heart. I want to apologize to you for what we put you through. You deserved so much better."

"It wasn't that bad."

"But it should've been so much better. Parents are supposed to lead by example. Jerome and I failed you miserably. I hope that one day you'll be able to forgive not only me, but your daddy as well."

"I do forgive you. I'm still mad with Jerome, though."

"It's okay to be angry with him but you will eventually have to forgive your daddy, Divine. I forgave him and I feel so much better now."

"I thought I had but I guess not. I'll try."

"I have no regrets about sending you to live with Reed. He and Phoebe have been good for you. I can see the strides you've made since coming here." She reaches over and grabs my hand, squeezing it. "Divine, I'm so proud of you."

"So do you have a new relationship with God now?"

Mom nods. "I'm working on it."

"What are you doing to work on it?" I want to know. "Are you going to stop singing?"

"No. Actually, I'm thinking about doing a gospel album and I'd like you to sing with me on a couple of songs. You and Alyssa."

I break into a grin. "Really?"

"Yes. You both have beautiful voices. But to answer your question, I'm reading my Bible. I'm going to start attending church services again. I'm going to put God first. The way it should have been."

Eyeing Mom, I say, "You're really serious about this, aren't you?"

"Your uncle's sermon really spoke to me this morning. Especially when he asked if we love Jesus more than we love other people. What do we love the most? The applause of the crowd or the approval of the Savior? I'm no longer going to allow another person to come between me and my God."

"So if we do wrong, then we don't love Jesus?"

"The true motivation for serving God is love—pure and simple, sweetie. If you're out there doing wrong, I can't say you don't love God, rather it's because you don't love God enough. Not enough to make Him first. Take me, for example. I have always loved God—never stopped loving Him. I just loved Jerome more. Now I've got my priorities in order. Think about your life, hon. Do you love Jesus above all else?"

"I'll have to think about that." It wasn't something I'd ever really considered.

"You don't have to tell me the answer," Mom says. "But think about it seriously."

Aunt Phoebe calls for Mom.

"Your aunt and I are going to the store. You want anything?"

"No ma'am." I follow her up to the living room where Aunt Phoebe is seated on the couch, tying her sneakers.

Since coming home from church, she's changed from her loud orange suit into a more conservative pair of khaki pants and a black sweatshirt.

She and Mom walk out of the house, talking about the stuff they need to pick up from the store.

I watch Mom from the window, my heart swelling with pride. She's really trying to get her life straight and in order. I think about our conversation and decide that I need to talk to Uncle Reed.

I find Uncle Reed in his office and knock on the door.

"Come in, sweetheart."

I take a seat in one of the chairs facing his desk. "Uncle Reed, can I ask you a question?"

"Sure."

"I listened to your sermon this morning and I don't know . . . I guess it's still with me. Will I go to heaven if I die right this minute?"

"Well, you have to recognize the fact that you are a sinner. Know that sin causes death. You have to repent and recognize that Jesus died for our sins. Ask God to forgive you because of what Jesus did and trust His word that He will."

Uncle Reed stands up and walks around his desk. "I'll pray with you, Divine. If this is something you feel you're ready to do."

"I'm ready. Mom and I talked earlier and she's ready to put God first in her life. I'm ready too. I'm not doing this for her. I'm doing this for me."

Uncle Reed takes my hand. "Repeat after me. Dear God, I am a sinner and need forgiveness. I believe that Jesus Christ shed His precious blood and died for my sins. I'm willing to turn from sin and I now invite Christ to come into my heart and life as my Lord and personal Savior. Thank you for this free gift of salvation. In Jesus' name I pray. Amen."

I repeat every word of his prayer, meaning them with my whole heart.

After we've prayed, I ask, "So what do I do now?"

"Pray and read your Bible to get to know Jesus better. This is God talking to you."

"Uncle Reed, I have to tell you now that I don't know if I can be this perfect little church girl. You know I like to have fun and I love listening to music and dancing. I'm just being truthful."

He chuckles. "Do you think my children's lives are boring?"

"No. Not really."

"Alyssa's not perfect. Neither is Chance. To tell you the truth, your aunt and I aren't perfect either. God knew us before we knew ourselves. He knows everything about us, but the good news is that He loves us just the same."

I relax. "Good. I just don't want to get up to heaven and God like shuts the door in my face. I'm going to try to be the best Christian I can be."

Uncle Reed laughs. "That's all any of us can be. C'mon, let's share the good news with the rest of the family."

"Divine has something she'd like to share with all of you," Uncle Reed tells everyone.

Mom looks at me with this puzzled expression on her face. "What's going on?"

"I was just talking with Uncle Reed . . . about what would happen if I died right now. I want to go to heaven so I asked Jesus into my heart. I want to be a Christian. It doesn't look too hard and Alyssa seems to enjoy being one. I figured I'd give it a try. I really want to go to heaven."

My mom bursts into tears, totally shocking me. "Mom, I didn't mean to make you cry! Did I do something wrong?"

"No, baby. You did the best thing you could ever do in your life. I'm just very happy for you."

Aunt Phoebe and Mom are happy. It amazes me that this means so much to them. I look over at Alyssa and ask, "Did Aunt Phoebe act like this when you got saved?"

"Girl, she cooked a big family dinner. I thought I was gon' die right on the spot."

"I hope she doesn't do that for me." I didn't want my being saved all over the news. This was something private to me. I don't want to share it with the world!

chapter 24

The next Sunday, Uncle Reed finishes his sermon and then asks if anyone needs prayer. Normally, I'm itching for service to end but not today. I'm planning to go up and join the church. Alyssa keeps telling me that this is the next step I should take in being Christian.

My uncle barely gets the words out of his mouth before I jump up out of my seat and head up to the altar. I have to do this before I lose my nerve.

I stand before the teddy bear in my black pantsuit ready and willing to be a servant of the Lord. I heard Aunt Phoebe say that before. I'm hoping I don't have to start wearing those crazy-looking hats the women in the church have on.

Uncle Reed smiles down at me. "Divine, are you sure this is what you want to do?"

"Yes sir. I've thought about it and I prayed. When I opened my heart for Jesus, you said I need to find a church home. I want to be a member of this church."

"Have you ever been baptized?"

"No sir." I make a mental note to find out what he's talking about.

He starts talking about me being a candidate for baptism. I have definitely got to find out about this. Maybe I should've talked to Uncle Reed at home about this before running up here.

After service, I ask Alyssa, "Okay, what did I just get myself into? What is this baptism Uncle Reed keeps talking about?"

"He takes you into a pool and dunks you in the water. That's your baptism. Remember, after Saul's encounter with Jesus on the Damascus road, he decided to accept Jesus and was baptized. Saul's name was then changed to Paul. And Jesus was baptized."

"I didn't know that."

"You should read your Bible and not just bring it to church."

I give Alyssa a jab in the arm. "Like you read yours all the time. The only time you read the Bible is right before you have to do something in church or when you get in trouble."

"Well, at least I read it sometimes. You don't even look at yours."

"I'm going to do better," I vow.

I can't wait to get home and call Mom. I want to tell her my news. I'm getting baptized.

Mom and I talk for almost an hour. She's so excited for me. She tells me about the time she joined the church and how her father, who was the pastor, cried.

"I'm going to do my best to be there when you get baptized. I have to be there."

"I hope you can come, but if you can't—I understand."

Mom changes the subject by asking, "So when am I going to meet this young man you've been talking to so much?"

"Who?"

"Now I know you're not gonna try to play me. By the way, I believe you have something you need to tell me."

I can't believe Aunt Phoebe busted me out like that. "Mom, I didn't want to upset you while you were trying to do your thing. I . . . I went to the movies and I met a boy there. Chance was there and so was Alyssa."

"All of you had dates? Or just you?"

"We didn't have dates," I say. "We were just hanging out."

"Is that what they're calling it now? 'Hanging out'?"

"It was wrong. To be honest, I didn't really enjoy myself. I kept worrying that we'd be caught. Maybe that's why we did get caught. I was thinking about it so hard."

"Well, I'm not gonna fuss you out like I want to. I'm sure Reed and Phoebe got you told."

"Aunt Phoebe was really mad. Probably because she caught Alyssa kissing her boyfriend. I would've died if that had been me."

"What were you doing?"

"I was trying to crawl out of there."

Mom busts into laughter.

"I was. Madison was the one who said we needed to just own up to what we did. He said he wasn't going to hide."

"That's mature of him. I'm laughing right now, but I want you to know that I don't think it's at all funny. I'm glad you told me."

"You already knew about it," I interject. "Aunt Phoebe told you."

"No, she didn't. She told me that you needed to tell me something. She never said what it was."

"Oh."

"Regret telling me?"

I laugh. "No ma'am. I'm glad I told you."

"I hope you learned something from all this."

"I have. I'm not trying to pull a fast one over Aunt Phoebe and Uncle Reed. They have some kind of direct connection to God. He tells on us all the time."

"He did the same thing to me when I was little," Mom tells me with a laugh. "But it's because He loves us so much. God only wants the very best for us."

"Mom, I'm sorry for what I did."

"I know you are, baby. Just slow down and stop trying to grow up so fast. I don't want you messing around and getting yourself a baby. I'm too young to be a grandmother. And you are definitely too young to be a mother."

"Why does this keep coming up? I'm not even thinking about sex. I'm waiting until I get married for that."

"I certainly hope so," Mom states. "I'll buy you a chastity belt if I have to."

"A what?"

"Never mind. Just know that you have to follow Reed and Phoebe's rules. You are in their house. Remember that. Now I have to go, but I love you, baby."

"I love you too. Bye."

* * *

It took me almost a month to get baptized. First, I spoke with Uncle Reed about the whole process, then I had to pray, read the Bible *and* take classes at the church on it. But now I know I'm ready.

I pull my hair into a tight bun at the back of my neck. I can't have my hair looking all whack after I come out of the pool.

Mom is here. I'm so happy she could make it. I didn't really think she'd actually come but she did. She got in around midnight and decided to stay in Atlanta. Mom's going to drive out this morning for the service.

"You look different," Alyssa comments when she comes into the bathroom.

"I don't normally wear my hair in a bun. I figure I'd do it today since I have to be dunked in water. Should I put on some makeup?"

Alyssa shakes her head. "Not unless you want it running off in the water."

Yuck. "I guess I'm ready then. Is Mom here yet?"

"Not yet."

I chew on my bottom lip, wondering where she could be. She should've been here by now. "Maybe I should give her a call."

"She'll be here, Hollywood. Don't worry."

I leave the bathroom. "I'm going to give her a call." Just as I'm about to dial Mom's cell number, I hear a car outside. "Is that Mom?"

A few minutes later, I hear her voice. I can relax now. Mom's here with me. I don't have to go through this without her.

I ride to the church with Mom. Every time she comes, people just stand around staring at her. Like always, Mom draws everybody's attention whenever she's around. She's still going to her meetings and Mom swears she hasn't touched marijuana or anything. She doesn't drink anymore either.

Right before service ends, I have to go get ready for my baptism. Mom is with me and helps me undress.

"I'm so proud of you, baby. I wish your daddy could be here to see you."

"You make it sound like I'm graduating college or getting married. Jerome wouldn't care about this. He's not into church."

"Have you written him?"

I shake my head.

"Have you read the letters he wrote you yet?"

"No ma'am. I'm not ready yet."

Mom sighs. "How long are you going to keep saying that?"

"Do you and Jerome still talk?" I ask.

"We don't really have anything to discuss," she tells me. "We're getting divorced. He's starting a new life with the woman he probably should've married in the first place. He ended their relationship because of me. It was wrong, but like I told you—you have to pay the price."

I think I know what she's trying to say to me. We talk about a more pleasant subject. Me.

Aunt Phoebe comes to get us.

The entire baptism is over so quick, I'm left wondering if I missed something. Uncle Reed dunked me into the water then lifted me back up in one smooth move.

Alyssa walks me back to the dressing area.

"I'm baptized," I state.

"How does it feel?"

I shrug. "Okay, I guess. I don't feel no different. Am I supposed to?"

"I didn't. But then we're baby Christians. Maybe if we were older, we'd feel something more."

I dry off and get dressed. "I almost invited Madison, but I'm glad I didn't." Standing in front of the mirror, I eye my reflection. "I look a sight."

I'm disappointed when Mom tells me that she has to fly out this evening. She's heading out shortly after we get back to the house.

At least I have spring break to look forward to. My cousins and I will be with Mom for a whole week in Australia. I'm looking forward to showing them what living in my world is like.

Right before she leaves, Mom tells me, "Oh, I have something for you." She gives me a piece of paper.

"What's this?" I ask.

"It's the number of Shelly's mother in Atlanta. I spoke to her and she's fine with you coming to see Jason. That's his name: Jason Jerome Campbell. She's expecting to hear from you. If you're afraid to call Mrs. Campbell, ask your uncle or aunt to do it."

Mom hugs me. "I'll see you in a few weeks."

"Thanks so much for coming, Mom. I really appreciate it."

"I've got my priorities back in order. I'll see you soon, hon. Be good and don't give your aunt and uncle any trouble."

"I won't."

I watch her leave, holding back my tears.

* * *

That night I have Uncle Reed call Mrs. Campbell. He arranges for me to meet little Jason this coming weekend. As Saturday approaches, I begin having second thoughts.

"I don't know about this," I tell Alyssa and Stacy during our lunch break on Friday. "I didn't really like his mom. She was causing problems for my mom and Jerome. What if I don't like him?"

"I think you're worrying too much about this." Alyssa grabs my hand. "Hollywood, he's your little brother. You have to be there for him. His dad can't be and his mother is gone. He only has his grandmother."

"He may have some other family. They may not live in Atlanta."

"He doesn't have another sister."

"We don't know that," I counter. "None of us knows if Jerome was faithful before Shelly. She may not have been the only one."

Stacy picks up a French fry. "Your dad is fine."

"Ugh. You're like grossing me out. Don't say that."

"Well, he is. If I was your mom, I wouldn't let that other woman have him. I'd be at that prison all the time."

"Jerome and Mom weren't good together. They tried. But it's better this way. Mom is so much more at peace. I like her relaxed and happy."

"She's gonna find a new man in no time," Alyssa utters. "Aunt Kara is hot."

"Not. I don't need a stepfather." I make a mental note to ask Mom if she's dating the next time I talk to her.

Uncle Reed and I leave at noon driving to Atlanta. I'm meeting my little brother today.

"You okay?" he asks me.

"Yes sir."

"You seem a little nervous."

"What if Mrs. Campbell changes her mind? Jerome killed her daughter. What if she tries to hurt me?"

"I spoke to her. She sounds like a nice woman."

"None of us expected that Jerome would be in prison for murder."

"I never cared much for him but I have to be honest, Divine. I think Jerome is telling the truth. He never meant for that woman to be shot. It was an unfortunate accident."

"It *must* be true if you believe Jerome."

"I'm just sorry things turned out this way for him. I pray for him constantly. I hope that this experience will encourage him to turn his life around."

"Me too." I close my eyes and sing softly along with the radio.

We pull up in front of the house around one-thirty. I sit in the car for a moment, trying to wait for my nervous stomach to settle. *He's a baby,* I keep telling myself. *He doesn't know anything about me or Jerome.*

When Mrs. Campbell comes to the front door, I get out and walk up the steps to the porch. Uncle Reed introduces me.

"Y'all come right on in."

We follow her into the living room. I see a playpen sitting over in a corner by the window. A little boy is curled up sleeping.

"Jason just fell asleep not too long ago," Mrs. Campbell tells us. "He don't sleep long. Too busy for that. He'll be up in no time."

I find my voice. "Thank you for letting me see him. I'm so sorry about . . ." I just can't say the words.

"Honey, you have nothing to be sorry for. When your mother called, I didn't know what to think. We talked for a while and then she told me you was living out in Temple with your uncle and that you wanted to see Jason. I'm glad you want to know your little brother."

I notice the picture of a little boy on top of her television. "Is that Jason?"

She looks over her shoulder. "Yeah, that's the little busybody." I can tell Mrs. Campbell adores him.

"He's got a head full of curly hair."

"I'm thinking about getting it cut off. I was going to do it for his first birthday back in January, but never got around to doing it."

I hear a moan and Jason begins to stir.

"I told you. He just takes catnaps."

Jason rises and his eyes get big as saucers when he sees me and Uncle Reed. He searches the room for his grandmother and smiles when he finds her.

"He's so cute," I whisper. He looks like Jerome. I don't say this out loud because I don't know if the mere mention of Jerome's name will cause this woman to go ballistic. I'm not taking any chances.

"You can go pick him up," Mrs. Campbell encourages.

"He won't cry?" I ask as I walk over to the playpen and bend over. Jason eyes me for a moment, then reaches upward. "He wants me to pick him up."

It's love at first sight for me. From the moment I lay eyes on Jason, I start feeling some weird sisterly emotions. At least that's what I think it is.

We play for a few minutes while his grandmother prepares

lunch for him. She even lets me feed him while she and Uncle Reed talk.

Jason pretty much grosses me out with his bad table manners. He sticks his finger up his nose, then in his mouth while I'm trying to coax him into eating the lukewarm mac and cheese.

I'm feeling the love and everything but when he decides to mess up his diaper—I had to draw the line. I may like him for a brother but I'm not changing diapers. Ugh.

We stay for a couple of hours. Before we leave, I present Jason with a teddy bear. "This was my very first bear and I'd like him to have it. I hope you don't mind."

"I don't mind, child. Bless your little heart. Look at him. He's holding it and patting his back. He must like it because he usually don't have much to do with stuffed animals."

Great. I give him something that he'll probably never look at again.

Jason wouldn't let go of the bear. Each time I tried to reach for it, he'd move and laugh. He's sitting here cracking up over this stupid game.

My heart nearly breaks when we stand up to leave and Jason starts to cry. I leave him with a hug, a kiss and a promise that I'll come back and see him very soon.

In the car, Uncle Reed tells me, "I'm very proud of you."

"This part is easy. He's innocent." I give him a sidelong glance. "You're not going to start on me about Jerome, are you?"

Uncle Reed shakes his head. "You know what you have to do. I don't need to say a thing."

chapter 25

Alyssa shifts her backpack from one side to the other as we stand near the doors of Sydney Airport. "This is so cool. Me and Chance have never been outside of the country. I can't believe we're actually here in Australia."

"I'm just glad to be off that plane," Chance mutters. "That was a long ride."

I agree.

"Where's Miss Stella?" Alyssa looks around. "I don't see her anywhere."

"She's probably arranging for transportation and getting our luggage."

"We should help her."

I laugh. "Alyssa, she's not actually getting the luggage. She'll have someone else do it. Relax. This week you're in my world, so just have fun with it."

Chance removes his backpack. "I'm ready. Bring on the babes."

"Yeah, right. All the way over here you didn't do anything but moan about Trina."

"I can still look. I'm only going to be here for a week."

"I wonder what Trina will have to say about that, big brother."

"You better not tell her, Alyssa. I mean it. And that goes for you too."

I fold my arms across my chest. "Boy, you better leave me alone. I got my own relationship to worry about. I don't have time to be all up in your business."

"Good."

Stella comes toward us with two men carrying the luggage following her. "Okay, kids. Let's go outside. The car will be here in a few minutes."

I slip on my sunglasses.

"All right, diva . . ." Alyssa murmurs. "Let me put mine on. I wanna be a diva for a day too."

"Girl, if you want to be a diva, it takes much more than a pair of sunglasses. You've got to dress like a diva. And you have to do everything with attitude."

"I know that. You got attitude for days."

"Whatever."

Stella tells us a little about Sydney once we're in the car.

"The airport is actually situated on Botany Bay, which was the landing point for Captain Cook," she says. "Did you know that Sydney was once a convict colony?"

"No," Alyssa and I respond in unison.

"What can we do in this city?" I ask.

"During the day, you can relax on the beaches. If y'all were a little older, you could . . . well, there's no point talking about it." Stella smiles. "Make the most of your daytime hours."

"I can't believe you just did that."

"Seriously, there are some wonderful restaurants in the area. And I know how Divine is about the mall. They have some really great malls here."

I'm excited already. All I need is a shopping mall and I'm good to go.

The studio rented Mom a beautiful villa near the beach. There are three double bedrooms in addition to the master suite, four bathrooms with underfloor heating, a huge dining room with ultra-high ceilings and a generous terrace off the living area.

Me and my cousins go crazy over the heated indoor swimming pool. Chance is especially thrilled to see the gym. Now that he has a girlfriend, he's trying to bulk up.

Mom loves the villa because of its fabulous views of the city. I especially like that the cafés and restaurants are all within walking distance. I don't want Stella having to go everywhere with us.

"Is this how you always live?" Alyssa asks.

"Yeah."

She nods in approval. "I could get used to this."

"Don't bother," Chance states with a deep laugh. "You'll never have a lifestyle like this. This is only for the superrich and famous."

"Just give me a plasma TV and I'll be happy."

"LCD is much better," Chance counters. "Plasma TVs burn out in three years or so."

Alyssa flashes her brother an angry look. "Let me dream, Chance. Okay?"

After we settle in, Chance borrows my laptop to send Trina an email. When he's done, I send one to Madison, my boo. Alyssa's not going to be outdone, even though she and Stephen had a big argument right before we left.

"I'm not speaking to him, but I will let him know that I'm in Sydney and how cute the boys are over here," she says.

"But we really haven't seen any boys."

"He doesn't have to know that."

Mom's movie is being filmed in the southern highlands, which are about ninety minutes away from Sydney, according to Stella. While she's away shooting on location, Mom has arranged for Stella to take me and my cousins to Bondi Beach.

I consult my travel guide for information on this must-see strip of golden sand.

"It says here that at the southern end of the beach is a public seawater rock pool," I read to the others. "The southern end is also popular with surfers as good waves break at this point. Hmmmm. Anyone want to go surfing?"

Chance and Alyssa both shake their heads and look at me as if I've lost my mind.

"Good, because I don't surf." I read on. "'Bondi Beach has a famous beach pavilion, which includes a café toward the northern end. A grassy reserve between Campbell Parade and Queen Elizabeth Drive, in front of the beach, is a popular location for those wishing to relax or picnic without venturing onto the sand.'"

Closing the guide, I ask, "So what do you think? Do we want to hang out around here and maybe have a picnic, or do you want to go swimming?"

"Let's just do some sightseeing and then have a picnic," Alyssa suggests.

I look to Chance for a response.

"I'm cool with whatever y'all wanna do. I want to take some pictures, though."

He's just like Aunt Phoebe. Always snapping pictures. I'm the wrong one to talk though. I've gone crazy with my digital camera.

We spend our first few days sunning on Bondi Beach and shopping. In between seeing the sites, we're able to go on location with Mom to watch the filming of her new movie.

We take a day to go to Darling Harbour to the Sydney Aquarium to see some of Australia's most spectacular fish. Not my idea or Alyssa's, but Mom said we had to go because Chance had been such a good sport about the shopping malls.

Sharks are his thing, so we're here. I'm amazed once I get inside. The sharks are swimming directly above us as we walk through the glass tunnels.

Alyssa doesn't like it. "I don't know about this," she whispers. "What if this glass breaks?"

"Then we'd better run fast. Real fast."

"You're stupid."

"And you're a scaredy-cat," I respond. Since I'm probably never going to visit the Great Barrier Reef, I have to settle for Queensland's reef fish.

We leave a couple of hours later.

"I'm so glad we're outta there. I didn't like having those fish swimming all around me like that." Alyssa puts on her sunglasses. "Chance, you better be glad that I love you."

Mom and Stella take us out for dinner.

"I'm so sorry I haven't been able to spend much time with y'all," Mom begins. "We're behind schedule so I have to work a little longer than usual."

"It's okay," I assure her. "I know how you work, so I'm not bothered by it. Especially since I have Alyssa and Chance here with me."

We give her a brief recap of our day, including Alyssa's fear of the glass breaking at the aquarium.

"You had to see it, Aunt Kara. It was really scary. Some of those sharks didn't look too friendly either."

I burst into laughter. "What did you want them to do? Smile and wave?"

Our laughter and teasing back and forth carries over to the house when we return home. Chance and Alyssa go swimming with Stella while I hang out with Mom in her room for a while. We haven't spent much time alone since we arrived.

"So, are y'all having a good time? It sounds like it, but I just want to make sure."

"Mom, it's been great. I love Australia. Well, Sydney anyway. I just wish I could've spent more time with you."

"Me too."

"I need to ask you something."

Mom eyes me. "What is it?"

"Are you seeing anyone? Do you have a boyfriend?"

"Why? Did you read something about me?"

"No ma'am." My eyes narrow. "Is there something I should know about?"

"*The Daily Gossip* is running a picture of me with Bobby Lowes on the beach and they're saying that we're having an affair."

"Are you?"

Mom shakes her head. "Divine, I'm not divorced yet. Besides, I'm not interested in jumping into something else right now. I need to work on me."

"Dad's seeing that Ava lady. Why can't you see somebody if you want to?"

"I want to do things the right way this time. I want to seek God first and just focus on Him. I have to make sure that you're okay and that you have everything you need. And then I have to straighten out my career. I messed up when I was messing around with the drugs and drinking all the time. I feel like I'm starting over again and I'm okay with that. I'm grateful for the chance."

"You sure sound a lot different than before. All you used to focus on was work."

"And Jerome," she adds. "I know. But I'm a different person now. Honey, you don't know how thankful I am that you don't hate me. I'm very blessed. I love you so much. There were times I wished parenting came with a manual. I never wanted to mess this up."

"You didn't. I think I turned out all right. I make mostly all A's. I'm cute and I have a great sense of style."

Mom laughs. "And you're so humble."

We're leaving in a couple of days and so I sit back in my chair, studying Mom's face. I miss her so much but I really do love living with Uncle Reed and Aunt Phoebe. I don't want to leave school and I most definitely don't want to leave Madison.

He's emailed me every day that I've been here—sometimes

twice. I'm going to miss Mom but I'm looking forward to seeing my boo when we go back to school next week.

I finally give in to playing Scrabble on family game night the
week after we returned from Australia. Actually, I lost a stupid
bet to Alyssa and this is how she wants me to pay up.

"You're part of our family—you need to start acting like it.
You have to play Scrabble. A deal's a deal."

"Fine. I'll do it this one time. I'm sure I can survive one
night of this torture."

"You'll have a good time if you let yourself. We always have
fun."

Whatever. "Let's just get this over with," I say.

When we enter the dining room, Aunt Phoebe has the game
all set up on the table and she's placed bowls of potato chips
and dip all around. I take a seat and reach for a napkin.

Aunt Phoebe looks surprised. "You're actually playing with
us tonight? I don't believe it."

"I lost a bet and this is what I have to do to pay up."

She laughs. "I'm not even gonna ask."

I help Aunt Phoebe bring in the drinks while we wait for the
others to join us. Alyssa was on her way up here until Stephen
called. I know she's not missing out on a game of Scrabble for
some boy. Not my cousin.

I'm about to go searching for her and Chance but they meet
me in the living room.

"I know you not trying to run away," Alyssa says to me.

"I was about to come looking for you." Pointing toward the
dining area, I add, "I was in there with Aunt Phoebe."

Uncle Reed is the last to sit down.

I read over the rules quickly. "I can do this," I declare. I have an extensive vocabulary.

"Stop cheating, Divine. E-n-n-u-i is not a word," Chance accuses shortly after we start playing.

"It is too a word," I argue. "Ennui is pronounced 'on-*wee*' and means boredom."

Chance reaches for the dictionary and looks up the word to challenge me. "Use it in a sentence."

"Chance was unhappy and filled with a sense of ennui."

Laughter rings out around the table. Even Chance can't help but chuckle.

"Okay, Miss Smarty-Pants. Where did you get this word?"

"From my Word A Day email. I learn a new word every day."

"Chance, I don't think that's a real word," I point out. "Moribund?"

"Like you, I learn new words too. Moribund means dying. Go ahead, look it up."

"Phoebe, we gonna need to start reading the dictionary or something. The kids are getting too smart for us."

"Daddy, you're one to talk. What was that word he used last time? Perfuddy or something like that."

"Perfidy," Uncle Reed corrects Alyssa. "Do you remember what it means?"

"Faithlessness, I think."

"You're right."

"C'mon . . . keep the game going," Chance fusses. "I don't want to be here all night. I told Trina I'd call her back."

He soon regrets sharing this bit of information with us.

"Did you two get married and not tell us?" I question. "Because it sure sounds like you have a wife."

Alyssa laughs. "Chance, who wears the pants in your relationship?"

"Y'all just hatin' 'cause y'all can't date."

"Whatever . . ." Alyssa responds. "Play the game. It's your turn, Chance."

I glance around the table, grinning. I really get it now. It's not just about a dumb game. It was never about the game. It's just about spending time with each other.

I think I'm beginning to like Scrabble.

I survived my first year in high school. In the fall, I'm coming back a sophomore and I can't wait.

Curfew will be extended and Alyssa and I will be able to go out on dates. That's if we can get Uncle Reed and Aunt Phoebe to change the age seventeen minimum requirement. We've been staying out of trouble just to prove we're worthy and that we're responsible. We're going to work on them this summer, right after they return from their honeymoon cruise.

"Aunt Phoebe . . . Uncle Reed . . . thanks so much for putting up with me," I tell them before boarding the plane for Los Angeles. "I can't tell you how much it means to be here with you. I've learned a lot."

Aunt Phoebe hugs me. "You've grown up quite a bit, Divine. I'm very proud of you."

"I *will* be back here for school in the fall."

"I know you will," says Uncle Reed. "Kara wants you to finish out your education here in Georgia. But not only that, we want you here with us because we love you. You've become very dear to us."

"I love y'all."

"Ooh baby . . ." Aunt Phoebe gushes. "We love you too. Let's pray right now for y'all to have a safe flight to California."

We bow our heads and hold hands while Uncle Reed prays. When he's done, I drop Chance's hand and check my watch. I have a few minutes before we board so I try to call Mimi. It's been a couple of weeks since I last talked to her. We don't talk as much now that I have Madison and she's got a mad crush on some boy named Wilton or something stupid like that.

I get her voice mail. "Mimi, this is Divine. I just wanted to let you know that I'm on my way to L.A. and I'll be home for the summer. Hopefully, I'll get to see you at some point. I'll call you when I get off the plane. Bye."

chapter 26

$\mathcal{I}$ thought Alyssa and Chance were going to faint from the shock of seeing our house.

"This is a mansion," Alyssa kept saying over and over. "Girl, you live in a mansion."

I laugh. "We definitely got to get you out more. Close your mouth before a bug flies inside."

"I've seen your house on TV and in magazines, but it didn't look this big. You're right. You *could* put our whole house right in the middle of your living room."

"We call it a great room."

"I can see why. It's a great big ol' room!"

Shaking his head, Chance tells me, "You can't take my sister

246

nowhere. Please don't let her see a celebrity. I'm telling you—she's gonna lose her mind for sure."

I give my cousins a tour of the house and grounds.

"This house is gorgeous. I see why you didn't want to leave it, Divine. I wouldn't either."

"It's a house, Alyssa. That's all." I can't believe I used to think that way. Before I left for Georgia.

The last stop on the tour is my bedroom, which I purposely saved for last.

Alyssa gasps. "Is that leather on your floor?"

I nod.

Chance kneels down to place his hand on the floor. "Leather floors? I've never heard of such."

Playing with one of her braids, Alyssa says, "Hollywood, you something else. You can't have regular ol' carpet on the floors like everybody else. You gotta have leather. Diva with a capital D."

"Mom picked out the flooring, not me."

"Wait 'til my friends hear about this."

I laugh at the way Alyssa's running around my bedroom, touching everything.

"Alyssa, you're going to sleep in the room across the hall and Chance, you can have the one next door. You each have your own private baths."

"Wow." Alyssa hugs me. "Thanks for letting us come out here with you."

"Stop bugging. We're family. My house is yours."

"I'm glad you said that." Chance takes my hand and leads me over to the love seat in my room. "Alyssa and I have a surprise for you."

"What?"

"Since you're going to be staying with us longer than we expected, Mama and Daddy came up with an idea. When you come back for school at the end of summer, the house isn't going to look the same."

I look from one to the other. "What do you mean?"

"We're getting the house remodeled. You're going to have your own room and we're getting two more bathrooms added."

"Are you serious?"

"Yeah. Aren't you excited?"

"Your parents are doing this for me?" I'm still in shock.

Alyssa's smile disappears. "You're not coming back to Temple, are you?"

"I am. I want to finish school there. And Madison's there. I'm just a little surprised that Uncle Reed would go to all this trouble for me."

"Dad's been talking about remodeling the house for a couple of years. Your mom offered to pay for the remodeling, but Dad refused. He said he wanted to take care of the cost himself. You know how he gets."

Tears run down my face. "You guys are so totally a cool family. I'm so happy to be a part of it."

Mimi comes over the next day to see me. She and Alyssa actually get through the visit without arguing or shooting daggers with their eyes. Mimi starts asking a lot of questions about Chance.

"He's got a girlfriend and you have a boyfriend," I remind her.

"He's old news. C'mon, Dee. See if he's interested. He keeps looking at me."

"That's because you keep looking at him. Mimi, his girl-friend is a friend of mine. I'm not going to do something like that behind her back. It's not right."

"I was your friend way before her," Mimi huffs. "What about showing me some loyalty?"

I shake my head. "Don't go there, Mimi. Don't."

"I can just leave you out of it then. I'll go over there and talk to Chance myself."

Whatever. I pick up my soda and walk over to where Alyssa is sitting. She's reading another one of her Christian romance novels.

She lays the book down when I sit down. "Is Mimi trying to get with my brother? Does she know that he's poor?"

"I don't know what she's doing. I told her that Chance has a girlfriend."

"He's not gonna go for somebody like her," Alyssa assures me. "She's way too high maintenance."

I steal a peek over my shoulder. "He's talking pretty hard."

"It's just talk, Hollywood. It ain't nothing to worry about. Chance really loves Trina. They're talking about going to college together and then getting married after they graduate. He cares for Trina."

Mimi comes over to where Alyssa and I are sitting on my chaise.

"I'm going to the premiere of Father's new movie tomorrow night. Why don't you all come too?"

Alyssa drops her novel at the invitation. "Are you serious?"

"Sure. We'll have a good time. Mother's hosting a party at our house afterward. We can have a slumber party. It'll be so much fun."

"I don't know if Chance will think so," I say. "And what about your parents? How will they feel with a boy in the house?"

"He won't be in my room, silly. We have plenty of bedrooms."

After Mimi leaves, I say, "We don't really have to go to this premiere. Those kind of parties can be so stuffy and—"

"I wanna go," Alyssa interjects. "This is my only chance for something like this."

"I don't," Chance tells us. "I don't know about that girl— your friend."

"We're not going to go and leave you." I can't believe these words are coming out of my mouth. There was a time I wouldn't dream of missing out on an event like this. "Besides, we're all going to the premiere of Mom's new movie when it comes out."

Alyssa shrugs. "I'm not crazy about Mimi anyway. We don't have to go. I just wanted to meet her daddy."

For dinner, Mom takes us to her favorite restaurant at the marina.

"I'd like for you to go see your daddy while you're here. We can drive out to Lancaster in the morning."

"Can't we wait until after Chance and Alyssa leave?"

"I thought it would be nice for them to meet him. He wants to meet them."

"Since when?"

"Since you're staying with them, Divine. Your daddy is still very concerned about you and what you're doing."

"I see that you're keeping him informed." I reach for my glass and take a sip of water.

"I wouldn't have to if you'd write to him."

I release a long sigh.

"Divine, give him a chance. He's your daddy."

"I thought you weren't going to push me about this. Mom, I'll talk to him when I'm ready."

"Well, make sure you're ready tomorrow morning. We're leaving at nine."

I hate when she goes into Mom mode.

Jerome hasn't changed much in appearance since the last time I saw him back in December. This time we're allowed to be in a contact visitation room, which means that we're allowed to visit with him in the visiting room or in the visiting patio area. Jerome wants to go out on the patio.

I'm not sure how he's going to react to Alyssa and Chance but I relax after a moment because he seems to be happy to meet them.

"I'm glad y'all came to meet yo' uncle. I'm just sorry it's in this place."

"It's nice to meet you, Uncle Jerome," Alyssa says. She's always so sweet. I give her a jab in the arm just because.

I'm shocked when we're joined by Ava, but Mom doesn't look surprised at all.

"I thought it was about time we all sat down and talked," Jerome begins. "Enough hurt's been done and I want to just start off fresh. I've been doing a lot of thinking in here. Got a lot of time to think about stuff . . . you know."

Mom and Ava won't even look at each other.

Jerome takes Ava's hand. "I guess you already know that Ava and I will be getting married. Kara, I want you and Ava to put aside all that bad stuff and try to get along. We all gon' be family."

Mom opens her mouth to speak but changes her mind.

"I want us to get along. Kara, I'm sorry for the way that I treated you during our marriage. I was wrong. I never shoulda disrespected you the way I did. I hope that one day you'll be able to forgive me."

"I already have," Mom tells him. "I'm sorry too and I ask that you forgive me for whatever I may have done to wrong you."

He smiles. "Already done." Jerome turns to Ava. "You and I done talked about this in private but I want everything to be open. I wronged you too and I apologize in front of my child, my niece and nephew and my soon-to-be ex-wife. I thank you for giving me this second chance to do right by you."

She takes his hand and kisses it. "I love you, Jerome."

Like, I'm about to be sick.

Jerome turns his gaze to me. I guess it's my turn now for words of love and I'm sorry's. Whatever.

"My sweet Divine. I know that you're very angry right now and that I'm gonna have to work a lil harder to show you I'm being true. Please forgive me, baby girl. I'm begging you for a second chance. I want so much to be a father to you—"

I cut in, interrupting him. "How? You're in prison, in case you've forgotten."

Alyssa nudges me. "Divine . . ."

"It's okay," Jerome says. "She needs to get this out of her system. Let her have her say. I brought her to this."

"I met your son," I tell him. "I met Jason and he's such a beautiful little boy. I hate that he has to grow up without a mother."

"So do I," Jerome says quietly. I see the glimmer in his eyes and know he is fighting back tears. "Do you know how much I hate that little boy growing up knowing that I'm the reason his mom is dead? It kills me. Divine, sometimes I wish they had given me a death sentence."

I gasp.

"Having to wake up every day with this on my heart. It tears me apart. I wish so much I could go back to that night and just start all over. I wish that I had just gone home. But the reality is that this is my life now."

In my heart, I know that Jerome's telling the truth. I reach over and take his other hand. "Uncle Reed told me something about forgiveness. He says we have to forgive ourselves even when we make mistakes or do wrong. Jerome, you have to forgive yourself."

"Divine's right," Mom contributes. "You have to forgive yourself and give this over to God. He's the only one who can give you peace."

"I never been much for the church, you know."

"Maybe it's time you changed that," Chance tells him. "Dad always tells us that God allows certain things to happen in our lives to get our attention. Maybe this is why you're here. God wants to get your attention."

"You might be right," Jerome concedes. "But me and God ain't never really been on speaking terms."

"We can pray with you," Alyssa offers. "If you'd like us to."

I look at my cousins. They are aware of Jerome's feelings for their father and yet they're sitting here offering to pray with him. They owe Jerome nothing, but they have welcomed him into their lives and ask for nothing in return. My heart overflows with love for them.

"I can use all the prayer I can get."

"Let's hold hands and bow our heads," Chance directs.

After Chance finishes the prayer, I say to him, "I didn't know you could pray like that."

"Thanks," Jerome says a little sheepishly. He wipes his eyes with the back of his hand. "I appreciate that. I really do." Leaning back in his chair, he asks, "You gon' follow in yo' daddy's footsteps? You gon' be a preacher?"

Chance shakes his head. "No sir. I plan on becoming a lawyer."

"Good for you."

Jerome glances over at me. He squeezes my hand. "You staying out of trouble?"

I cut my eyes at Alyssa and say, "Yeah. I am."

Alyssa moves her chair away from mine. "I don't want lightning to strike me."

Everybody laughs. Even Ava relaxes and we're able to have a pretty good visit. Mom's nice to Ava but I can tell she's still a little steamed about having to give the woman a million dollars.

Ava's wearing it well. She went out and bought herself a nice big rock for her engagement ring. I hope she's not planning to ask me to be a bridesmaid because I'm not walking down nobody's aisle at the prison chapel. They're going to have to do that without me.

Mom tells me that Jerome won't have to serve the entire sentence and that he'll be going up for parole in another year. Maybe Ava will wait until then, but I hope she isn't planning to have any babies because she's old.

At home, Alyssa and Chance talk about meeting Jerome as we eat the pizza Mom ordered for lunch.

"He seems nice," she tells me. "Maybe the drugs messed him up."

I agree. He does seem kind of normal now that he's been off the drugs for a while. I'm still not crazy over his decision to grow dreadlocks.

"I like his dreads," Alyssa says.

"You like everything about him," I argue. "I hope you don't have a crush on Jerome."

"No. Girl, that's my uncle. I can't believe you said that to me."

"Chill. I was only kidding with you." I pick up another slice of pizza. "So what do you think of Ava?"

"Ice queen," Chance states. "I hope she thaws out some before they get married."

"I think Uncle Jerome still loves Aunt Kara. Did you see the way he kept looking at her?" Alyssa downed the rest of her soda. "I know that Ava lady saw him. She almost burst into tears when he said he wished he'd just gone home that night Shelly died. You know that means that he wouldn't be with her."

"I hate that my parents are breaking up but they weren't good for each other. It's better this way."

"How does Aunt Kara feel about it?"

"I think she's okay, Chance. She seems to be more at peace. I think Mom still loves Jerome. I think she'll always love him."

"That's so sad." Alyssa takes a bite of her pizza. "Maybe one day they'll get back together."

"*Not,*" I utter. "It's time to move on."

"Are you feeling better about things now between you and your dad?" Alyssa questions. "It looked like y'all made peace today."

"It's a new beginning for us. I'm giving him this second chance. We'll just have to see what happens."

We spend our days shopping at the Beverly Center, sightseeing and sunbathing on the beach, and Mimi and Rhyann came over a couple of times.

When I talk to Madison he tells me he's worried about whether I'm returning to Temple. He misses his boo. He emails me daily to say how much he loves me. This boy is definitely going to be my husband one day. I can feel it.

The days fly by and before I know it, it's time for my cousins to go home.

Alyssa is thrilled to be taking home pictures of her with some of her favorite singers. Mom had taken us to a couple of concerts and we had backstage passes.

Mom kept her promise and allowed Alyssa and me to sing background on a couple of songs with her for her new gospel album. I think Uncle Reed's more excited about this project than anyone.

Too soon the day arrives for them to leave. I cry most of the way to the airport. I plan to give Madison a call later on today. Talking to him will take my mind off the fact that my cousins are not here anymore. Mom's already planning on taking me out to the Cheesecake Factory, but I'm feeling too depressed to enjoy myself.

Alyssa starts crying when we park the car and get out.

"Stop it," I tell her. "You're going to get me started again if you don't quit."

She wipes her eyes. "I'm sorry. I'm just gonna miss you so much."

I help Chance take the luggage out of the car. "I'll be back in a few weeks, Alyssa. Summer vacation never lasts long. You know that. I'll be back before you know it."

Alyssa scans my face as if trying to see whether I'm telling her the truth. "You're not gonna come back. Just tell me now. I don't want to read it in a letter."

"I am coming back," I promise. "Mom's not going to let me stay in California. She's so busy now with recording two new albums and working on three new movies—she thinks I'm better off going to school in Temple."

"What do you think?" Alyssa sniffles.

"I think she's right. The Hollywood life is nice and all, but it can be crazy too. I kinda like the quiet life I have there."

She hugs me. "I love you, Hollywood."

"I love you too."

Chance walks up on us being emotional. He embraces me. "Hey girl, I hope you come back to Temple."

"I will. I'll be back the week before school starts."

"We need to get y'all checked in," Mom announces as she walks up. "I've enjoyed having y'all out here. I hope you had a good time and I hope you'll come back to visit me from time to time."

"We really enjoyed being here too. We'll be back. Oh, Aunt Kara . . . I don't want to leave."

I shake my head. Alyssa's so emotional. She's over there holding onto Mom and crying like she's never going to see her again.

I wipe away the tear that slips down my cheek. I really love Alyssa and Chance. They're the siblings I never had. We fuss and fight from time to time, but I wouldn't trade them for anything in the world.

I found something I never expected to find in a small town: I found love and family and I learned about God and what it means to have a relationship with Him. I learned how to forgive, even to the point that I was able to sit down and write Jerome a letter last night. The first one but not the last. He is who he is, but he's still my father. He's asked for a chance and I owe him that much. It's not my place to judge him. It's just my place to be his daughter.

Still, as I watch my cousins head toward their departure gate, I realize that I'm missing them already. I wave until I can't see them anymore. Before we leave the airport, I send up a prayer request asking God to keep them safe.

I can't wait to go back home. Then it suddenly strikes me that while I grew up on a fabulous estate in California, the only place that ever really felt like home to me is a little house in a small town called Temple, located in the heart of Georgia.

Reading Group Guide for
simply *divine*

A Conversation with Jacquelin Thomas

Q. **You've written several novels for and about adults. In *Simply Divine*, why did you decide to focus on a teenage girl?**

A. I wrote about a teenage girl because of my two daughters, who are now twenty-six and twenty-two. When they were in their teenage years, I wasn't sure any of us would survive. However, with much prayer and open lines of communication, we made it through. Being a teen is hard enough without having to deal with your parents' issues—it's too much added pressure. While *Simply Divine* was written for teens, I'm hoping parents will take note that children watch us. How we respond to situations helps to shape their views on life.

Q. **Music plays an important role in *Simply Divine*. Has music been a significant influence for you? Do you have a favorite song or musician?**

A. I love gospel music because it really ministers to my soul. There have been several times in my life when only the soothing words of gospel music could reach me like no sermon or spiritual living book could. It was as if those songs were written just for me and my situation at the time. Classic R & B music is also a favorite of mine. Patti LaBelle, Regina Belle and Whitney Houston are my all-time favorite singers. With gospel music, I love Nicole C. Mullen, Yolanda Adams and Mary Mary.

Q. How did you conceive of your main character, Divine Matthews-Hardison? Did you know from the outset what her story would be, or did she evolve as you wrote?

A. Divine was conceived out of my wondering how children of celebrities handled the pressures of having parents who are constantly in the media because of legal and drug problems. Then I began to think about how they would respond if taken out of their Hollywood environment, and suddenly I had a story for Divine.

Q. Why did you choose to write the book in the first person? Was it difficult to adopt the mind-set and vocabulary of a fourteen-year-old girl?

A. I wrote *Simply Divine* in the first person because I really wanted readers to experience Divine—her emotions, her pain and her joy. I'm forty-six, so it was a challenge to adopt the mind-set of a fourteen-year-old. But as I pulled from my experience of raising two teenage girls and talked with a few teen girls at church, it became a little easier.

Q. **At the beginning of the novel, Divine is not exactly a lovable character, yet we do want to know what happens to her. Was it difficult to create a character who is deeply flawed but to whom readers can still relate?**

A. I'm deeply flawed too, so some of Divine's character came to me naturally. Divine is spoiled and a little full of herself, but we all know someone like her. She's human and I believe there's a little of Divine in all of us.

Q. **The importance of good parenting is a major theme in *Simply Divine*. What qualities make a good parent?**

A. I'd love to know the answer to that myself! Seriously, in just looking back to raising my daughters and now my eleven-year-old son and three grandchildren . . . it's important to listen to children. You have to really listen and hear what they're saying. You also have to know when to draw the line between being a friend and being a parent.

Q. **There are many important messages for young readers in *Simply Divine*. Is there one that you consider the most important?**

A. It's so important to keep the lines of communication open. Teens should talk about what they're feeling—not just with their friends, but with their parents or another adult they trust.

Questions for Discussion

1. How would you describe Divine at the beginning of the book? What details most clearly reveal her character?

2. Divine and Jerome have a complex relationship. Describe the different feelings Divine has toward her father at different points in the story.

3. After she has been in Temple for a while, even Divine notices that she is changing. "I'm not the same girl that left Pacific Palisades back in March. Thankfully, I'm still cute. Some things just never change." In what ways has Divine's personality altered and in what ways is she exactly the same?

4. Why do you think Divine is initially reluctant to sing in front of the church? Why does singing ultimately become so important to her?

5. Compare Reed and Phoebe's parenting style to Kara and Jerome's. What differences do you observe? Do you see any similarities?

6. After she is sentenced to eight months in rehab, Kara tells Divine, "I committed a crime . . . and I have to pay for it." While Kara seems to understand that her actions have consequences, learning this lesson is difficult for Divine. Describe a few of the episodes in which Divine struggles with taking responsibility for what she does. Does she ever learn this lesson?

7. What factors led to Divine joining the church? How does this decision affect her and those around her? Were you surprised by her choice?

8. Describe Divine and Alyssa's relationship. How does it change as the story progresses? In what ways do the two girls affect each other?

9. Describe Divine at the end of the book. What details reveal the kind of person she is now? What has she learned?

10. By the end of the novel, the character who caused the most damage—Jerome—is shown in a more sympathetic light. Why is it so important that Divine forgive him?

11. What does the future hold for Divine? Do you think she will pursue her dream of becoming a model? Will she go to college? What about her relationship with Madison?

Activities to Enhance Your Book Club

1. Bake homemade Southern biscuits to serve during the discussion. For recipes, try www.recipes.com.

2. Music plays an important role in *Simply Divine*. For your next meeting, make a CD of songs Divine would like or of gospel music that reminds you of the book.

3. Temple, Georgia, is a real city. First, find it on a map. Then do an Internet search and see what you can discover about the setting for *Simply Divine*. Compare Divine's reaction to Temple to what you've found out. Is the city different than you thought it would be?

POCKET BOOKS

Proudly Presents

Divine Confidential

Coming in February 2007

$\mathcal{I}$ spot Uncle Reed standing near the street entrance of the baggage claim in Atlanta. As I walk over to him, I say, "All right, the diva is here. Divine Matthews-Hardison is back."

I remove the loaded-down Gucci backpack from my left shoulder, praying the weight of it didn't leave a bruise because I intend on wearing the new halter top Mom bought me in Martinique.

"You won't believe what I had to sit beside on the plane." Tossing my hair over my shoulders, I huff, "They let anybody buy a first-class ticket these days."

I stiffen, momentarily distracted as my aunt approaches wearing a neon green shirt and matching pants that don't quite reach her ankles. They're wide-legged pants at that. My aunt stands almost six feet tall and glowing in this outfit the way she is—people can't help but notice her. Here I am looking all fly and she's dressed like . . . I am so totally embarrassed.

"Aunt Phoebe, you can't be going around here wearing stuff like this," I blurt out. "I can't believe you actually wore this out of the house. Uncle Reed, why'd you let her come to Atlanta looking like that? I see we need to do some serious shopping to get you a new wardrobe. And just so you know, Aunt Phoebe, neon colors are out."

"It's good to see you too, Divine," Aunt Phoebe says with a chuckle.

Only then do I realize I've temporarily forgotten my manners. "Oh, I'm sorry!" I wrap my arms around my aunt, giving her a hug. "I didn't mean to come out here fussing, but that thing on the plane . . . he really gave me the creeps. Aunt Phoebe, I was afraid to close my eyes the entire trip, so you know I'm tired."

I embrace Uncle Reed next. "Sorry for being rude." I put on a big smile and say, "I'm back!"

Uncle Reed gives me a smile. "So, how was Martinique, Miss Diva?"

At the mention of the island where I spent the last couple of weeks, a grin spreads across my face. "Oooh, Uncle Reed, I had a great time. Mom and I didn't do anything but hang out on the beach, eat a bunch of good food and shop."

"Child, I'm so glad you're here," Aunt Phoebe interjects. "Alyssa's been worrying me to death about when you were coming back."

"I told her that it would be a couple of weeks before school started." School starts August fifteenth, ten days from today. I pick up my Gucci backpack and continue, "I have a couple of suitcases. Mom said I didn't need to bring much more than that. I don't know who she's trying to fool. Mom carries this much luggage for an overnight trip."

"You still got a lot of clothes back at the house. A whole closet full. I don't even know if I've ever seen you in the same thing twice."

Running my fingers though my hair, I point out the obvious. "Aunt Phoebe, you know how I am. I'm a trendsetter. Besides, a girl can never have enough clothes."

She cracks up with laughter.

"C'mon, let's get your luggage," Uncle Reed says, his eyes bright with humor.

"Let's get them quick, because we need to stop at the first mall we find. Aunt Phoebe definitely needs a new outfit."

"Never you mind, Miss Diva. I'm comfortable in what I got on. Besides, I just came out here to get you. If your plane had come on time, I probably wouldn't have gotten out of the car."

Looping my arm through my aunt's, I say, "Aunt Phoebe, you know I love you, so I hope you don't take this the wrong way. Please, never *ever* wear this outfit again. It's so done."

Fingering her collar, Aunt Phoebe responds, "Oh, I was actually thinking about wearing it to the back-to-school dance. You know I'm going to be one of the chaperones."

Tilting my head back, I peer up at her face to see if I can tell whether she's joking or not. I can't, so I say, "I'm staying home that night."

Laughing, we follow Uncle Reed over to the slowly revolving conveyor belt laden with a mixture of suitcases and garment bags ranging from supercheap to top of the line. I hope those bag throwers were careful with the new Hartmann luggage Mom got me.

Ten minutes later, suitcases in hand, we make our way to the parking deck and Uncle Reed's car. I keep telling him and Aunt Phoebe that they need to upgrade to a Mercedes S600 sedan. My friend Mimi's dad just got one and it's tight.

As usual, Aunt Phoebe and Uncle Reed think they're down

with the people or something by driving a boring black Cadillac. I have to admit it's cooler than the Nissan Quest Aunt Phoebe drives. The Quest has all the tight stuff like DVD screens and a navigational system in it, but vans are just not cool. She should get an SUV.

Despite my relatives' poor taste in cars and clothing, I can hardly contain my excitement over being back with them. It's so obvious that they really need me.

I spent the first part of my summer at home in Pacific Palisades with my mom up until a couple of weeks ago. That's when Mom decided we should do some serious bonding, so we escaped to Martinique, French West Indies.

During the drive from Atlanta to Temple, I reflect on how upset I was last year when, in true Hollywood style, Mom was sentenced to a court-ordered rehab program for abusing drugs and alcohol and sent me to Georgia to live with relatives I'd never met.

I was so totally against leaving sunny California for some hick town in the middle of nowhere. But I've changed my tune.

I still love California but it really doesn't feel much like home anymore. Not like Temple does. Maybe it's because my mom, R & B singer Kara Matthews, is away most of the time. As one of Hollywood's most sought-after actresses, she spends more time starring in movies than in the recording studio.

Mom still owes Sony one more album. But after that, she plans to focus on acting. We decided that the best place for me right now is with Uncle Reed and Aunt Phoebe. I don't mind because my boo, Madison Hartford, lives in Temple. It was really hard not seeing him over summer break but we are determined to make our relationship work, no matter what. We kept in contact via email and phone calls.

Alyssa was looking out for me too. She made sure that Madison didn't get stupid and cheat on me. As far as she knows, he's been a good boy. *That's my boo. He's crazy about me.*

I pull out my compact mirror to check my makeup. I can't be caught looking whack. After all, I'm still a celebrity. I touch up with my favorite lip gloss, Dior Addict Euphoric Beige. When I look up, Uncle Reed is pulling up into the driveway.

"Oh my gosh!" I exclaim. "The house . . . it looks so different." Gone is the small, aluminum, matchbox-looking house and in its place is a sprawling ranch-style home with red brick front and sides. "Wow. You even have a two-car garage. This is nice."

"We've had a lot of work done to it," Aunt Phoebe tells me. "We have all this land out here. We decided to make the house bigger."

I rush out of the car. "I can't wait to see what it looks like on the inside." I slip out of my jeweled thong sandals to feel the crisp, green grass tickling my bare feet.

It feels so good to be home.

My cousin Alyssa runs out of the house, screaming, "You're back! You're finally back . . . Girl, I have so much to tell you."

We hug each other, jump up and down and then hug some more.

"I told you that I was coming back."

"I thought you might change your mind. Divine, I'm so glad you're back. I have something to show you," Alyssa sings. "I can't wait until you see it."

"You must be talking about my room."

"Yeah. Divine, wait 'til you see it. I just know you're gonna love it."

We rush inside and down the hallway.

"I have my own bedroom! Praise the Lord!" I scream. "*Yes.* Yes." I am beyond thrilled to have my own room and a full-size bed, but I am *ecstatic* that Aunt Phoebe didn't decorate my room in that Pepto-Bismol pink she's so crazy about.

"Calm down, Hollywood . . . I mean, Divine. You act like you've never had nothing before." Alyssa apparently has developed a case of short-term memory. She was acting as hyped up as me not more than five minutes ago.

"You don't know how much this means to me," I tell her. "Don't get me wrong—it wasn't too bad sharing a room with you." I stop for a moment. "Okay, I'm lying. I *hated* sharing a room with you. I love you, Alyssa, but I just need my own space."

"Hey, it wasn't no prize for me either, having you for a roommate. You kept hogging up all the closet space. Even after Mama got you that armoire."

"Well, now you don't have to worry about it anymore. I have my own room and my own closet. A walk-in closet at that. Yes." I run my fingers along the scalloped edge of my new dresser. "I love it."

"I have a walk-in closet too." Alyssa takes me by the hand, leading me back toward the front of the house. "You'll see my room later. First, you need to see Mama and Daddy's room. They have a sitting room now. And a big Jacuzzi tub."

I glance over at my uncle, who looks like a big teddy bear. "And why do you and Aunt Phoebe need such a big tub?"

"None of your business," he replies smoothly before giving Aunt Phoebe a wink.

"Gross . . ." I utter. The last thing I want in my mind is an image of my Amazon-looking aunt and uncle being all hugged up . . . or worse, being all lovey-dovey. "You two are way too old to be . . . you know."

Uncle Reed and Aunt Phoebe laugh, but Alyssa looks about as grossed out as I do.

Aunt Phoebe's comeback makes me shiver. "The only folks in this house that should be doing anything is us. *We're married.*"

"TMI, Aunt Phoebe," I say. "TMI."

Christian Novels for Teens!

From #1 *Essence* bestselling author
ReShonda Tate Billingsley

Three interconnected novels about a group of teen girls who form an unlikely friendship when they meet in a church youth group.

Nothing but Drama
Coming November 2006

Blessings in Disguise
Coming January 2007

With Friends Like These
Coming April 2007

From bestselling author
Jacquelin Thomas

A glamorous Hollywood teen is sent to live with devout relatives in rural Georgia, where she learns the importance of family and finds strength by turning to God.

Simply Divine
Coming October 2006

Divine Confidential
Coming February 2007

Available wherever books are sold or at www.simonsays.com.

POCKET BOOKS
A Division of Simon & Schuster
A CBS COMPANY